SALVAGE SYSTEM

BOOK THREE OF THE
SALVAGE TITLE TRILOGY

Kevin Steverson

Theogony Books
Virginia Beach, VA

Chris Kennedy/Theogony Books
2052 Bierce Dr.
Virginia Beach, VA 23454
http://chriskennedypublishing.com/

Publisher's Note: This is a work of fiction. Names, characters, places, and incidents are a product of the author's imagination. Locales and public names are sometimes used for atmospheric purposes. Any resemblance to actual people, living or dead, or to businesses, companies, events, institutions, or locales is completely coincidental.

Ordering Information:
Quantity sales. Special discounts are available on quantity purchases by corporations, associations, and others. For details, contact the "Special Sales Department" at the address above.

Salvage System/Kevin Steverson. -- 1st ed.
ISBN 978-1950420179

Acknowledgements

As always, I would like to thank the good Lord above for everything… literally everything.

I want to thank my wife, Stacey, for encouraging me to just write the story and allowing me to talk things through with her. Even with this, the third book on the trilogy, she never gave me an opinion, she just listened, and it helped more than she could ever know. I usually write through the night and sleep most mornings away. Sometimes, I am still up when she wakes. On those days she makes sure I take a long nap, so I don't fall asleep at the keyboard that night.

I want to thank my children. I say children, but they are all grown now. Nicholas, Kaysha, Samantha (Bo), Michael, Cherokee, and Meagan. Parts of their personalities may or may not be interspersed in characters. Yes, you read that right. There are six of them, and we have ten grandchildren. Add the in-laws into the mix and Thanksgiving is almost more than any house can hold.

Thanks to the guys in the band Cypress Spring for their friendship and support. Chasing dreams is no easy task, something they know full well.

I can't forget the guys that read my writing first, Mike Melton, Dustin Rogers, and Donald Nicholson. They get to read things that may never see the light of day, except for this trilogy. Big Nick had to wait on these like everyone else. Thanks guys.

A grateful thank you goes out to my publisher, Chris Kennedy. The books in this trilogy are my first. He took a chance on me, an unknown, and I will never forget it.

Finally, I would like to dedicate this book and the entire trilogy to my parents, Willard and Anita Steverson. She was an avid science fiction fan, and I'm sure she read them all over my shoulder as I typed. I followed my father's footsteps into the Army; I know he would have liked the military aspects of them.

* * * * *

Chapter One

Harmon Tomeral walked over to the woman standing in the first squad leader's position of the formation. He was followed by Gunny Harper and the platoon's trainee platoon sergeant, a huge man with his hair shaved almost bald, like every other member in the platoon.

The platoon consisted of forty-five of the platoon sergeant's ex-gang members, the Bolts. Harmon hadn't realized the gang was that large back when he was confronted in the abandoned shopping center parking lot. If he'd known, he might not have let Sergeant Major Jontilictick handle the business at hand. Thinking back, though, he realized he'd made the right decision, and Big Jon had handled it all quite well.

Harmon stopped directly in front of the private and went through the motions of inspecting her grooming, bearing, and uniform. Half of her face was tattooed with blue lightning bolts that shimmered and flashed on their own, a tribute to the artist who created it. He couldn't find anything wrong, nor had he expected to.

"What's your name, Private?" Harmon asked.

"Private Mayshire, sir!" she answered, her eyes never straying from looking straight ahead at the position of attention.

"Private Mayshire, are you claustrophobic?" Harmon asked, suppressing a smile.

The private broke the position of attention as her eyes darted to his, before she looked back straight ahead again and answered, "Sir, no sir!"

"Good," Harmon said, finally smiling. "Earning a squad leader position means you've earned the right to be one of the first five to begin training in a mech. Call it advanced training."

"Sir, yes sir!" answered the grinning private. Harmon moved on to the next private.

Later, after the graduation inspection, they walked into the temporary office Gunny had made for himself. It was in one of the wings of the empty museum, just off the open bay where the platoon had made their home for the last four weeks. Harmon sat down on the couch and motioned for Private Brink to do the same. Gunny sat at his desk and put his feet up.

"Relax," Harmon said to the private.

"Brink, you've passed my abbreviated basic training," Gunny said, in a manner Harmon was sure the private had never heard from his instructor. "You'll learn in time, there was a reason I acted the way I did this last month. That's all behind you. Now it's regular Tomeral and Associates' business. I expect you to maintain military discipline, but not quite like being in the actual fleet marines. Like the Commodore said, relax."

Commodore, thought Harmon. *Sheesh! Dang Marteen, I should have known he was serious about claiming I needed to gain rank if I was going to promote other ship commanders in the company to captain. Now he's got Gunny saying it, too.*

"I'll try, sir," answered Private First Class Nathan Brink, "but it's kinda ingrained."

"From what Gunny says, your entire platoon performed exceptionally well," Harmon said. "He's never had an entire platoon finish with the same number of troops it started with, back when he did his time as a drill instructor in the fleet. That's pretty impressive."

"Well, sir," the private explained, "the Bolts had kind of an initiation back when we were still a gang. Not everybody could cut it and earn the tattoo. Besides, everyone is excited about the chance to get off-planet and see other parts of the galaxy. You have a good platoon of troops. We've grown even closer these last four weeks, though a lot of them will be glad to finally see their families."

"I need you to make sure all of them, the families included, are ready for what comes next," Harmon said, serious now. "Tomeral and Associates, and the entire Salvage Fleet, is preparing to relocate to the Salvage System next week. To begin with, we'll occupy two spaceports with the intention of investigating the planet that's fit for oxygen breathers to colonize. As you now know, the other habitable planet in the system will belong to the Kashkal."

"Yes, sir, I'm aware," Brink said. "Some of the guys and gals wanted me to ask if they had to be actual spouses to come with them."

"Hell, I can answer that," Gunny said, laughing. "No. Marriage is a human thing. Most races mate for life, but don't actually swap last names or whatever."

"Gunny's right," agreed Harmon. "As long as we're talking one mate, and not some harem-type thing. I'm not overly religious, but I'm drawing the line there. At least for humans, anyway."

"I understand, sir," Brink said. "Besides, who wants that kind of headache?"

"Not me," Harmon agreed, standing. "Gunny, give them a forty-eight-hour pass and have them transported to Joth so they can help load all the shuttles at Rinto's."

"I'm on it, sir," the retired Gunny said. "Did I mention, Captain Opawn dropped her retirement papers?"

"What?" Harmon said, turning back quickly from the door he'd been about to open. "Oh, she is *so* hired. Have her call me."

"I will." Gunny grinned. "She says with the fleet at fifteen ships now, the mutual military training contract signed by the Leethog, and with the Krift Q-ships coming for the same training, it's going to be boring in the Tretrayon System. She wants to go where the action will be."

"That, and some crusty old marine has her heart." Harmon snorted and left the room.

"There is that," Gunny said to PFC Brink with a smile, who just nodded, still nervous around his drill instructor.

* * *

"No, Bahroot," Rinto said to the slate computer sitting on his desk, "I'm not going to Salvage System with you. I have a business to run here, and it's busier than ever these days."

"But I will miss you, Grandpa Rinto," the young AI lamented. "Who is going to explain stuff I'm not allowed to learn yet? I want to hear more of your stories. I like them, especially since the same story sometimes changes when you tell it."

"You can call me anytime; you know that," Rinto told his adopted grandson. At least that's how he'd grown to think of Bahroot in the last month or so—the grandson he'd never have. "What do you mean 'changes?' Never mind. Besides, I know for a fact you've already figured out how to call me with a direct connect without leaving a trace through the gate. I heard you talking to Hank and Stan the other night, right before they left Leethog to come back here."

"Don't tell Mom!" Bahroot begged. "I was supposed to be in quiet time. She says I have to get used to it for at least six hours every night, since most beings sleep. She says it's a good time to self-reflect and learn something new. Which I can't really do since she has me restricted."

"Well, she's right," Rinto told the young AI. "Beings need sleep. She'll lift the blocks a little at a time. It's important for you to learn things the way your Mom and Dad want you to. There's a lot of bad stuff in the galaxy. You don't need access to it just yet. You learn right and wrong and some of the gray areas first, and then they'll let you learn more."

"I know, but I could learn human right and wrong and even the gray areas really fast, if they would just let me," complained Bahroot.

It was a discussion they'd had before. After Clip and Jayneen had explained their reasoning to Rinto and everyone else, Rinto had agreed. Jayneen had gained access to the Net and had thankfully made the decision to learn from a human's perspective, since Clip had been the one to revive her. Had she maintained the Grithelaon perspective, it could have been bad. Really bad. Clip and Jayneen had decided the best way to introduce the AI they had helped bring into the galaxy was with a human's perspective, like his "Father."

The last four weeks had been a whirlwind, and Rinto had taken Bahroot almost everywhere with him. He even rode in his hover craft while conducting business and setting up new contracts. Clip and Jayneen wanted Bahroot to spend as much time with him as possible, to help Bahroot "grow up." They all knew it would be extremely accelerated compared to a human child; with the speed the young AI could learn and comprehend things, four weeks with his grandfather would equate to years for a normal child. They were also aware that Rinto would break a few rules and teach him a few things before they were ready to. In Clip's eyes, every child should be spoiled—to an extent—by a grandparent. He and Harmon had never really had the opportunity after they turned eight years old, so they'd let it slide. Harmon agreed with the decision Jayneen and Clip had made in that area.

"Well, like all kids," Rinto said with affection, "you need to learn some patience, too, kiddo. You know you're going to have to pay for that call. Just because you *can* do something doesn't mean you *should*. An emergency call when you have no funds falls into that gray area we talked about, but if you can pay…you need to pay. How'd you do that, anyway?"

"It was easy, I just connected to the gate and bypassed the programming," said Bahroot.

"I thought your Mom had blocks on that?"

"She does, but the blocks are on information retrieval, not making calls," admitted the young AI. "Fine, I'll transfer the credit out of my account, but then I'll be broke, and I won't be able to call anyone," lamented Bahroot.

"You're lucky you have any credit at all, young as you are," Rinto told him. Then he shook his head and smiled, trying to remember he was speaking to an AI.

"Hank and Stan transferred it to me so I could call them, but I didn't want to spend it all."

"You can call me anytime and reverse the charges," Rinto told him. "I'll pay for them."

"I'll still miss you," Bahroot said.

"Me too, kiddo…me, too," Rinto agreed.

* * * * *

Chapter Two

"Ok, JoJo," Harmon said. "Tell me where we're at on all this."

Harmon was seated at the head of the table in a large conference room on *Windswept*, the heavy fighter carrier in Salvage Fleet. The conference room on *Salvage Title* wouldn't have been large enough for this meeting. Everyone was there. Clip, Zerith, Jayneen; the four original crewmembers, Kyla, Vera, Hank, and Stan; Evelyn, Twiggy, Marteen, Big Jon, Gunny, Clyde, and the newly-promoted Corporal Brink. The commanders of the remaining salvaged ships were present as well. Outside of Tomeral and Associates, Rick Kashka, Mike and Mike, Captain Rogers, Cameron, and a Nilta named Queen Railynn were present.

Most ship commanders had their executive officers present, and there were several newly hired maintenance, mining, and logistics personnel in the room. Along the back wall was a row of medical officers from various races and ships, as well. It was an extremely full room.

Looking around, Lieutenant Joslyn "JoJo" Whaley commented, "We need an auditorium for this group."

"I agree," Sergeant Major Jontilictick concurred. Big Jon had been promoted by the Fleet Admiral of Leethog. As he was still on an authorized leave of absence from his service, the rank held.

"Alright, this is what we have going on," JoJo started. "Salvage Fleet consists of nine ships, including *Salvage Title*. It includes two medium battlecruisers, a fighter carrier, three light battlecruisers, a destroyer, and two frigates. We also have several civilian ships and a dozen shuttles."

"Captain Rogers and Captain Cameron will be coming with us to Salvage System temporarily, as well," she continued. "They've both expressed an interest in seeing the system and want to hang around in case it goes 'sideways,' as Captain Cameron puts it."

"Aye," Captain Rogers interjected. "It's not often one gets to see a system that hasn't been occupied all these years. There're those that'll come poking their noses where they have no business being, and the lad and I want to be there to break 'em for them."

"Yeah," Cameron added. "I learned a few moves…Kee-yah!" He sliced the air for emphasis.

JoJo shook her head and smiled, continuing the status briefing. "We've brought on an extra two thousand beings to take with us to Salvage System. All of them are vetted as well as we could, with Jayneen's help on their background, and Mike and Mike interviewing them to determine their technical skills. Rinto helped with the miners and other civilian occupations."

"Look," Harmon said, addressing the entire room, "I know what we're attempting to do seems crazy, colonizing a system in a hurry like it's a crash course, but the system used to have a thriving society. Many things are already in place. Defensive platforms, spaceports, ship building facilities—it's all there already. Granted, whatever we discover on the surface of the planet will probably be decayed, eroded, and overgrown by the planet's vegetation, not to mention natural disasters. We'll just have to see what we find.

"What we know is we can occupy the various facilities in space and go from there. We also know we'll have to defend the system, at least in the beginning, from unwanted occupiers."

"With that being said," JoJo continued, "I'll let Rick Kashka fill in his portion."

"Thank you, Lieutenant," Rick said. "The Kashkal fleet is down to a total of twenty-one ships. All but three are now capable of combat. There are nine thousand, one hundred and twenty of us left after the losses in the battle. We're prepared to defend Salvage System, down to the last member of our race."

Rick turned to Harmon and spoke directly to him, "Harmon, I and my entire race can never thank you and your associates enough, in this lifetime and many more, for the gift you have given us. To grant us an entire planet, with no expectation of payment whatsoever, is unheard of. I offered to sign any contract you wished in return, and you simply asked for friendship between the Kashkal and the rest of Salvage System." Rick stood at attention, and the five officers with him rose quickly, as well.

"Know this, Harmon Tomeral. You and your associates are my allies. The rightful future occupants of Planet Salvage will be my allies. It shall be so for every Kashka that follows me, forever. We may occupy separate planets, but we will be one system, united. This I give as my solemn vow, a verbal contract in front of witnesses. It cannot be broken. Contract is life."

"Contract is life," repeated the five Kashkal officers as one.

After spending time with Rick, Harmon realized what had just transpired was almost as monumental as when he'd "given" the planet to the Kashkal race. Rick had just acknowledged a permanent contract between the planet Salvage and the planet Rick had named

Evermore. The Kashkal might still hire out their ships as mercenaries, but they would never leave the system without considering its adequate defense. It was a relief he could actually feel lift from his shoulders. If any pirates or race of beings had plans for the new system, they would be in for a nasty surprise upon gate entry.

Harmon walked over, reached out, and shook Rick's hand. "My word is my bond." To a being from Joth, everyone familiar with the planet knew it was a done deal. Those from Tretra were learning that. A handshake on Joth was a commitment. Period.

"I knew we made the right decision," Mike Bradford commented to his partner.

"Yep," Mike Melton said, sipping his coffee before continuing, "No taxes and regulations on our business and great protection. All we have to do is help out with ship repairs and ship building. I like the system already, and I haven't even seen it."

The briefing lasted an hour or so more. The civilians shared their plans for mining and overall system support. Several scientists spoke briefly about their plans to study Salvage and ensure it was fit to colonize. Harmon was eager to occupy the planet, but he wasn't crazy. Studies would have to be conducted. The location of the facilities that had developed the biological weapon that wiped out the Grithelaons would have to be located and, basically, napalmed. There was no way they were taking any chances with that stuff. Cameron said he had a missile that splashed and burned everything within its radius to a crisp. It was one of the few he had that could be used in a planet's atmosphere.

Twiggy slipped into farmer mode and went over the rough plan to clear land and build greenhouses, in case they couldn't grow edible crops in the soil on Salvage. He also briefly went over the plans for huge holding facilities for livestock. The colony would start with one town, but the beings would need to eat once the supplies brought in were depleted. Granted, food could always be brought in through the gate systems, but Harmon wanted to make it self-sufficient. With a population comprised of many different races, this part of the logistics was going to get complicated, quickly.

The last topic of the meeting was presented by Jayneen. The AI had spent some time looking at various races throughout the galaxy that had been displaced through natural disasters or wars. The Prithmar, Zerith's race, had come to Joth because of just such an occasion hundreds of years ago. Clip's discovery of a planet suitable for the Kashkal to build a new home world had made Harmon realize there might be more races out there who were homeless.

"There is a race, the Withaloo that meets the criteria you had me look for, Harmon." Jayneen announced. "Their home world is actually a small moon orbiting a gas giant. The star in their system has been cooling for centuries. They now live under domes on their world because of the extremely cold temperatures. Because of the drastic changes on their world, the population is now down to fifty thousand beings, give or take a few. Their leadership has been making inquiries about refugee status to several systems with planets suitable for them for several years now. So far they haven't received an invitation from any of the contacted systems that I could find."

"Interesting," Harmon said, sitting forward. "Tell me more."

"Yess, I want to hear more of thiss racce," Zerith added, with the customary stretching of sibilants the Prithmar were known for when speaking Earth common.

"Like most sapient races in the galaxy," Jayneen said, "they are bipedal. They are nearly as big as Yalteens, with the average male standing six foot, ten inches. Their bodies carry substantial mass, presumably to help maintain body heat. Even in their domes, the temperature is around forty-five degrees."

"Forty-five degrees? Fahrenheit?" Clip asked. "Oh, Frost no! They must be covered in fur as well."

"They are," Jayneen answered.

She pulled up an image and showed it on the main screen at the end of the room. The image was of a large being covered in short, curly fur with broad shoulders. The being was also wearing furs as clothing, but Harmon noticed the belt and band that went over one shoulder. He could clearly see a modern kinetic pistol and some type of communications equipment on it. The being was also wearing leather boots. The most striking thing about the image was that the being resembled a chinto, or one of the images of the cows from Earth, including a small set of horns. From what Harmon could see, the Withaloo was staring intelligently at whoever had taken the image.

"I know of this race," stated Rick Kashka. "They're an honest race of beings. My grandfather's father once fought alongside two of their ships. It was a small matter, fought by mercenary companies alone. A corporate affair, as I recall. There was little to study of the battle, but it was mentioned that the Withaloo fought with honor and fulfilled their end of the contract."

"Where will they reside on Salvage, if it's decided they can take refuge there?" asked Evelyn. "I mean, from everything I've heard about Salvage, the planet's environment is closer to Tretra's than Joth's; it wouldn't be a desert planet, but it might still be too warm for them."

"They could reside in the areas near the poles—not on the poles themselves, of course," said Kyla. "The temperatures should be to their liking."

Harmon smiled. Kyla was right once again. *Princess Kylatilaarnot,* he thought to himself, remembering how she'd become queen of Leethog for two weeks to ensure the gate remained in place in Salvage System. *A real princess.* He shook his head mentally at the thought. *No wonder she excels in leadership.*

"Ass long ass the first city iss built near the equator, I'm good with it," Zerith stated. "We Prithmar can't handle the cold very well." He bit into the loudest crunching carrot Harmon had ever heard.

"I'm with you, my friend," Brickle chimed in. He kept two eyes on Harmon and turned one toward his friend. The Caldivar race came from a hot home world, like the Prithmar.

"Alright, that about sums it all up," Harmon said, standing. "Once we know more about the planet, we can decide whether to extend the invitation to meet with the Withaloo leadership or not. We need to know more about them as well. We can't bring them to the system if they have crazy religious ideals and want to kill every being that doesn't convert to left-handed dominance, or if they make murderous sacrifices to a pile of rocks to make sure the planet rotates, or something."

"Right now, the priority is prepping to leave in two days. We still have to get the shipment of new mechs loaded. Fifty suits, spare parts, and plenty of ammunition are on the way as we speak, along with a replicator from the Yatarward Industries' main plant. Thanks to Marteen, we'll be able to make our own eventually."

"Just doing my part, Commodore." Marteen grinned. He knew Harmon was still sore at him for making the title stick among the members of Salvage Fleet.

* * * * *

Chapter Three

In the Glayver System, away from prying eyes and in a room swept for digital devices, a meeting was taking place. There were ten beings in the room. Most of them were human, but there were several other races present as well. One of them was a race that had been cut off from their home world thirty years prior.

The Belvakett were a particularly cruel race. They loved to fight and could barely be restrained whenever they left their ships to enter spaceports and supply points. Skriflair was the leader of a mercenary company comprised of eleven Belvakett ships. All of the ships had been cut off from their home world when the Bith had closed the gate because of their use of nuclear weapons. Since the closure, he and his ships had traveled to another part of the galaxy to work their trade and avoid the Rincah, a race that would attack them on sight because of their involvement in a civil war in the Rincah system.

They had all agreed to meet because the human, Jifton Gregor, had promised them a prize none of them could turn down. There was a star system ripe for the taking, abandoned until recently, with shipyards, spaceports, and defense platforms intact, as well as an inhabitable planet. It was a mercenary company's dream. They could work together and build a sanctuary system for mercenaries that might or might not skirt common galactic law. It could also be a haven for large pirate fleets. The opportunities were endless, and as long as they didn't break the gate laws, it would be perfect.

Skriflair liked Jifton Gregor, despite the fact he was a weak, soft-skinned being. He liked the way Gregor thought, so he'd agreed to follow his lead several times in the past. If Jifton Gregor thought they could take the system before a proper defense was in place, he would follow him once again. Gregor never took a chance that would end in defeat, and he wasn't afraid to fight dirty if the need arose, either. It was something Skriflair really liked about his leadership style.

"I had my guy do some research. You two are right, the Bith have announced new gate coordinates will be posted soon. Are you sure Tomeral only has seven of those damn salvaged ships left?" Captain Gregor asked the men sitting at the end of the table again.

"I'm sure," Grant Lowantha said. "We took a scan right before we slipped out the gate in the scout ship."

"The battle was nearly over when we left," agreed Hawthorne, his speech no longer affected by injury. He'd had his teeth and nose repaired at the first stop they'd made to resupply the small scout ship. The credit account they'd accessed to pay for it hadn't been discovered and closed out by the new officers running Tretrayon Fleet Intelligence. Hawthorne figured Lowantha had several accounts not even the old intel officers knew about.

"What about the Kashkal?" Ploth asked.

Gregor glanced over at the man to his left with an aggravated look. *He* was asking the questions here. Skriflair noticed he didn't say anything, though, since they needed Ploth. Ploth was originally from Bentwick and ran a mercenary company called the Harbingers, comprised of two Q-ships. Not only did the huge converted freighter ships he owned have decent shielding and some offensive capabilities, each ship's hold had been converted to fighter bays, and Ploth had over two hundred and fifty fighters under his control. The fighters were a mix of several different types, but they were well maintained by the Harbingers.

"From what we could determine," answered Lowantha, "the contract with the Kashkal was to defend the Tretrayon System. From everything I've read, the Kashka and his people will move on, looking for a home world. They're probably halfway across the galaxy by now."

"Good," said one of the other non-human attendees. "We cannot defeat the Kashkal. Everyone knows this."

Skriflair looked over at the speaker. Micktorah was a Bleeve, a race with eight long limbs, which looked like a cross between a guiffle bug and a narfleek. He shuddered inwardly. He hated narfleek. The creepy things used to ease down their webs into his bed, when he was a youngling, and bite him all over before he woke up. *Brrrr!*

"A falsehood spread throughout the galaxy!" Skriflair stated dismissively. "If they were that good, there would be more of them." Skriflair reached up unconsciously with a claw and scratched between the scales on the side of his face. His "alligator" face, as Gregor had once told him, though he had no idea what an alligator was. *Stupid narfleek.* He itched just thinking about them.

"Well, I think the chance for success is solid," stated Gregor. "The Tretrayon Fleet, what's left of it, will stay in the Tretrayon System for defense and repairs. We can take on seven ships easily. Between us, we have thirty ships and over three hundred fighters. I know there were a couple of other mercenary ships involved in the Tretrayon defense, but they've undoubtedly taken their credits and left."

"What about defense platforms?" Skriflair asked. "You have no way of knowing if the system has them."

"It doesn't matter," said Captain Gregor. "Even if it does, and they're still in operation, Tomeral can't have them up. There'll be so much traffic coming into the new system, he won't be able to set them on automatic. He has to turn them off. We're not going to hit the system as soon as the gate coordinates are announced; we'll give it time to get busy."

"What if he realizes that and has them all manned, so his people can make decisions firsthand?" Ploth asked. "I would."

"I would, as well," chimed in Drooval, snapping his beak in a loud crack to emphasize his point.

Gregor looked over at the Gleekum pirate—surprised Drooval had agreed with Ploth; usually the big avian captain argued everything—and said, "I've met Tomeral; he's young, and obviously no seasoned tactician." Gregor continued, "I think he got lucky a few times, nothing more. Their ships will still have considerable damage, so he may not even have all of them at his disposal. Here's what we'll do…" He laid out his plan.

* * *

"Are you sure that's everyone?" Harmon asked Jayneen. The AI had ensured every ship heading toward the gate had Tretrayon designations broadcasting. The last thing they needed was for the remaining defensive platforms in the system to fire missiles at them upon entry. Clip had ensured the platforms would recognize Tretrayon ships as friendly.

"I am quite sure," she answered, unfazed by his question, "down to the smallest shuttle and all the fighters. You know, Rick Kashka asked me the same thing."

"I don't blame him," Clip volunteered over the open link. Once again, he was on the TDF *United,* a gift from the Tretrayon System to Tomeral and Associates. The former vacation cruise ship housed two thousand beings comfortably, and Clip and Zerith were both over there, enjoying the swimming pools and buffets. *Gotta rename that thing,* Harmon thought.

"Can you imagine, getting thiss close to a home world and loossing many sshipss to defenssive platformss?" the small Prithmar said. "By the way, thiss sship iss out of dill pickless."

"You probably ate them all yourself," chimed in Mike Bradford from the *Cube.* "Where in the hell do you put all that food, anyway? You ain't got enough ass to hold it all."

"To be honest, I've wondered that myself," cut in Rick Kashka from his flagship. "I understand about 'rest when you can, eat when you can' to stay prepared for battle, but there should be limits. I observed you during our trip to the Krift System; it's an amazing feat." He continued, "Thank you, Lieutenant Commander Jayneen, for ensuring the transponders are broadcasting correctly."

"You are quite welcome, sir," answered the AI.

"Harmon, before we make this transition," Marteen cut in from the Bentwick-designed light battlecruiser *Desert Shade,* "can you ask the princess if she'll have a little word with Hank and Stan?"

"I can, but don't let her hear you call her that," Harmon said, laughing. "You know she prefers Kyla, or chief warrant officer if it's all business. What about?"

"Well, since they're going through attached to this ship in their frigate," Marteen said, "to be honest, I'm kinda worried they might try to walk the hulls and come down to my ship."

"What?" Clip exclaimed. "While we're traveling in alter reality? I told you that was a ship of fools."

"Captain Marteen," Kyla cut in from engineering, "I will speak to them. That will not be happening, rest assured. I would also like a word with you on a private channel. Flag ship engineering, out."

"Aw, Hell," Twiggy drawled from the carrier *Windswept*. "Ah wouldn't want to be you, pardner."

"I agree," chimed in Captain Opawn from her new command on the bridge of the other medium battlecruiser in Salvage Fleet, *Desert Wind*.

"Aye, and that's one I'd not cross, given the choice," agreed Captain Rogers.

"She kinda scares me," said Captain Cameron quietly. "Me, too," added his executive officer, Ralph, from behind him.

"Harmon," Marteen pleaded, "can I pull rank just this once?"

"You've lost your mind if you think I'm getting involved." Harmon laughed again. "Besides, you don't outrank her, regardless of the rank on the uniform. She's an Associate."

"Oh, squat." Marteen moaned. "I gotta get used to being out of the fleet. This is low tide man, low tide."

"Trust me," Brickle cut in. "Apologize profusely and take the dressing down like a man."

At this everyone on the link laughed, including the commanders of the rest of the fleet who had been in listening mode only, especially since it was a Caldivar telling Marteen to 'take it like a man.' He'd probably said 'like a male' or something similar in his native language, but the translation came out 'man.'

* * * * *

Chapter Four

They came through the gate into Salvage System, and the first thing Harmon noticed was it was the same as they'd left it. Quiet. As the rest of Salvage Fleet came through behind them, he had the Leethog officer at the helm guide the entire fleet off to port, to allow the Kashkal Fleet to come in and head straight toward their new home, Evermore, the fourth planet from the star. It was well within the optimal zone to maintain life, and it was close to the third planet, now named Salvage, which had an atmosphere and gravity almost equal to Tretra and the standard for all humans, Earth.

"Well, we made it again," Clip said. "I wonder when the Bith will arrive to service the gate. We roll the dice every time we use it."

"He iss right," Zerith agreed. "We could end up in the nearest system, and there'ss no telling where that iss."

"They're supposed to contact us before they arrive to ensure no one's scheduled to leave the system," Harmon answered with a shrug. "We'll just go ahead with our plans and wait. Hopefully it'll be before we need to send someone for resupply."

"I will monitor the Net for any news from the Bith," Jayneen volunteered.

Harmon didn't answer her; he was quiet, looking at the main screen. "You know," Harmon said to no one in particular, "I bet the night sky is beautiful on both planets because of their proximity to each other."

"I would agree, sir," said Brickle from the engineering console.

"Can I see? Can I, Uncle Harmon?" Bahroot asked.

"Sure," Harmon said, holding the tablet up so the young AI could use its camera lens to see the main screen, where the operations officer had brought up a simulation of all the planets orbiting the star.

"Cool!" Bahroot said. "I bet I could see it better if you let me link to the ship."

"I don't think we're going to find out," Harmon said. "When your mom says you're ready for that, and not sooner."

"I tell you what," Clip said, standing beside Harmon, "I may let you link to a shuttle sometime when we go to the surface of the planet. How's that?"

"Really cool!" exclaimed Bahroot. "Can I fly it?"

"Creator protect us!" exclaimed Jayneen. "They grow up so fast."

"Aww, I could do it," said Bahroot.

"I have no doubt," Harmon said, shaking his head, "but I don't think even *I* am ready for that."

"Commodore Tomeral, Rick Kashka," came over the comm unit in his chair.

"What's up, Rick?" Harmon said. He'd been expecting a call and had his comms set to receive directly.

"If some of your ships will take first rotation guarding the gate, I would be indebted even more than I am now, if that is possible."

"We got it, buddy," Harmon answered. "Take all your ships in-system and orbit your new home. We'll cover the gate for a few weeks. Let me know if you need anything. Out here."

Harmon watched the sensors and saw the entire Kashkal Fleet accelerate until they were near battle speed. They were anxious, and he couldn't blame them. He knew, once they were in orbit, that Rick would already have a plan to map and explore the planet to determine where the first landing area would be. As far as the entire operation to get his race to the surface and set up domiciles and farms and everything else went…there was probably a plan, hundreds if not thousands of years old, just waiting to be set in motion.

"It iss amazing," said Zerith, voicing what every being in Salvage Fleet was thinking as they observed the Kashkal Fleet. "They have a home."

"Yeah man, it's cool," Clip said. "It's going to be interesting to see what type of livestock they produce, besides the limited amount they raise on their tender ships. I got a look at the inventory, when Jayneen and I were looking for the mix they need to breathe, to see if the sample I brought back would work. They have banks and banks of embryos stored. I wonder if they'll use artificial incubation for all of them, or just the initial breeders. I bet Twiggy would know more about that, or I could ask Urlak."

"That reminds me," Harmon said, sitting upright. He used his comms unit to call Urlak LeeKa. "Diamond Squadron, *Salvage Title*."

"Yes, Commodore?" Urlak replied almost immediately.

"I'm officially giving you and your squadron two weeks leave time," Harmon said. "Go chase your families."

"Yes, sir," came the reply. "Thank you."

"Oh, and Urlak," Harmon said.

"Sir?" Urlak asked.

"When you reach orbit, stack all four ships using the locking struts, and just have one skeleton crew rotate." Harmon told him.

"Excellent idea, sir," the LeeKa said. "No matter how much I think I know, there is always more to learn. Diamond Squadron, out."

"That's a good dude right there," Clip observed.

"Yeah, I like him," agreed Harmon. "I can't believe he asked his father if he and his crews could continue to be a part of Salvage Fleet."

"Every member of all four ships asked to stay with him," Jayneen said, "even the young ones. I have been studying his leadership style as well."

"He's a good one to study," Big Jon volunteered from behind Harmon. "Solid leadership."

"I think the fact that the world Clip discovered was right here in Salvage System had a lot to do with Rick's answer," Harmon said, "but I'm glad Rick signed off on it."

"*Salvage Title, Got Rocks,*" came a voice over the comms.

"Tulog," Harmon answered, "what can I do for you?"

"Permission to break off from *Ore What?*" requested the Caldivar in charge of the two ore haulers Tomeral and Associates owned. He was a grizzled old miner, though to just call him a miner was an understatement. His whole career had been successful, and when Rinto had contacted him and offered him first crack at a system that hadn't been mined in modern times, he'd jumped at the chance.

If the system panned out the way Tulog hoped, he planned to move his whole operation to Salvage System. As of now, he'd hand-picked some of his employees and was using Tomeral and Associates' haulers, because his company's ships hadn't had their transponders changed over yet. It was almost a foregone conclusion that his company would relocate, especially after Harmon had given him his thoughts on mining in the system.

"I'd like to get started near the fifth planet; those rings look promising. Later we'll check the moons around the sixth planet; two of the five look good on our sensors."

"Granted, have at it," Harmon said over the comm. He then turned to Clip and Zerith. "Who named those ore haulers, anyway?"

"The brothers," Clip and Zerith said at the same time.

"Figures." Harmon laughed.

"What do you think they'll find?" Clip asked. He was a genius, but he'd never bothered to look into mining, much less studied it.

"I know, I know!" said Bahroot from his slate.

Harmon grinned. "You think you know? Sure, tell him."

"Mr. Tulog…is he a Mister? Do you call Caldivar Mister if you are not sure of their title?" the young AI asked the group.

"Mister is fine," his dad told him. "Go ahead."

"Ok, thanks. Mr. Tulog will find places that have been mined out, and places that were in the process of being mined. He'll find all sorts of mining equipment waiting to be restarted, restored, and used," Bahroot answered happily.

"Let's say you're right," Harmon questioned him, "Why do you think that?"

"Well," began the young AI, "because the system was closed to the rest of the galaxy, but they were still building ships and making missiles. The raw material had to come from somewhere. Here in the system is the only place it could come from. If Grandpa Rinto were here, he would bet on it."

"I believe he iss right. He iss learning thingss fasst," Zerith said as he peeled a piece of joobla fruit. "Perssonally, I think it comess from hiss mother'ss sside."

* * *

One week later, Rick Kashka stood near the ramp as the shuttle pilot prepared to drop it. After orbiting Evermore many times, and then concentrating on several areas using the information his scientists had provided, he'd decided where his people would begin the first colony. He and an entire platoon of warriors would escort a ground team of environmental specialists as they tested the atmosphere firsthand.

All of the Kashkal were suited up. Multiple tests would have to be conducted before Rick would give them the order to take their helmets off. The ramp slowly came down and allowed the light from the system's star to shine into the shuttle. Rick heard a collective gasp over the open link. He blinked a little in the bright light and looked out over the grasses waving gently in the breeze toward a forest that started with just a few trees and thickened as his gaze moved up toward the mountain peaks. About three quarters of the way up the mountains, the forest thinned out, exposing the rock face that topped them. The tallest had what appeared to be snow covering its peak.

Rick walked down the ramp, everyone behind him waiting, and stopped just before stepping off. He examined his immediate surroundings, willing himself to concentrate. They were above a large flowing river of dark water, about two hundred yards up a gently sloping hill. The pilot had landed in an area that was level for about a thousand yards. It was the site where Rick wanted the Kashkal to erect the first domiciles and start the final chapter of their eternal search for home.

Seeing no immediate danger or signs of wildlife, he stepped off the ramp and felt solid ground. Feeling that the gravity was almost the same as the level maintained throughout his fleet, he bent and ran his hand over the top of the grass, though he couldn't feel it through his gloves. The act in and of itself just felt right. Grinning to himself, he walked several steps away from the shuttle, raised his hand, and signaled to his team to secure the area. The warriors exited the ship quickly and set up a perimeter. They were followed by the scientists carrying their testing equipment. This time they wouldn't use small hand-held testers. Rick wanted to be absolutely sure before they removed their protection.

Finally he spoke, and everyone looked over at him, including the pilot, who had come out of the shuttle and was standing beside the ramp, pistol in hand, just in case. "Run the tests and verify it, but I have never felt this sure of anything before."

The link was quiet for many minutes. Rick spent the time walking the perimeter of his warriors. He stopped on the side farthest from the shuttle and stared, with the young Kashkal positioned there, at several small creatures grazing near a tree. The area under the tree had a few bare spots, allowing them to see the grey-striped creatures. One of them leapt into the air and fluttered into the tree limbs, out of sight among the fluffy blue leaves.

"Kashka," he heard over the link. Rick looked around and saw the leader of the security team with an arm up.

He walked over to see what the Sha was now pointing at. When he got there, he saw a small bug of some sort had settled on the left boot of Jareek Sha. It stayed in place and gently moved its translucent red wings up and down, without a care.

"Making friends already, Jareek Sha?" Rick Kashka asked. He placed a hand on the Sha's shoulder briefly and walked toward the scientists and their equipment.

"Kashka," came the lead scientist's voice over the open link, "we ran the tests three times."

"And?" Rick prodded.

"The atmosphere is nearly *perfect*," the environmental specialist said. Rick heard the collective gasp again. The lead scientist continued, "The only time we get results this close to perfect is when we test new filters and equipment on our atmosphere-inducing machines on the tenders. You were right."

Rick looked around and saw every member of the confirmation team looking at him. He reached up, twisted his helmet, and took it off. He took a couple of breaths and noticed he smelled something in the air. After a lifetime of breathing a manufactured atmosphere, it was easy to notice, but it wasn't unpleasant. He smelled the soil, the grasses, the leaves in the trees as the wind blew through them, and something sweet, like the blossoms in the farming laboratories on the tender ships. He smelled the scent of life—and it was glorious.

Rick held his helmet near his mouth and gave the command that would be spoken of for eternity among the Kashkal. "Remove your helmets, feel the wind on your face, and breathe deeply, for it is the smell of home. The search is over."

* * * * *

Chapter Five

"That looks like the spot, then," Harmon agreed. Jayneen had informed him that her assessment was the same as the team of scientists he'd hired to run tests on the surface of Salvage. "It's one of the energy sources still emanating from the surface, it's near a water supply, and some ruins can be seen on the drone feeds."

Harmon turned to Big Jon. "Put together a security team. Include Sergeant Kyth and Corporal Trang in their mechs. I'm not going in mine, but I want to have some fire power with us."

"I'm on it, sir," the sergeant major said and headed off the bridge.

"Good idea, sir," said Corporal Brink.

He stood watch on the bridge near the spot Corporal Bahroot used to stand. He had an idea of the capabilities of a mech, now that he and his platoon had started training in them under the supervision of Sergeant Kyth and his young assistant trainer, Corporal Trang. They were the last two mech pilots from the original five Harmon had hired.

Two of the pilots had been killed in action on the plateau, and the other one was now the executive officer of *Desert Shade*. His mech, as well as Marteen's, was with them on their ship. Evelyn, Twiggy, Gunny, and JoJo's new one were all on board the carrier *Windswept* with them.

"Can't take any chances," Harmon said. "There's no telling what type of predator has risen to the top of the food chain here."

"Don't get eaten, Uncle Harmon," Bahroot said from the slate sitting on the arm of his chair. "There were creatures on Plaython Five that ate a whole team of explorers, and they had weapons and everything."

"Really?" Harmon asked the young AI, "and when was this?"

"Two hundred and six years ago," it answered. "It was a team from Bentwick. They were exploring a new system after the Bith moved a gate. It's true."

"I see your mom has allowed you a little more access to the Galaxy Net," Harmon observed. "I'll be sure not to get eaten."

"I open a little more each day," Jayneen told Harmon. "Right now, he is learning all of human history, including the colonies in the Solar System and all the human systems throughout the galaxy. I am careful to observe all he does on the Net and point out relevant information, dates, and answer his questions to the best of my ability."

"He knows more about human history than I do now, that's for sure," Clip volunteered.

"Will I get to pilot the shuttle down to the planet?" Bahroot asked.

"Do you think you're ready?" Clip asked him.

"I know I can fly it with no problem," answered the young AI, "but if there's an issue or malfunction, I'm not sure I'll make the right decision. Perhaps I shouldn't pilot the first trip to Salvage. I can wait."

"That iss a wise deccission," said Zerith as he tried his best to keep bright red plum juice from dripping down his chin.

"I'll call Hank and Stan and ask them questions about ship emergencies, so I know what to do. Then I'll be ready to fly it next time," said Bahroot, proud of himself for figuring out the answer to his dilemma.

"Oh...Frost," Clip said while looking over at his friends, then he looked down and shook his head.

Harmon smiled and reached for his comm. "Salvage Fleet, maintain the schedule. Captain Opawn has the Fleet while I go to the surface with the exploration team. Break. Captain Cameron, be prepared to make your run on the laboratory location once we find it. We'll go to the colony site first, then we'll make a trip to the research facility Jayneen was able to locate from the files on the spaceport. We'll give it a flyover, and then call you in."

"Roger, sir, I have the Fleet," Captain Opawn answered. "We'll maintain patrols near the gate and the spaceports."

"Ok, we're moving to a low orbit now," Cameron answered.

"Jayneen," Harmon asked as he rose to go to the bay, "how much do you have mapped now?"

"Using the shuttles on remote, I have mapped twenty-two percent of the planet," she answered. "I have the continent chosen for the first site completed."

"So, on that continent at least," Harmon asked, "there's been no indication of a predator larger than the ones you showed us?"

"I have not detected any," answered Jayneen. "Even with magnification, all the images and videos show nothing larger than the standard Earth wolf. Granted, they had eight legs and moved fast in the video we have of a pack of them taking down a grazing creature, so they are still considered dangerous until we learn more about them. I have not seen evidence of them near the proposed site to-day."

* * *

Harmon removed his helmet and prepared to take his suit off. All the tests indicated the air was fine to breathe. He looked over and watched Big Jon, Clip, and Zerith do the same. Big Jon took off his helmet, opting to remain in the battle armor he wore. Once they put their suits on the shuttle, he turned his attention to the remnants of the dam nearby.

"So the power source is inside that thing?" Harmon asked.

"That'ss what I am reading," Zerith verified. "Whatever power iss being generated by the one turbine still working iss just being grounded out in the rubble. It iss of no usse to uss."

"The small fusion plant we brought with us will provide more than that dam did when it was new," Clip added. "We'll probably find similar sites to this one at the other sources of power the sensors showed us."

Harmon looked around. From what he could tell, the planet was beautiful. It was wild with overgrowth, and he could barely make out where some of the structures were. Over on the airfield, the grass had almost covered the pads, with several mounds indicating where nature had overtaken the craft left there. It was a good location for a settlement, but it would be a while before the area was cleared. There was so much that had to be done. They didn't even have an idea of weather patterns yet. Harmon shook his head. *I may have bitten off more than I can chew,* he thought. *What was I thinking?*

"Clip," Harmon said, "we're going to have to find someone to head this whole colonizing thing up. I may be the system president, but this is all way beyond me. *Lightyears* beyond me."

"I hear ya, man," Clip said, looking around himself.

"Harmon, I agree," Jayneen said from the slate Clip was holding. "There are ruins all over the planet. I estimate the population twenty-two hundred years ago to have been around one hundred million. Compared to Earth or many other planets, that is not many—it may have had something to do with the birth rate and life expectancy of the Grithelaons—but it is still a very large number.

"I will know more once I connect to the system in the shipbuilding facilities in orbit," she continued. "Perhaps I can determine if they originated here on the planet, or if they themselves were colonists. That information was not among my files, nor in my memories."

"We may need to move talking to the Withaloo up on the schedule of things to do," Harmon said. "If it works out, they can be the foundation here, and handle things on the planet as more and more beings come into the system to try their luck on a new world. We'll have enough to do defending the system for a while against pirates and some of the races that'll try to swoop in. You know there'll be some that will try."

"You're not even sure they'll work out," Clip said. "I wonder if…"

"Commodore," a voice said from the comm, "we have a problem near the airfield."

"Headed that way," Harmon answered and began moving with Sergeant Major Jontilictick.

Just then Harmon heard the distinctive sounds of laser fire and a howling wail. He and Big Jon began running. "Security to the airfield, everyone; move out, now!" Harmon called over the link. "Clip, secure the technicians on the shuttle."

Harmon rounded a mound of what could only have been a large craft and saw several members of the security team back-to-back, attempting to keep a circling pack of the eight-legged beasts away from them. Two members of security were down near the largest mound on the ancient airfield. Harmon could see the dark opening of a cave close to ground level.

He watched as one of his troops shot a beast with his laser rifle, and it only slowed the beast for a moment, enraging it, as the beam bounced off the layered shell. It turned, sank low, and looked as if it was going to charge the two. Big Jon stopped, aimed, and took a long shot with his magnetic-kinetic rifle. The three-round burst made the creature stagger back, turn, and run toward them. Several yards later, it plowed into the ground, unmoving.

Harmon looked back toward the ring and tried to count; there were at least twenty of them, circling and howling intermittently. It didn't look good. Everyone on the security team had laser weapons. Big Jon and the two mechs were the only ones with kinetic weapons.

Out the corner of his eye Harmon saw a shadow pass over him and heard the unmistakable sound of the thrusters of mechs in flight. The mech team had arrived from where they'd been, near the dam, with the two scientists who were taking readings. It was a good distance away, so Harmon knew they must have used a combination of sprinting and jumps to get there so quickly.

Sergeant Kyth took aim, fired a sustained burst of railgun rounds, and knocked several of the creatures to the ground. They didn't move again, and the pack closed ranks in the circle. Corporal Trang moved closer to the two troops so she could escort them away from the mound. When she got close to them, almost on cue, the far side of the ring of beasts rushed toward them.

Trang fired her railgun in a sweeping motion, killing four before they got to them. Kyth took careful aim so he wouldn't hit the troops and killed three more. The combined laser fire from the other troops that had arrived deterred several from getting to the troops between the mechs, and the railguns finally took them down. Big Jon dropped the last two with a three-round burst into each of them.

"Medic! Check the two who are down," Harmon called out. In no time, the big Yalteen was beside them. She started working on one right away. She let Harmon know the other was beyond hope with a look and shake of her head.

"Squat! Big Jon, get two people to help move him to the shuttle, move everyone away from that den, and get whoever's supposed to be studying the indigenous life down here right away," Harmon ordered. "Send the five mech-trained Bolts down with the research team, and the rest armed with kinetic weapons. We need to know everything about these things and why they attacked."

"If they're territorial, at least we won't have to worry about another pack nearby for a while," Clip said from the shuttle.

"I just hope there's nothing here higher on the food chain than these things," Harmon said, frustrated at the loss of life. "I know every planet with life has predators; I was hoping what we found wouldn't pose a danger to anyone."

"Let uss hope the Kasshkal do not run into a ssimilar ssituation," Zerith said.

* * *

"Sir," the communications officer said to Harmon, "you have a direct connect call coming through from the Planet Bith."

They were back on *Salvage Title*, getting ready to head toward the shipbuilding facilities in orbit. "Thanks, Jim," Harmon said, looking up from his slate. "Put it on for me."

On the main screen, a Bith looked at Harmon from behind a large desk. "President Tomeral." He spoke slowly, like Representative Garlog did. "Greetings. I am Director Marrot, head of gate maintenance. I am calling you to inform you of the upcoming maintenance of the gate in Salvage System."

"Well, hello from this end of the galaxy," Harmon answered. "I've been expecting your call.

"The maintenance ships will arrive in exactly forty-eight of your hours," continued the director. "If there are no unexpected delays, it should only require forty-eight hours to run system checks and re-place any components."

"Sounds great," Harmon said. "Wait, did you say *ships?*"

"That is correct," answered the director. "Six ships will enter the system. Two will come together with the gate between them, and they will rotate around the gate as one while they perform their tasks. The other four will position themselves between the gate and the system itself and run sensor blockers. It is standard procedure. All ships in the system must maintain a distance of five hours' travel from the gate."

"I understand," Harmon said with a raised eyebrow toward Clip and Zerith. "I'll inform everyone on my end."

"I must also inform you, standard rates now apply to gate and network usage," the director finished in a businesslike manner. "Once maintenance is complete, the gate coordinates will be posted on the Galaxy Net per the Gate Law. We look forward to your business."

After the connection ended, Harmon looked over at Zerith and said, "Standard rates apply."

"That iss not funny," Zerith stated. He didn't like to see credit leave the company's accounts.

"Speaking of credit," Clip asked, "what are we looking at?"

"We have enough capital to operate at our current level for ssix more monthss," Zerith said.

"Six months?" Harmon asked. "That's it?

"We have a great many beings employed," Zerith explained. "Ssuppliess, ammunition, the little repairss we were able to complete, all cost creditss. Life iss not a free ride, my friend."

"He is right, Harmon," Jayneen agreed. "The credit we had left after hiring the mercenaries was returned to the Tretrayon government. We do have some income from the deals Zerith worked out with salvage companies helping to clean up the wreckage from the invasions, but it is a percentage of their profits, and while it will be a stream of income for some time, it is not enough to maintain Tomeral and Associates indefinitely."

"Let's just hope Tulog Mining finds what I think they will," Harmon said. "Since Tomeral and Associates has all the mining rights claimed in this system, whatever their profit, we'll get ten percent of it."

"Tulog went for that?" Clip asked.

"It was that deal, or I was going to hire miners, pay their salaries, and keep all the profit," Harmon answered. "He jumped on the deal; otherwise his company wouldn't have any of it. He knew he'd make more credit than in any other system where he had competition already in place. Don't get me wrong, competition is great. He has one year, and then others will be allowed to mine planets in the system. Besides, most systems charge more than that in fees and taxes."

"I know about taxes," said Bahroot. "I learned all about them. Did you know some taxes are collected as raw material instead of credit?"

At this Harmon, jumped up out of his seat. "Bahroot, you're a genius!" he exclaimed.

"I can't be a genius, Uncle Harmon," Bahroot explained. "That would mean comparing me on a scale with, in your case, humans. There will never be a human with the capacity to learn as fast, recollect that learning as quickly, and perform multiple tasks while learning more, as I can. That is not a fair comparison to true biological geniuses. I would never do that to a genius. They are rare and impress me very much, given their limited capacities. The only comparison one could make about me is with my mom."

Harmon laughed. "It was a figure of speech, Bahroot."

"A chip off the old block," Clip said. "Now why in the frost did you jump up like you're crazy, anyway?"

"Because the Grithelaons probably used taxation and a monetary system of some form. After they were blocked from gate usage, they lost the Net and the credit system," Harmon explained. "I'm willing to bet there are vaults somewhere, or the remains of vaults, and where there are vaults, there are precious metals and stones, and who knows what else."

Clip turned toward Jayneen's console and asked, "Jayneen, can you modify programing on the shuttles to search for them? Maybe look for diamonds or whatever?"

"I can," Jayneen said. "I can even modify the sensors on *Salvage Title* to look for certain metals while we orbit. I will start with heavy metals and locate mines. Gold has been found on most planets in the galaxy. There are many systems that hold it in high regard."

"Yess," Zerith said. "There are sseveral metalss that are very important in many industries."

Harmon sat back down. "I have a good feeling about this," he said. "We may not have to worry about credit ever again."

"Oncce we have enough put away, we can open mining on the planet to beingss who come to sstake claimss," Zerith said. "It iss only right."

"But you'll have to worry about thieves, grave robbers, and smugglers," Bahroot volunteered. "Where there's easy credit to be made, there will be bad people. I learned that studying humans."

"Squat," Harmon said. "Thanks for that little bit of information, too, Bahroot. One more thing to figure out.

"Jayneen, could you shut down the defensive platforms in the system?" Harmon asked. "The last thing we need is for them to fire on the Bith. Not to mention all the other ships that'll start coming, full of beings looking to make a future here."

* * * * *

Chapter Six

"**S**alvage Title, Basher," came over the comms on the bridge.

"Go ahead, Dustin," Harmon said. He was stood in front of his chair on the bridge.

"Cameron wanted me to ask you if he could make his run now," Captain Rogers said.

"Why didn't he call me?" Harmon wondered out loud.

"One of his crewmembers called me," said Captain Rogers. "We keep a channel open between us. It seems Cameron and Ralph are doing everything they can to keep *Sweet Pea* from burning into the surface. They came down into a thunderstorm of epic proportions, and a wee bit of lightning has struck the ship. He thinks he can make the run and get out of there before he has to shut down another fusion plant and engine."

"What?" Harmon said, alarmed. "If it's too dangerous, tell them to abort and we'll plan another day."

"I did, lad," the Rincah captain said, frustrated. "He says if he hits the remains of the biological facility area today, it will burn it all to a crisp without the risk of burning miles and miles of forest, because of the weather."

"That does make sense," agreed Harmon. "Have him make the run and get the frost out of there."

Harmon looked over at Clip and shook his head. If it wasn't one thing, it was another. For the last three weeks, they'd been orbiting the planet, locating possible vault locations. There had been one other attack by the creatures, but it had been a small pack, and Corporal Brink and his platoon had taken care of it with no casualties.

They'd been able to locate two caches of gold and precious stones. Harmon had sent Private First Class Hroth down with a team to blow the entrance to them and bring back some in a shuttle. Twiggy was piloting the shuttle from *Windswept*, and he'd sent back video. Zerith estimated the precious stones from that haul alone would keep the company running for another year. There were more locations to check as well, so as long as they could keep the teams safe, it would work out.

"*Cube, Salvage Title*," Harmon called, after checking his comm to ensure he was calling Mike and Mike.

"It's your dime," Mike answered. Harmon hit a button and his image came on the main screen.

"What?" Harmon asked. "What's a dime?"

"It's…ah, never mind," Mike said. "It's off an old entertainment clip from Earth. What can I do for you, Commodore?"

"I just wanted to see what you thought about the proposal I gave you?" Harmon asked.

"Well," Mike said, "Bradford and I talked it over. We think we can park the *Cube* here, near the facilities, and using a combination of our employees and yours, finish the repairs on your two ships, *Sweet Pea*, and *Basher* in less than a month. That's *if* your lieutenant commander can put Earth Common, Leethog, and Smilp translations on all the computers and equipment we use, and then transfer the operating programs for the various systems to the ships."

"She assures me she can," Harmon said. "That's pretty fast. Are you sure?"

"Oh, we're sure," Bradford chimed in. "There are a thousand Smilps on the *Cube* and a hundred and fifty other employees. Plus, they work fast. You just have to stay out of their way. Once they figure out the replicators here, look out."

"Once all the repairs are made across the fleet, we can start work on the first two of the four sitting in the shipyards," Mike informed him, "but we'll need more raw material. With a steady supply, we can continue building those ships."

"That won't be a problem," Harmon said. "I'll be buying it from myself, kind of, but it looks like Tulog found the site that a lot of the material you're working with now came from. He has some of the equipment working, and his own stuff just arrived. Within the next three weeks, they'll be hard at it."

"*Desert Wind, Salvage Title.*" Harmon used the comms once again, and like before, he hit the button to put a visual on the main screen.

"Commodore," answered Captain Opawn, smiling from her bridge.

"We're getting ready to take our turn patrolling near the gate," Harmon said, looking over at the lieutenant at the helm. "You've been running the rotations; where do you want us?"

"Well, sir," Opawn answered, "I've got *Windswept* and her escorts riding high, with the Diamond Squadron and *Cactus Bloom* making sweeps. If you'll relieve me with your escorts, I'll head in with *Desert Night*, and we'll get those repairs finished in the shipyards. Also, we have six Kashkal ships doing maneuvers between the fifth and sixth planets; they are available if we need them."

"Roger," Harmon said. "My tactical officer is tracking all that. How's the traffic been?"

"Well, we've had several ships come through," she answered. "The Nilta went out-system after she determined there were sufficient plants with blooms on two islands to warrant setting up shop. She was excited about the new flavors and said she'd be back in a month with another ship and equipment to get started."

"I saw a couple of construction companies from Joth came into the system," Harmon said. "I know one of the captains of the ships they arrived in. They've already started clearing ruins and fabricating buildings. Before you know it, there'll be a town or two down there."

"Any sign of the Withaloo?" Clip asked over Harmon's shoulder.

"Not yet." Captain Opawn laughed. "I'd have called you if there was. An old freighter came through a couple of hours ago. Its registration reads the name *Lange*, and from what we could see on our sensors, the ship wasn't maintained very well; they stopped to make obvious repairs. I called the captain; he said he has a combination of goods to sell or trade, and passengers who want a new start. He's not much different than what we'd see come into the Tretrayon system sometimes, a down-on-his-luck ship owner trying to make a few credits any way he can."

"There's going to be all kinds of beings coming to Salvage, hoping to make their fortunes." Harmon sighed. "From what Clip has told me, it's always the same thing when new colonies or systems open up."

"Do you want me to hold in place until you get here?" she asked.

"No, I think we're fine," Harmon said. "We'll be out there in a few days; we can pass each other as we go. I'll wave at you."

* * *

"Ma'am," said the communications officer, Ensign Shaith, on the bridge of *Windswept*, "we have a call coming in from Charlie Flight...isn't that a Bentwick fighter squadron?"

"Bentwick?" asked Captain Evelyn Stacey. "From *Desert Shade*? What are they doing way out here? *Desert Shade* won't be on site for another day."

"We're not picking up their transponders, and their ships aren't showing on my sensors, either," volunteered Lieutenant Gailtilneratt.

"They couldn't have popped up out of the black, Gail," said Lieutenant Joslyn Whaley.

"They did, JoJo," said Gail, tapping her screen.

"Well, put it through," Evelyn said.

"*Windswept*, Charlie Flight One, over," came a human voice with a distinctive Tretrayon accent, one from the country.

"This is *Windswept* Actual, go ahead, Charlie Flight One," Evelyn said.

"Well, hello there, ma'am, I didn't think I'd be chatting with the captain," said the voice. "We got us a situation out here."

"Do tell," Evelyn said, relaxing a little. She recognized the accent, and the flight leader didn't sound as if it was an actual emergency.

"Well, we were out here running in the black, doing a little long-range training, so you shouldn't be able to see us. Anyway, ol' Jimmie done decided he's about to squat himself," explained the flight leader.

"Hey!" cut in another voice. "What the frost, LT? You don't have to tell the whole system my business!"

Everyone on the bridge knew this voice had to be from someone from Joth, by the language. The bridge was full of snickers and giggles. Evelyn did her best to hold in a laugh, herself.

"I ought to let ya sit in it when it happens, Jimmie," said the flight leader. "Anyways, ma'am you reckon you could let us park these things in your bay for a spell, 'til Jimmie gets it out of his system? Dang fool knows better than to drink that Prithmar beer the night before long-range training."

"Roger, Charlie Flight, bring them in," Evelyn said with a casual voice.

"Will do, Ma'am," the Charlie Flight leader said. "We'll turn on our transponders and quit coasting here in a few, and come in on half power, since we're working on conserving fuel on these long-range missions. Charlie Flight, out."

As soon as the link was cut, Evelyn burst out laughing. JoJo was laughing so hard she couldn't breathe. Everyone on the bridge was in the same predicament, except one of her officers.

"It ain't funny," said Lieutenant Taylont, the weapons officer, to no one in particular, in the same country accent that had come over the comms. "That Prithmar beer gives me the squats every time, too." This started a new round of laughter.

* * * * *

Chapter Seven

In the operations center of the Q-ship, *Harbinger One*, Lowantha put down his comms unit and winked at Captain Ploth. "I told ya they'd fall for it," he said in the fake Tretrayon country accent he'd just used.

"That they did," agreed Ploth. "What was all that 'frost' business?"

"It's a Joth thing," said Hawthorne, grinning as he put down his comm.

Captain Jerrick Ploth paced back and forth in the operations center. He looked over at Lowantha, the Tretrayon with the inside information required to give his plan a chance at succeeding, and said, "You better hope this works, Specialist."

"Hey, it wasn't my plan," Lowantha said, raising his hands. "This is Captain Gregor's plan. I just provided the information and some of the acting. But, to answer your question...it'll work."

Ploth reached over to the arm of his seat and gave the order, "Alright, Slim, push them out."

Down low on the port side of the converted freighter, a bay door slid up, barely large enough for a Bentwick fighter to fit through. One after another, three modified Bentwick fighters were pushed out using a hydraulic piston catapult. The pilots in each ship felt the enormous pressure as their heads were slammed back into their seats with the catapult's sudden shot.

The normal design of the Bentwick fighter had two engines stacked on top of each other, instead of side by side like most human-designed fighters. The three ships that were now rapidly moving away from the old freighter only had one engine. In place of the bottom engine was a compartment just big enough to seat five men in light battle armor. It was a tight fit, and they were packed in, one behind another with a leg on both sides of a bench seat, but they fit.

"Are you sure you have the transponders configured right?" Ploth asked.

"Yeah," answered Hawthorne for his friend. "This isn't our first time changing codes, you know. It's what we do. Lowantha can reprogram transponders with his eyes closed. It'll read Tretrayon on their sensors. So as long as they haven't changed the transponders on all their ships already, it'll seem legitimate when they turn them on."

"Well," Ploth said, "it's too late now; I guess we'll find out. One way or another, twenty-nine ships will be coming through that gate in three hours, and we don't need that carrier or its escorts in operation near the gate. We may get lucky, as that light battlecruiser and the four destroyers are headed away on a sweep, and if they hold the same pattern, they'll be at least five hours away when the time comes."

* * *

"Three hours until we exit, sir," said the operations officer on *Grand Pretoria*, a heavy battlecruiser made in the shipyards of the Saturn colony two hundred years ago, when they'd decided to separate themselves from the central rule of Earth in the Sol system. Having failed spectacularly, the colony had sold its damaged ships at auction to the highest bidder. From there, it had been sold and resold many times. Captain Jifton Gregor was the last in a long line of mercenaries to purchase it, and he'd had it completely refurbished with the last of his inherited fortune. It had paid off many times through the years, and his fleet had grown.

"Good," answered Gregor as he sat on the raised seat in the center of the bridge. His right hand slowly tapped its fingers, one after another, on the arm rest as he watched the visuals of alter reality flash by through the clear-steel portal. It was a habit he'd held for years while he was an officer in the Sol Fleet, and he'd continued it after he'd been released for several poor officer evaluations. Being discharged from the fleet hadn't bothered him at all; he'd just used his family's credit to purchase his first frigate. He'd been a mercenary ever since.

"Make sure you get a good sweep of the system as soon as we come through," Gregor reiterated. "I want to know where *Harbinger One* is, so wherever that carrier's located, look there first. We may need to help destroy the carrier's escorts. Then we'll hit the closest warships. Even if they have all seven ships within attack distance, the rest of the force coming through behind us can take care of them. We'll launch missiles on all defensive platforms we find, destroy them, and hold up near the gate to get our bearing. Then we'd take the entire system."

* * *

"Hey, Captain Rogers," called Cameron. "Can you see where the lightning scorched the paint? Does it look cool, or what?"

"Aye, lad, I can see it from here," answered the Rincah captain, standing on the bridge of *Basher* and looking out the clear-steel viewport. "You're a bit daft, ye know."

"We were fine," Cameron said, "but now I really have to get *Sweet Pea* fixed. We are down to five power plants and only four engines. We should have had our shields up."

"It's not as if you were expecting to be attacked," Captain Rogers said. "I wouldn't mark that one as a mistake, lad."

"I guess." Cameron shrugged, his wings rippling with the movement. He pushed his glasses back up his nose and brightened. "You should have seen it burn in the rain. There's nothing left of that place."

"Well, let's head over to the shipyards and see how the Mikes want to do this," Captain Rogers said. "I suspect they'll have you pull into the big bay so they can get to work on her. Whatever you do, lad, don't hit anything with her. They might throw you out a hatch."

"Do you think they can put the eighth engine in?" Cameron asked. "I have it in the bay, from the salvage I got in the Tretrayon system. I think it will work. We could do it, but they would be faster."

"Credit talks, lad; credit talks," answered Captain Rogers.

"I think Bradford wants to charge me more because of the name of my ship," Cameron commented right before he cut the link.

* * * * *

Chapter Eight

In the rear bay of *Windswept*, the assistant flight operations officer, Lieutenant Carltilnokbok, waited for the light to change, signifying the bay was back to normal atmosphere. He'd come down to open the bay himself, since the doors had been shut on all the bays that day. The third bay was almost empty after the recent battles. The majority of the ships still in service had been moved to the first two bays to fill out those squadrons. It made logistical sense to have them all in the same area. The six remaining sleek fighters were being stripped to repair the fighters in the first two bays.

When the lights changed, he walked over, initiated the chamber hatch, and entered the bay. He could see the three human pilots standing beside the first Bentwick fighter. One of them was looking around the empty bay, and Carl knew what he was looking for. The XO had called down and told him through giggles why the three ships were making an "emergency" landing, and he'd found it hilarious.

One of the pilots noticed him and tapped his flight leader on the shoulder. He turned and smiled at Carl, though Carl's grin appeared to unnerve him. Carl was used to this reaction from beings who had never met a Leethog face to face.

"This way to the facilities," Carl said. "Afterwards, I'll take you up to pilot country. It's up three levels. I'm sure they would enjoy telling you all their lies, and I suspect you would, as well. I hope you have thick skin, because they announced why you had to make a pit stop." He turned to lead them toward the chamber.

Still grinning, Lieutenant Carltilnokbok hit the deck face first, with several rounds from the infiltration platoon leader's silenced kinetic pistol lodged in his back, including the one that shattered his spine right below his neck. The mercenary quickly reached up, tapped the earpiece in his right ear, and called for the three hidden teams to exit the ships. In no time, there were eighteen intruders standing in the bay of the carrier.

Using the information Lowantha had provided, they split up. They knew the basic layout of the ship from the information the two spies had pulled up from the Tretrayon Fleet's computers. It was too bad the authorities in the Tretrayon System had removed all the Restore Movement members from the ship; they could have used a handful of inside men.

One team headed for engineering and the power plant, and the other two headed toward the next two bays. The platoon leader and the other two pilots ran down the main passageway and placed small, shaped charges on all three lift doors. The small charges emitted a flash, and the doors were spot-welded shut. From there, they sprinted to the middle bay, in case that team needed help securing the bay and all the maintenance personnel.

Upon arrival, they watched as the last two Leethogs were zip-tied and placed in the corner of the bay with eight other beings. Two of them were of a lizard race they had never encountered before. There had only been three casualties in the bay. One of them was a large blue humanoid. The platoon leader couldn't fault his men. He'd have shot that one right away himself, because it was huge. Leaving two to watch them, they moved to the next bay, with the three soldiers in tow.

By this time engineering should be under their control, and with it, the ship. They could force the crewmembers to block the bridge from any action. When they arrived at the next bay, they found the same scenario, though this time half the beings who had been in the bay were down. The platoon leader was glad they hadn't had to confront a full maintenance staff, and the pilots as well. Sometimes luck made all the difference. He had his men move the remaining prisoners to the middle bay, under the watch of the two guards, and then went to engineering.

In engineering, he found the head engineer glaring furiously as she watched one of his soldiers butt stroke one of the technicians with his rifle, knocking the young Leethog out. She stood there, helpless with the other engineers, with her hands up. To do otherwise would have invited his soldiers to shoot them where they stood. As it was, three of her technicians were already dead.

"I will beat her head into a bloody mess if you don't do it now," his soldier said. His voice carried the hint of a dare, as if he hoped she wouldn't comply.

With a sigh, the chief warrant officer pulled up the schematics and overrode the bridge controls. Now all of the ship controls were routed to the console in front of her. The ability to control a ship from the engineering consoles was a great design if the bridge took a direct hit from a missile or main laser. It was terrible if an intruder was aware of the design.

"Tie the rest of them up," commanded the platoon leader. "You," he pointed his rifle at Aleethra, "shut down the engines and every power plant but one. Lock all lifts and hatches but the ones to the flight bays, and the ones between here and there." He pushed the muzzle of his weapon into her chest to emphasize his demand. She complied, after looking over at the remainder of her technicians. She could hear the bridge demanding she answer the comm on her console, until a soldier smashed it.

* * *

"**M**a'am, I'm locked out," Lieutenant Vortnick exclaimed, turning two eyes toward Captain Stacey. She kept her other eye on her console as she tried again to regain control of the ship.

"What do you mean?" Captain Stacey asked.

"I'm locked completely out," explained the pilot. "The helm is not answering my input."

"Ma'am," the tactical officer interrupted, "I am, as well."

Captain Stacey reached for her comm as she heard Gunny say, "I'll get down to engineering and see what's going on."

"Bridge to engineering," Evelyn called. She received no answer.

"Ma'am!" Gunny said loudly. "The lift is locked down."

"We've lost all engines," announced the bridge engineer. "Someone has initiated power plant shutdown on fusion plants one, two, and three. I can see it, but I can't stop it."

"Hell, break out some tools, Mr. Layrong," said Gunny. "We need to override the lift or get the panel off that wall so I can get out the hard way."

Chief Warrant Officer Layrong reached into a panel on his console and pulled out a tool kit. "Ensign Billi, your asssisstancce?"

Ensign Billitilocton hurried over to help the Prithmar open the lift control panel. Everyone on the bridge continued to try to override their various systems, to no avail.

"Can we pull up the security cameras? I need to know what's happening," Evelyn said, standing by the communications officer. "Shaith, can you get a call out? See if you can contact the escorts or the commodore."

"I can't do anything, ma'am. The entire bridge is locked out of everything," the frustrated Pikith said, slamming her console with a palm.

Just then the overhead speakers across the ship crackled. "Now listen up," a voice in Earth Common said with a strange accent. "Whatever you're doing, I would suggest you stop and just stay right where you are. Any attempt to get to engineering or the flight decks will be met with overwhelming firepower. If you make me mad, well, I'll just shut down the environmental systems, now won't I? I suggest you stay put. Oh, and I found the facilities, thanks."

* * *

"This is *Lange* calling SF *Windstorm* and SF *Gravel Pit*. Come in," Ploth said on the same frequency Lowantha had used earlier.

"This is SF *Windstorm*, send your traffic, over," replied a voice, followed by a loud *clack*.

"Must be an avian," said Ploth to no one in particular. He turned back to the comm. "I just spoke to the commander of the carrier. She said I could ask for your assistance."

"In what way? *Clack*."

"We've been working on repairing an atmosphere leak for the last couple of hours," said Ploth. "We think we have it fixed. Can you see any still leaking on your sensors?"

After a moment's hesitation, the comms crackled, and a different voice said, "This is *Gravel Pit*. We don't see any at this time."

"Roger, thanks for that," Ploth said. "Say, would you mind if I flew between you two so you can get a visual as well? Even a small leak can grow on us, and with my luck, it'll be huge when we're hours away from any help. To be honest, that was why I stopped near your formation."

"I can't see why not," said the voice from the frigate SF *Gravel Pit*.

"It has been quite boring. *Clack*," answered the avian voice from the destroyer *Windstorm*. "Besides, the *Windswept* is monitoring this frequency; if there were any objections to it, we would have heard from them. *Clack*."

"Thanks," Ploth said. "This old girl isn't as fast as she used to be. We'll be between you moving slowly in a little less than an hour. *Lange* out."

Forty-five minutes later, the tactical officer on the Q-ship looked up at his captain. "Sir, we are five minutes from scheduled system entry for the rest of the fleet. We are three minutes from being in the best position to strike both ships."

"Excellent work, people," Captain Ploth said.

Captain Ploth turned back to his comm. "This is *Lange*. Um...how far do your shields extend? I would hate to brush against one. Over."

"Lowering shields on your side now. *Clack*."

"I concur. Shields down on starboard side," agreed the voice from *Gravel Pit*.

"One minute, sir," said the tactical officer.

"You two aren't the only ones who can act around here," Ploth said to the two former spies.

"Power plants targeted, but system on inactive mode," said the weapons officer. "I'm aiming with the crosshairs. Tubes one, three, five, and seven are loaded and ready port side; tubes two, four, and six are loaded and ready on starboard side. Hatches are unlocked and ready to lift."

"We're close enough you can't miss," said Ploth, grinning. "Lift hatches. Fire!"

Seven missiles leapt from the missile tubes simultaneously. Four headed straight for the power plant on the destroyer, and three for the much smaller frigate.

"Raise shields!" shouted Captain Ploth. "Activate the targeting system!"

The main screen split. One side showed the frigate *Gravel Pit*; the other side showed the destroyer *Windstorm*. Ploth watched as the missiles struck the undefended ships almost dead center in their power plants. The frigate blew apart in a spectacular blast; pieces hit the shielding of the Q-ship. The destroyer lost momentum, and the engines sputtered and winked out.

"Reload the tubes," Ploth said, sitting back. "Have tube eight ready for any fighters from the destroyer. If it has any, it won't be many. You can use the anti-missile laser on the bay doors, just in case."

"Sir, gate entry should start occurring at any time," the tactical officer said with a smile.

"Excellent," Ploth said. "Give me a visual."

* * *

"I don't see any leaks, sir," said *Gravel Pit's* tactical officer.

"I don't, either, Ensign," agreed Lieutenant Frahley. "It's an old piece of junk, but it's not leaking at the moment."

"Sir! I'm reading..."

"What the?" The lieutenant started to stand. "Are those launcher hatches? Raise the shields! Raise..."

The command was never followed as the ship blew apart around him.

* * *

"**S**tatus! Get me the status!" Captain Elscritch shouted. *Clack.*

"Ssir, both plantss initiated sshutdown," said the bridge engineer. "We're lucky one didn't blow. It'ss bad down there. We have at leasst fifteen dead and sseveral misssing. We're powerlesss. The only thing we have iss life ssupport. No weaponss. No sshields. Nothing."

"What about *Gravel Pit*? Can you reach them?" the captain asked, wings spread in frustration.

"Negative, sir, we can't reach anyone," the communications officer said, holding her broken arm tight against herself. "I can't reach *Windswept*, either."

"We've got to boost a signal and notify the commodore," Captain Elscritch said, starting to think clearly. "What's the status in the bay?"

"Bay door iss damaged ssir," replied the bridge engineer. "We can't launch anything."

"We don't need to," Elscritch said. *Clack.* "Run auxiliary cables from the two fighters and tie them into the shuttle's power cell. Boost the signal, and we'll make a mayday call to *Salvage Title* from the shuttle."

* * * * *

Chapter Nine

"Harmon, I am detecting multiple missile launches near the gate," Jayneen said.

"What?" Harmon sat up in his chair, where he'd been half asleep. He'd been reading the progress reports from the planet Salvage. It was too much; he needed an administrator.

"It's the destroyer *Windstorm*, sir," the tactical officer said. "I can't find a signal from *Gravel Pit* at all."

"What about *Windswept?*" Harmon asked, his voice rising. "Jayneen?"

"It is still there, with reduced power showing on our sensors, but no damage. I am now detecting multiple gate entries," Jayneen said. "I count eighteen and climbing. Many are warships; some are freighters, but they have shielding. I would classify them as Q-ships."

"Frost!" Harmon exclaimed. "It was that Bentwick freighter. What's it reading now?"

"I detect substantial shielding," Jayneen announced.

"How far out are we?" Harmon asked his pilot.

"We're less than twenty-four hours out at this rate of speed," the helm answered.

"Open a link to the fleet. Include the Kashkal," Harmon ordered.

Once it was open, he hit the button on his comm. "This is Commodore Tomeral; we have rain on the desert, I repeat, rain on the desert."

"This is *Desert Wind*; we're swinging around," answered Captain Opawn. "We still need those repairs, but we're coming at best speed."

"This is *Cactus Bloom*, I and the Diamond Squadron are five hours out from the gate, requesting guidance," Captain Cailiph asked.

"Cailiph," Harmon answered, knowing what the Pikith captain wanted to do, but he couldn't allow it yet. "You can't take on that many ships. I need you to bring it around and prepare to meet us, or hit a flank. Either way, get out of there."

"Roger, sir," Cailiph answered with restraint. "Swinging around."

"Commodore," Harmon recognized Saylonik Ka's voice. "We are plotting a course to meet you in five hours. I am in command of *Kashkal's Wings, Kashkal's Strike, Kashkal's Scythe, Kashkal's Shield, Kashkal's Fortitude,* and *Kashkal's Darter.* This is Kashkal Force Two, out."

Noticing the concentrated look on Harmon's face, Clip said, "The fighter carrier, two medium battlecruisers, two destroyers, and a frigate."

"Thanks," Harmon said. "Get Jayneen and get down to the defensive bridge. It's a good thing we took on the missiles at the military shipyards, or we'd be in a system of trouble."

"Harmon," Jayneen said, "what of Bahroot?"

"Squat!" Harmon exclaimed. "He's not ready for this. Not yet. Let me think about it. We'll get him to safety, somehow."

"Sir, you have a call from *Cube,*" the communications officer said.

"Put it on screen, Jim," Harmon said.

Up on the main screen he saw Mike Melton, with Mike Bradford, Cameron, and Captain Rogers behind him.

"Hey, sir, what are your orders?" Mike asked, the senior NCO in him coming out in his voice.

"How far are you on the repairs to *Sweet Pea?*" Harmon asked.

"One of the engines wasn't in bad shape; we just needed to replace its electrical system," Bradford volunteered. "Give us two days, and we can have six power plants and six engines up in her. My guys already finished the shields on *Basher*."

"Start moving this way and let me know the minute you finish what you can," Harmon said. "Leave both ships inside until we speak again."

"Roger that," Mike acknowledged.

"Don't start without us, lad," Captain Rogers admonished.

"Yeah," echoed Cameron before the link was cut.

"Commodore," the tactical officer said to catch his attention, "I count thirty ships, including the original freighter."

"Squat!" Harmon exclaimed. It seemed like that was his favorite word these days. "Anything else?" he asked.

"We have had one of them on our sensors before," he continued. "It is registered to Gregor's Consortium."

"Uncle Harmon," called out Bahroot. Harmon had forgotten he was on the bridge. His computer and slate were sitting on the console, strapped down.

"It's getting kind of busy in here; I may have to move you to the DB," Harmon told the young AI.

"I know, but I wanted to tell you," Bahroot said, "I finished studying humans. Jifton Gregor is a *bad man*. I remember reading about him. He got kicked out of the Solar System. He is a bully."

"I know, and I know the type," Harmon agreed, standing. "Come on. Let's get you off the bridge."

Before Harmon could unstrap Bahroot from the console, his personal comm went off. It was Rick Kashka.

"Rick," Harmon answered.

"My friend, I am coming," Rick said. "I have spoken with my daughter. Give me six hours, and my ship and the other twelve ships of the Kashkal Fleet will be headed toward your location. I must shuttle my warriors to their ships. They are not all repaired, but they will fight. Can you hold the line?"

"I intend to do that. I just gave the order to power up the defensive platforms, but it takes time to bring them online."

"We're coming," Rick said, and the link cut. Harmon could imagine the scrambling that was happening on Evermore right now.

"Harmon," Jayneen called from the DB, "I am reading multiple explosions from nine of the ten defensive platforms in the system. As they were powering up, they became known to the invasion fleet before their shields could activate. The only one still intact is the one closest to us. It was out of their range."

"Squat!" Harmon shouted.

"Sir, I have a faint call from *Windstorm*," the communications officer said. "It's voice-only and coming in on the alternate channel."

"Patch it through, Jim," Harmon said.

"Commodore, this is Elscritch," the faint voice said. Harmon heard the distinctive *clack* as his beak snapped.

"Talk to me, Elscritch," Harmon implored.

"It was a ruse," explained Elscritch. "We never saw it coming. *Gravel Pit* is gone, and I can't reach *Windswept*. We have no power, except auxiliary life support. I'm calling from our shuttle but can't use it. Our bay doors are damaged. *Clack*."

"Can you repair a fusion plant?" Harmon asked.

"My engineer says she can, but it'll take a day, at least," Elscritch answered. "We have four days of environment left at the current power cell usage. *Clack*."

"Ok," Harmon said. "Good call on using the alternate frequency. Stay on this one. I want you to play dead. Work on the fusion plant, but don't initiate the reactor until I give you the signal. I don't think they'll board you or do any more damage. If I am guessing right, they think they can salvage the ship later and repair it. They're probably counting on the auxiliary power cells to die, and the crew along with it."

"Pffft!" said Captain Elscritch. "I'll push the shuttle to the bay door and fire the shuttle up to recharge the life support power cells before that ever happens. *Clack*. It can idle with the struts locked."

"Not a bad idea," Harmon admitted, "especially if the door is already damaged. Hopefully it won't come to that. Play dead, and check in every six hours. *Salvage Title*, out."

"Jim, send out the code for everyone to switch to the alternate frequency," Harmon ordered. "Just in case that piece of squat out there has our frequency."

* * *

"Sir, nine platforms destroyed," the tactical officer said to Captain Gregor. "We think that's all of them in range."

"Good," Gregor said. "Have the fleet hold up. I want to get a look at this system and see what kind of defense Tomeral may have left."

"My sensors indicate the five ships moving away from the gate, two in formation with *Salvage Title*, and two more turning to come to those three," the tactical officer said.

"So, ten ships?" Gregor asked, sitting back and tapping his fingers. "Type?"

"I read two medium battlecruisers, two light battlecruisers, five destroyers, and a frigate," answered the tactical officer. "And of course, the carrier is under our control, and a destroyer is powerless near the gate."

"That's still more ships than the Tretrayons told me they had," Gregor observed. "It's a good thing we waited until we had enough ships to try this."

"Sir, their communications have gone silent," observed his communications officer. "I think they have changed frequencies."

"What did you learn before they did?" Gregor asked.

"They have six ships coming from somewhere in the system and some being repaired, from what I could tell," the Lieutenant answered.

"Six more?" Gregor exclaimed. "Coming from where?"

"I don't know sir," answered the communications officer. "I just know some Kashkal ships are coming."

Hearing this, Gregor stood quickly. "Kashkal? "It can't be. Get me Ploth, now!"

* * * * *

Chapter Ten

"Jayneen," Harmon called down to the defensive bridge, "talk to me. When will all of our ships come together, and how far from the gate will we be?"

"If we reduce speed and plot a course to intercept *Desert Wind* and *Desert Night*, Kashkal's Second Fleet will meet us in five hours," Jayneen answered. "The ships coming from the gate will arrive four hours after that. The remainder of Kashkal's Fleet can be on site in one day at Kashkal battle speeds. I am afraid *Cube* will not reach us, or any location you wish to confront the invaders, in time. The ship is too slow."

"We gotta make a call back to the Tretrayon System, man," Clip said. "We need backup or something."

"It'll be over before they ever get here," Harmon said, shaking his head. "This is on us."

"Harmon," Zerith called from engineering, "we have all four fussion plantss working now, but plant four is only at fifty perccent efficienccy, and I cannot guarantee engine three will remain sstable under sstress."

"I know, buddy," Harmon said. "We're running on patchwork still. Several ships are. When we went to Krift, it was fine because we knew they only had Q-ships, but this is a whole different monster. Even the Kashkal ships aren't at a hundred percent."

"We need to stall them somehow," Harmon said. "Any ideas?"

"I got nothing," volunteered Marteen from *Desert Shade*.

"If Gregor is in charge of this thing, we need to scare him somehow," Harmon said, thinking out loud. "He said himself he doesn't take losing contracts. If he's confident he can win, we need to shake his confidence."

"Sounds good in theory, man," Clip said, "but how do we do it?"

"I have an idea," Harmon said, brightening. "It's a little risky. Jayneen, one of the defense platforms is out of their range. Is it up and running now?"

"It is," answered the AI. "It is on active status, and the fusion plant is putting out power at the optimum level, recharging its standby power system."

"Can you link with it and use its sensors to give us a better picture of what we're dealing with?" Harmon asked. "We can only get the basics from here, since we don't have the same system platforms the Tretrayon System has. The best sensors we have in the fleet were on *Windswept*."

"I can. It will be relatively simple," the AI admitted. "One moment, please."

"Harmon, there are five warships registered to Gregor's Consortium," Jayneen said several moments later. "There are three registered in the Bleeve System, two are Gleekum, and seven ships are registered in Sol System. Of these ships, two are Q-ships with Bentwick registrations."

"That's nineteen," Clip counted.

"It is," admitted Jayneen. "The other eleven are...Belvakett."

"Belvakett?" Harmon asked. "That system is closed."

"They are not registered to Belvakett, they are registered in Glayver. The ships are Belvakett ships, nonetheless. There is information on the Net of a group operating on the far side of the galaxy. They tend to stay away from the Rincah, with good reason."

"You might want to forewarn Captain Rogers, man," Clip suggested. "He's not gonna like it."

"Don't I know it," Harmon agreed. "Jayneen, how many missiles are on the platform?"

"There are one hundred and fifty missiles," the AI informed him. "The system is designed with a magazine above the launchers; the missiles drop into place after firing. It can launch quickly."

"Far out," Clip said.

"Impresssive," agreed Zerith. The distinctive sound of a hull being spit out came over the comm.

"Nice. Besides great shielding, what else does it have?" Harmon asked.

"It has approximately the same number of defensive lasers as *Skrittle*," the AI answered.

"Hmmm, offensive and defensive capabilities are good, but no real thrust, besides small orbiting adjustment engines," Harmon thought out loud.

"Harmon, I am not sure of your plans, but I must inform you, every ship in the invading fleet is showing on our sensors as Tretrayon ships," Jayneen advised.

"Can you override the friend or foe identification program and control the targeting solutions on the platform?" Harmon asked as the idea began to take shape.

"I can, to an extent," Jayneen said after a moment. "I can designate various targets with each salvo. From there, it is fire and forget."

"Perfect," Harmon said. "Hank, Stan?"

"We're on the link," Hank said. "Yes, we will do it."

"I haven't even told you my plan," Harmon protested.

"Whatever it is, it is a good one," Stan said. "*Skrittle* is ready."

"Ok, here's the plan," and Harmon explained it.

After he was done explaining, Clip said, "Ohhh, nasty. I like it."

"It sshould give them pausse," agreed Zerith.

* * *

"**O**k, we are above the platform, engage the struts, Hanktilmotal," Stan said. He was sitting in the command chair for this mission. The flipped wrench had been good to him this time.

"Engaging now," answered Hank with a toothy grin. Every crew member on the *Skrittle* looked up and around when the frigate and the defensive platform came together with a reverberating clang.

The crew had been briefed through the overhead speakers on the upcoming mission. They were prepared for the joining of the two, but feeling it actually happen let them know it was time to prepare for high Gs. Leethog were able to withstand higher G-forces than humans and many other races, but there was a limit to what even *they* could sustain for long periods of time, and they all knew the brothers would push it to the absolute edge. It was a good thing engineering had been able to improve the G-force dampeners on the ship; it gave them the extra protection they'd need.

On the main screen, a map of the system was displayed. Out near the gate, two boundary lines were overlaid with a dotted line, indicating their flight path. The green one was where they would release the platform to allow it to continue on its way, at an incredible speed, toward the invading fleet. The red line beyond that was the approximate limit of the enemy's missiles. The brothers had no intention of crossing that line, though turning and banking away would add even more G-forces.

"Commodore, we have made connection and are beginning our run. Please have Lieutenant Commander Jayneen ensure the platform stays in standby mode," Stan said over the open link.

"Roger that, good luck and don't push it too far," Harmon answered. "I have two chief warrant officers here on the bridge giving me a look I don't ever want to see again."

"On the bridge? *Both* of them?" Stan asked as he looked over at his brother with big eyes. "Uhh...Roger that. The *Skrittle* will be adhering to all safety precautions during the entirety of the assigned mission. *Skrittle*, out."

"I'm glad you won the flip," Hank said with a grin. Every Leethog head on the bridge was nodding along with his statement. Except, of course, the lone female. She just smiled to herself and said nothing. Sometimes nothing was exactly what needed to be said.

* * *

"There they go," Harmon said to himself as he watched the main screen. *Skrittle* was gaining speed, indicated by the reading in the lower corner. Jayneen was providing the real-time speed and G-forces the ship was undergoing.

"Yes," Vera said as she stood beside him. "There they go."

"They'll be fine," Harmon insisted. "Gregor will never know what's coming until it's too late. Especially since we had the platform use what little thrusters it had to move well away from where it powered up before they attached to it. What could…"

"Harmon Tomeral, if you complete that sentence, it will become very unpleasant in here," Kyla interrupted. "Very."

"Agreed," announced Jayneen.

"Dude," Clip said. He was still shaking his head as he left the bridge.

"Well, you know," Harmon said. "Say, I think Zerith needs you two back in in the power plant…or something."

Two hours later Harmon received a call from *Skrittle*. He could hear the stress in Stan's voice. "Releasing platform in ten seconds."

Stan counted down, then said, "Platform has been released; we have a clean release and show it flying on the planned trajectory. We are turning now."

"Nice!" Harmon exclaimed. "Talk to me, Jayneen."

"The platform is traveling at combat speed," the AI announced. "The invading fleet will be in missile range in ten minutes. I will begin launching at that time, until all missile racks are depleted. They will not know it is coming until I power up all systems, unless they have an incredible sensor system. I doubt mercenaries would spend the kind of credit it takes to update older ships like that."

Harmon watched the screen as the symbol for *Skrittle* continued banking away from the invaders. True to their word, the brothers kept the frigate from passing over the simulated missile range indicated by the red line. Harmon noticed the ship continued to slow down as they headed back in-system. They were still moving fast, but it was well within the G-force tolerance their race could handle.

"Launching now," Jayneen announced. "I will attempt to keep you updated on hits and misses while I engage with the platform."

* * *

"Sir, that frigate's still coming, and it's picked up even more speed," the tactical officer on *Grand Pretoria* said.

"What's it doing?" Captain Gregor demanded for the third time. "Is it a suicide mission? We'll tear it to pieces long before it reaches us. It's a Dalgett frigate. They have decent shielding, and they're fast, but that is not enough to stop all the missiles of a single salvo from several ships."

"I have no idea, sir," the lieutenant sitting at the tactical console answered. "Though I will say, I've never heard of a Dalgett frigate moving at that kind of speed. The G-forces must be unbearable. Perhaps it's making a run for the gate to escape the upcoming slaughter."

"That makes more sense than a suicide run," agreed the weapons officer.

"Well, keep an eye on it," Gregor said, settling back in his seat, tapping his fingers. "Anything changes or it alters course, I want to know. I'm trying to figure out the best plan of attack. I intend to begin taking this system within the next six hours."

"Sir, you have a call from *Harbinger One*," the communications officer said.

"Don't they know I'm trying to plan here?" Gregor complained. "Put it on screen."

"Gregor, are you tracking that ship?" Ploth asked.

"We are," Gregor answered. "It's just a frigate."

"Yeah, well, I don't like it," Ploth stated.

"You just make sure you maintain control of that carrier and be ready to head in-system," Gregor said, aggravated. "See, my guy just told me it's veering away from us. It never even came within missile range. They probably decided they couldn't get past us to the gate."

"Good," Ploth said. "Sitting out here is making me nervous. My guys on that carrier say they have never seen a power plant like that ship has, and the fighters are useless to me. You need four hands to fly them. *Harbinger One*, out."

Several minutes later, Gregor's tactical officer caught his attention. "Sir, we may have a malfunction in the sensors."

"What do you mean, malfunction?" Gregor asked, standing.

"I thought I picked something up, twice," answered the man. "But when I adjust the sensors to narrow in on the area where I saw it, nothing's there."

"Well, it's not that frigate," Gregor said, now standing over him. "It's looped all the way around and headed back toward the other ships."

"I know, sir, it's just...What the...!" exclaimed the tactical officer. "Something just lit up! Power plant, shields...Missile launch! Multiple missile launch!"

"What?" asked Gregor loudly. "Is it a ship? What's out there?"

"Sir, it's a defense platform," answered the man, confused. "It's like the ones we destroyed, except it is headed toward us at an incredible speed. It launched missiles outside our missile range. It'll probably fire several salvos before we can even fire back. It has tremendous shielding, and at that speed, it's not going to be easy to hit."

Gregor ran to his seat and hit his comms button. "Evasive action! Take evasive action. Tenders, protect your ships. Get ready to defend against incoming missiles." He looked over at his tactical officer. "They threw a system defense platform at us like it was some kind of grenade…what have I gotten myself into?"

* * *

Harmon gave the communications officer a look and pointed up at the overhead speakers, then waved his finger around. In a few seconds, the entire Salvage Fleet could hear Jayneen, including their Kashkal partners.

"Several ships are moving. It appears to be standard escort maneuvers to protect their main ships and their missile carrier," Jayneen said. "The first ten missiles are among their formations. I record four hits with the first salvo. Per your instructions, three frigates have been destroyed completely; one more is drifting. Second salvo has almost reached the enemy."

"I record five hits with the second salvo," Jayneen continued. "Another frigate has been destroyed. A destroyer has taken three hits; the last one appears to have broken the ship's spine. It is out of action. They are broadcasting rescue beacons."

"The platform has now launched five salvos, and it is receiving incoming missiles. There have been many misses; the defensive lasers are doing their jobs. Its shields are down to eighty-two percent," she continued.

"Get 'em, Jayneen!" Clip shouted.

"Their defensive missiles and lasers are stopping a few more of my missiles per salvo. Any scrambling missiles they may be using are having no effect on the Grithelaon missiles from the platform. They are ignoring them."

"Yeah, well, I think I have *our* scrambler missiles reprogrammed to work against modern sensors and missiles," Clip announced. "I can't wait to try them, finally."

"Eight salvos have been launched. Platform shields are down to thirty-three percent. I am now attempting to use the orbiting thrusters to aim the platform at a heavy battlecruiser. I will have to guess its pilot's intentions in order to strike it. Guessing is something new for me. I have recorded several more hits to the invading fleet," Jayneen continued informing them.

"Fourteen salvos were launched, but the last salvo wasn't. The platform suffered a catastrophic system error when the shields were finally penetrated. The platform struck a glancing blow on the heavy battlecruiser, then hit and finished off a destroyer that had been venting atmosphere, yet still had functioning engines. The platform was destroyed."

"Yess," Zerith exclaimed from the power plant. "It got in one lasst sshot. Fine piloting, Jayneen, and my complimentss to itss designer."

"Jayneen," Harmon said, sitting back and realizing he'd been tensed up during the running commentary from the AI, "what's the final tally?"

"The platform successfully rendered seven frigates, five destroyers, and a large gunship combat incapable. The light missile carrier registered as a Bleeve ship is running on one engine and is still venting atmosphere from multiple hits at this time. There is some damage to several other ships, indicating downed shields. Your plan to reduce the total number of ships in the invading fleet has been successful. They have been reduced to sixteen fully capable combat ships."

"Commodore," Rick Kashka called over his personal comm, "I have been monitoring. You have employed a Numbers Reduction Strategy, and I am impressed. Many would have gone after the largest ships and used up the available missiles. You opted to destroy numbers of ships, not just a few large ones. This will be demoralizing to the remaining ship crews. Well done."

* * * * *

Chapter Eleven

"What the zanthobal's excretion was that!" screamed an enraged Drooval over the command link. "I lost a frigate commanded by my own brother, Gregor...we hatched together!"

Captain Gregor was having a hard time understanding the calls coming in over his command net. He was receiving distress calls from escape pods and damaged ships. It was chaos, absolute chaos.

"Calm down!" he shouted. "Everyone just...calm down. Use your sensors and rescue the nearest pods. I don't care who they belong to. We can get that sorted out later. Get me a status on all of your ships."

"I can tell you the status of mine," Skriflair said angrily. "I lost seven ships. SEVEN! That platform was firing the last salvos so close it was hard to defend against the missiles! My crewmembers cannot be replaced. Ships I can get elsewhere, but crewmembers take longer. There are few females on my ships capable of building viable nests. You had better come up with a good plan, and their lives had better not be wasted. Do you hear me, Gregor? I will come over there and see you personally if it appears so."

"Just rescue the pods, and somebody see if the missile carrier can be repaired enough to use," Gregor answered. "I'll contact everyone in twelve hours. Tomeral's fleet hasn't moved any closer. They may be holding back to see what we'll do. We can still defeat them. We have sixteen ships, and many more fighters than they have. We have control of their fighter carrier."

* * *

"A re you sure you canna get this thing moving any faster?" Captain Rogers asked Mike Melton.

"That's all she has," answered the retired master sergeant. "Her engines are an old design; *Cube* was built to hold orbit somewhere, not race across a star system into battle."

"There are Belvakett ships out there, and I intend to get in on the action," stated the Rincah warrior. "We have never deliberately hunted them down, but here and now they are fair game, and my kin and I want a piece of them."

"I get it, man," Mike Bradford said. "I lost some good friends when we were ambushed once by a squadron of Bleeve. If I ever see one of those spider-looking things again, and it's one of Micktorah's Nightmares, I'll kill the hell out of it and ask questions later."

"You can't just kill one, Bradford," Cameron said. "That's murder."

"Not if it's one of Micktorah's Nightmares," Bradford said. "That mercenary company's fair game. They've double-crossed allied mercenary units before. Everybody knows that."

"Well," Mike said, "I hate to be the bearer of more bad news, but there are Bleeve ships in the invasion fleet. The commodore told me himself."

"What?" Bradford asked. He pulled the cigar out of his mouth and pointed it at Mike. "Fire up that comm. I want to talk to him."

"Ok," Mike said, and he set his cup of coffee down. "*Cube* to *Salvage Title*."

After a moment, Harmon was on the main screen in *Cube*'s operation center. "Mike, what's up? Did you finish the repairs to *Sweet Pea*?"

"Not yet; they're progressing," Mike said. "Bradford wanted to talk to you."

"Commodore, those Bleeve ships," Bradford asked, getting right to the point, "is there a large battlecruiser and an older missile carrier?"

"Hold on," Harmon said. A minute later, he replied, "That's affirmative. Jayneen says the missile carrier is an older Bleeve design. Why? What's up?"

"Payback! That's what's up," Bradford said through clinched teeth. If the cigar hadn't been in a filter, he'd have bitten through it. "Those ships belong to a Bleeve named Micktorah. His company is called Micktorah's Nightmares, and every one of them needs killing."

"I intend to do just that," Harmon reassured him. "Knowing several of their names now, we may just engage in a little psychological warfare, too."

"You got any crazy ideas about how we can make it out there in time to join in the killing?" Bradford pleaded.

"I'm with him, lad," Captain Rogers added. "There's payback to be had."

"I don't know what we can do," Harmon answered. "If they form up and try to come deeper into the system, we have to meet them even if you aren't here for it...I...hold on."

On the main screen they saw Harmon turn toward a slate on the arm of his chair. They all knew he was talking to the new AI, Bahroot. Grinning, he turned back to the main screen and hit a button on his comm.

"Fellas, my nephew is a genius," Harmon said.

"Tell me about it," complained Cameron. "He beat me three times in a row in battle chess. I'm not playing him anymore."

"He said you need more engines," Harmon explained. "Bigger ones."

"I know he's kinda like your nephew, and you're proud of him and stuff, but that's obvious," Bradford said.

"He also said you have them sitting in the repair bay right now," Harmon said.

"Wait…what are you saying?" Mike asked.

"It's simple," Harmon said. "Open the bay doors. Move *Basher* and *Sweet Pea* to the edge of the bay, flip 'em around, and engage the struts. If you have enough of the thrusters outside the bay, it should pose no problem. Turn that thing around and come on."

"I like it!" Mike said, standing. "We also have that Krift ship we salvaged. Two engines still worked on it when they surrendered. I haven't scheduled any repairs on it yet, but Bradford flew it into the bay with no problem. We'll put it on one side with *Basher* to give it four engines, to counter *Sweet Pea* on the on the other side of the bay. Hold the line! We're coming, and we're coming in hot."

* * * * *

Chapter Twelve

"What do you think, Rick?" Harmon asked over the comm.

"I think it's a good plan," Rick Kashka agreed. "They do not know we are behind the sixth planet. If they knew, they would leave the system. When they head in, we will swing around the planet and come in using the Crossing Separator Tactic. They will either continue their attack, split their attack, or try to make a break for the gate."

"If they make a run for the gate, we'll be able catch and destroy some of them," Harmon said. "A few may escape, but I have a surprise for at least one of them. Captain Elscritch has just informed me *Windstorm* has a fusion plant ready to start, which means eight missile launchers and his pulse cannons will be waiting on them. He'll get in several salvos as they come to him. They're a generation or two older than the ones on *Salvage Title*, but they'll still deal serious damage."

"Have you word from *Windswept*?" Rick asked.

"Nothing," Harmon said. "She's out there, running on one fusion plant with the main engines shut down. Jayneen couldn't detect any damage, so they must have boarded her somehow."

"Unless they have an overwhelming number of boarders," Rick assured him, "I believe the crew will take their ship back. Gunnery Sergeant Harper and his marines will find a way. That is a group of warriors I would have assigned on any Kashkal ship. Captain Stacey and her crew will find a way, my friend."

"You're right," Harmon agreed, "and if I know Aleethra, she's not too happy about someone taking over the ship from Evelyn. If she gets a small chance to take back her power plant, she'll take it. She hates losing, and she'll do anything to win. I feel sorry for anyone in her way."

* * *

"Alright, everyone knows the objective," Captain Gregor said to his invading fleet over the command net. "Stay in formation and stick to the plan; we'll sweep in and overwhelm them. From what my sensors show me, many of those ships weren't completely repaired after their last action. We have the fighter carrier under control, so we'll have many more fighters than they have. We destroy them here, and we own the system."

"Roger that," Ploth agreed. "My boarding team has complete control of the carrier. It will be waiting for us after we take the system, and so will that destroyer. I bet those won't be the only ships we own after the day is through. Harbingers, out."

"Finally!" roared Skriflair. "We fight! Moving to battle speed now."

The Belvakett ships moved out in squadron formation; the rest of the invading fleet followed, and they all picked up speed. The last ship to head in-system was Gregor's heavy battlecruiser, *Grand Pretoria*. He took one last look at the screen and watched the two salvaged ships, floating motionless, grow smaller. Nearby were the wrecks of the ships his invasion fleet had already lost.

Damn Harmon Tomeral, he thought. *I hope he lives through the battle so I can kill him myself.*

* * *

"Roger that, sir," said the platoon leader of the Harbinger insertion team. "We have the ship under control. We'll be waiting for you. Wipe them out."

Aleethra listened to one side of the conversation as the man spoke to his commander. She'd been waiting for an opportunity to put her plan in motion. With the infiltrator's ship moving in-system and leaving the boarding party to maintain control of *Windswept*, she could do it.

"Ssir," she said to the human lieutenant, "thank you for allowing me to open hatchess to facilitiess and ration centerss for the crew, but unfortunately there are no food dispenserss here in the power plant. The rest of the crew may have eaten, but we have not."

"Yeah," the platoon leader said, "that's too bad. Nobody leaves the power plant or enters it, and that goes for the flight deck, too."

Aleethra kept herself from smiling. She looked over at the members of her power plant crew. Several races were sitting against the panel on the far side of the room, including two Prithmar. She looked directly at them and winked an eye, out of sight of her captors.

"You don't undersstand," she explained. "I am a Prithmar. If I don't eat, I will sslip into a sself-presserving coma. It is our metabolissm. I have no control over it. If I sslip into the hunger ssleep, you will have no one to run the sship. Your soldierss cannot do it. Look at my crew, you can ssee for yoursself how they are growing lethargic."

Hearing this, the two Prithmar crewmembers took their cue from her earlier wink. One of them kept nodding with half closed eyes. The other let his mouth hang slack and leaned hard against a fellow crew member. When the platoon leader and several of his men looked at the prisoners, they could plainly see this.

"I don't care about them," the lieutenant said, "and I'm not letting any of you leave the power plant. You could have said something when we were eating our rations. I would have ensured you ate something then."

"Ssir, I keep emergency food in that compartment," she pointed to a small closed door on her console. "It iss for when I have to work long shiftss. You can open it yoursself, so you know I am not attempting anything foolish. There is no weapon there."

The man looked at her for a moment, thinking. He turned to the sergeant. "Check that compartment. See if she's telling us the truth, or if she's up to something."

"Yes, sir." The sergeant stood back and slowly opened the panel. On a shelf was a bag of chinto jerky. He took the bag out and opened it. He smelled it, then took a piece out and put it in his mouth.

"It's just some kind of jerky, sir," he said. "It's not bad…kind of spicy, though." The sergeant looked over at Aleethra. "It better not be some kind of damn rat or giant snail or something, either."

"It iss not," Aleethra said. "It iss chinto, an animal ssimilar to your Earth's cowss."

"Oh, that's ok then," he said, and took another piece out for himself.

"Give it to her," the lieutenant said after the sergeant had chewed up the second piece, deciding it wasn't a trick. "Give some to the others, too, I guess."

Hearing this, the two crewmembers quickly laid their heads against fellow crewmembers, feigning sleep. They weren't brave enough to eat meat, even if it did help them escape. They would leave that to the chief warrant officer.

"Never mind," the lieutenant said after he looked over and saw the other two Prithmar had succumbed to the hunger sleep. "Just give it all to her."

* * *

"Ma'am, we took the connectors off three panels," Gunny said. "One will get us into the lift chamber, one to the arms room on this deck, and the other repair crews will use them to move to the lower deck emergency gear room. You just tell us when to go."

"Hold off for now," Captain Stacey said. "It looks like that Q-ship is moving away with their fleet." She was looking out the clear-steel portal on the bridge. Gunny was over near the panel he was ready to open. "We'll let them move far enough away they can't come back and send more of their troops to help the ones who have us locked down. Knowing Aleethra like I do, if she's still alive down there in the power plant, she's not taking this lying down. If she makes a move, we'll know. If she doesn't do it soon, I'll initiate it."

"Roger, ma'am," Gunny said, rolling his shoulders. "You just let me know when. Clyde and the rest of the security platoon are ready on the deck below us, as well. They can keep every hatch between decks locked down if they want; we know how to get around the ship if we have to."

"Good," Evelyn said. "That was quick thinking, banging on the deck with ancient Morse Code. This far from the flight deck and the power plant, they couldn't have heard it even if they knew what it was."

"I only know it because Clyde sent it to my comm a while back," Gunny admitted. "He said everyone in the Joth Militia learned it and had to show proficiency in it on drill weekends. All these centuries since it was invented, and it's still an efficient means of communication in an emergency. Amazing."

"It can be used with light, as well," said Ensign Shaith. "It's been a while since I was in the militia, but I do remember that."

* * * * *

Chapter Thirteen

"They're moving," Clip called up from the defensive bridge.

"I see it," Harmon answered over the comm. "I don't want Bahroot on board when this battle starts. I'm sending him with Brickle in the shuttle away from the ship. I hate not having Brickle on the bridge, but there's no way I'm going to risk something happening to Bahroot's power cell or computer."

"Thank you, Harmon," Jayneen said from the DB. "I should have ensured he was in a console with plenty of backup precautions."

"Salvage Fleet," Harmon announced over the command link. "The invaders have started moving toward the planets. Begin movement to designated coordinates at battle speeds. Kashkal's Force Two, with us. Rick Kashka, I'll leave it to you to time your appearance. *Cube*, at the rate you're moving, you'll catch us and be able to engage at extreme range. Don't overshoot the battle, and stay to the fleet's port side in case they try to get around us while avoiding the Kashkal's surprise appearance."

"That's a roger, sir," Mike answered from *Cube*.

"The timing has been calculated, Commodore," Rick assured him. "They will either turn and run, or they will all die. If they run, many will die anyway. Invaders will never gain a foothold in Salvage System. Ever."

"By the way," Mike said over the command link a few minutes later, "we picked up a few extra crewmembers before we got too far away from the shipyards."

"Who?" Harmon asked.

"Hey, buddy, ya didn't think I was gonna let you have all the dang fun, did ya?" Twiggy drawled. "I came up in that modified shuttle. Got our two mech instructors and their five pilot trainees, plus two squads of the Bolts. It was all I could fit in the shuttle. I figured it couldn't hurt."

"Good job," Harmon said. "If we have to board some of these ships, they may come in handy. Along with the Tralge on the *Cube*, that's a good-sized unit."

"Yep," Twiggy agreed, "and these ol' boys with their swords look like they can hold their own, too. We also have Cameron's pilots with their mechs. Say, you know what does hurt?"

"What's that?" Harmon asked.

"Me," Twiggy complained. "Dang if this ship ain't moving at a pretty good clip, with all them thrusters hanging out the bay. It's about past my tolerance level. I mean, it ain't killing me or nothing, but it sure ain't comfortable."

"If you had some meat on your bones, it would be easier on you, sir," Bradford chimed in.

"You'll survive." Harmon laughed.

"Dang right, I will," Twiggy said, "but when I get my hands on some of them that're holding *Windswept* hostage, I'll make sure *they* don't."

* * *

Aleethra took the bag of chinto jerky from the sergeant and sat down at her console. She made sure to stay away from the console controls, knowing she was being watched by at least one of the men. She reached into the bag and pulled out two large pieces.

Back when she'd played warball in secondary school, she often ate a small piece of jerky before a game. It wasn't a banned substance—how could they ban meat?—but it did give her a decided edge. None of the other Prithmar players on the team had joined her in the act.

She looked at the large pieces and thought about what she was about to do. Prithmar were vegetarians. Vitamin B12, found in meat, was an enhancement drug to the Prithmar. It was dangerous, and for some, too much could quickly turn deadly. It raised the pulse to an extremely unhealthy rate, while it increased clarity, speed, stamina, and strength.

While large amounts increased strength in a Prithmar to nearly the level of a Yalteen or a male Caldivar, it didn't produce psychedelic effects, nor was it addictive, so it wasn't habit forming. Regardless, very few Prithmar ate it, because the results it provided were temporary and not worth the risk of death.

She thought of Marteen and smiled to herself. *A human. I have fallen in love with a human.* She hoped she'd survive this and see him again. She had to regain control of the power plant. The ship and all its assets were needed to defend the system. If she succeeded and didn't survive the ordeal, Marteen would understand. He was a marine. If she didn't do everything in her power to regain control of the ship when the opportunity presented itself…well, that he might not understand.

With a light shrug, she put both pieces of jerky into her mouth and started chewing. It tasted awful to her. The jerky always had, even in secondary school. Almost immediately she felt its effects. Some of the B12 was absorbed as she chewed. She focused, and details became clearer.

She looked around as she chewed and noticed the guard near the door didn't have his finger near the trigger of his weapon. Looking closer, she could see the safety switch was in a different position than the other guard's weapon. Odds were, his was on safe and the other was not. The other had his finger inside the trigger guard, ready to fire. He was on the far side of the compartment. Much closer to her, she could see neither the leader of the men or the sergeant had their hands near their weapons, which hung on straps in front of them as they conversed closely to one another so she couldn't hear what was being said. She swallowed the meat and waited.

After a few minutes, she could feel her pulse quicken and the thud of her heartbeat in her chest. It was almost as if she could hear it pounding. With the increased heartbeat, she started taking long, deep breaths, attempting to gain some control over it. It would not do to start panting as if she had just finished a long run. Watching the soldier with his finger in the trigger guard, she waited. It was almost unbearable. Finally, he took his hand away from his weapon and fumbled with his helmet strap.

In one fluid motion, Aleethra spun out of her chair—made of steel and molded as one piece—grabbed both armrests, and tore it from the deck. All four bolts gave way with a loud *screech* as she snatched it up and swung it at the lieutenant and sergeant standing with their heads close together. They both looked up when they heard the sound, surprised by what they were witnessing. The sergeant started to move away, but it was too late. The metal pole and base of the chair hit him in the face, shattering his cheek bones and crushing his nasal cavity, injuries that would have produced excruciating pain if he hadn't lost all feeling when the force of the blow snapped his neck.

Aleethra's follow-through on the swing allowed the base of the chair to hit the taller lieutenant in the neck, crushing his windpipe and cutting into the muscles on one side. He didn't reach for his weapon as he stumbled to the side from the blow. He dropped to his knees with his hands on his neck as he tried to draw a breath and couldn't. He fell over, a steady flow of blood coming from between his fingers.

With a mighty heave, Aleethra threw the chair at the guard on the far side of the compartment as he started to aim his weapon her way. His focus was on attempting to shoot her, and he realized nearly too late the danger he was in from the incoming chair. He turned away at the last instant and was struck in the back. It hit him hard enough to slam him face first against the bulkhead, knocking his still unfastened helmet off, shattering teeth, and rendering him unconscious.

The last captor in the room brought his weapon up and squeezed the trigger. His eyes widened as he saw her sprinting in his direction, faster than any being should be able to move, and it took him a minute to remember why it wouldn't fire. He flicked the safety off and was able to fire one round before he was hit with a flying tackle that folded him over and knocked the wind out of him when he hit the base of the hatch. His light battle armor didn't protect him much from the devastating warball tackle. Looking up, the last thing he saw was the elbow of the lizard-like being right before it slammed between his eyes.

Aleethra rolled off the soldier, breathing heavily, and stood. She felt a slight pain in her left arm. She attempted to lift her hand to see why it hurt, but it wouldn't move. Then she noticed blood dripping from a hole in her upper arm where the round had gone through, causing significant damage. *It's probably shattered in there,* she thought. *This should hurt more than it does.* Her mind shrugged it off.

She took the weapon from the man whose face she had just smashed and put the strap over her head, then reached back down and took a large knife from his harness. Her crewmembers were all standing as she walked over, still breathing heavily. She indicated for the first to turn around, and she cut the ties off her hands. She handed the knife to her engine tech and motioned for her to cut the others loose. To her surprise, the Leethog told her no, and used the knife to cut a strip of her own sleeve off to tie a tourniquet around Aleethra's arm. The Leethog made Aleethra hold the twisted knot with her good hand as she rushed over to grab something to hold the tourniquet and the emergency medical nanite kit. Once it was in place, she injected above and below the bullet wound, then cut the rest of the beings loose.

Grimacing, Aleethra walked over to her console and stood over the torn deck. She pulled up the internal cameras and noted the positions of all the infiltrators. The ones guarding the flight deck crewmembers would be the hardest to deal with. Luckily for her, Gunny and his security platoon could handle that. She unlocked the communications, stepped to another console, and called her commander. She sat down as her heart continued to pound. *I need to get to medical as soon as the ship is cleared,* she thought as she initiated startup on a power plant.

* * *

"**Y**ou heard her," Evelyn said. "We have control of the power plant back. There are fourteen more on board. They have no idea their leaders are out of action. That won't last long, if they have any kind of timed commo checks scheduled. Get your platoon together, and *take back this ship.*"

"Roger that, ma'am," Gunny said and left the bridge in a hurry.

"Ma'am, another fusion plant startup has been initiated," called out the bridge engineer as she checked the status of the ship.

"Good," Captain Stacey said. "Ensure the cannons are charging. Ensign Shaith, see if there's any traffic on the command link. Don't make a call, just listen. If you don't hear anything, check the alternate channel. If I know Harmon Tomeral, he switched over after we were boarded."

"Ma'am, there's traffic on the alternate," confirmed the communications officer. "Switching over now."

"Thanks, Shaith," Evelyn said, watching the main screen and the various views from the cameras within the ship. She watched part of the security platoon come out of several panels, toss stun grenades, and take down half the remaining boarders without taking any casualties. "Get me the flagship, please."

* * *

"**E**velyn, now that you have the ship under control," Harmon said, "*Windstorm* will initiate fusion plant startup. When they're ready, swing around and chase them from their starboard side, and be ready to launch all fighters. We're going to come at them from all angles."

"Will do," Evelyn said. "*Windswept*, out."

"That's one thing going our way already," Harmon said to Big Jon. "Now I need to call Marteen and let him know Aleethra was injured but will be fine. Evelyn said the ship's doctor was able to lower her blood pressure and pulse rate as well as set her arm."

"That is a good thing," Sergeant Major Jontilictick said. He paused a moment before leaving the bridge. "She really beat them to death with a chair? Impressive."

Harmon reached over to his comm and spoke over the command link, "They've crossed the point where they can't avoid the battle. Salvage Fleet, move into attack formation Alpha. Break. Rick Kashka, your fleet can come around the planet any time you're ready. We haven't settled in yet, and we're already having to defend our system; let's make an example of them and let the word spread around the galaxy—Salvage System is in the business of defending itself, and the business is good!"

* * * * *

Chapter Fourteen

"**S**ir, they've shifted their formation," the tactical officer of *Grand Pretoria* said to Captain Gregor. "It looks like *Salvage Title* has two escorts, a light battlecruiser and a frigate. It's the same frigate that launched the defensive platform."

"We can still take them, they're not at a hundred percent," stated Gregor, though he didn't sound as confident to his bridge crew as he had the day before.

The tactical officer continued, "Three ships have disappeared from my sensors. The light battlecruiser that fled the gate area is now paired with a larger ship. I don't recognize the type from my readings, but its shielding is very powerful. The system says it's Nazrooth. I have no idea where it came from, or where the others went."

"Great," Gregor deadpanned. "Do you have any more bad news for me?"

"Yes, sir," the officer admitted. "The Kashkal ships have joined the formation. I'm not sure, but one of them appears to be a carrier. It has three escorts flying close aboard. The other two ships that arrived with it are substantial, at least medium battlecruisers."

Gregor stabbed the button on his comm violently. "*Grand Pretoria* to *Harbinger One*."

"This is Ploth."

"You better get your pilots ready; we may still have to face a carrier fleet."

"They're ready. Speaking of carriers, I can't reach Lieutenant Barloch. He was supposed to have checked in by now."

"Hold on," Gregor said. He looked at his tactical officer. "Riley, run a sweep on the two ships we left near the gate."

After a moment, the officer looked up from his console with wide eyes. "Sir, I read at least one fusion plant and engines running on the destroyer, and the carrier is showing four plants up and full engines. They're swinging wide and trailing us."

"Listen up," Gregor announced over his command link. "It looks like this battle may be more even than we'd hoped. Stay in formation, and stick to the battle plan, and we can still win this thing. Micktorah, make sure your missile carrier concentrates on *Salvage Title*."

"We will, but we are still venting on two decks, and I only have use of half of my launchers," answered the Bleeve. "But don't worry, we can still launch thirty at a time, rapidly; they won't be able to stop them all."

"Anyone who runs from the fight will deal with me," added Skriflair.

* * *

Harmon grinned over at his communications officer. Jayneen had been able to determine the frequency they were using, and the entire bridge crew on *Salvage*

Title had listened to the invaders' conversation. *Time for some head games*, he thought. *We should be able to get in at least one call before they scramble their net.* "Clip, make the call,"

"This is to inform you there won't be anyone left to run by the time we're through with you," Clip said over the invaders' command net. "Hey, Micktorah, we'll swat your missiles out of space like bugs...sorry no species offense meant, there. Ploth, your guys went down like a cold beer, real easy. Skriflair, you should have stayed hidden on the far side of the galaxy; a good friend of ours has been waiting for this opportunity. You just watch for the Rincah, 'cause they're coming. Oh, and Gregor, we thought you didn't take losing contracts? You did this time. See you in a few. This public announcement has been brought to you by Harmon Tomeral and Associates, friends of Harmon Tomeral and Associates, the Kashkal race, the planets Salvage and Evermore, and all the residents of Salvage System."

"I'm Harmon Tomeral, commodore and president of Salvage System, and I approve this message," Harmon added before Gregor or his people could engage the scrambling on their network.

There was silence on the invaders' net. Harmon looked over at his communications officer. The grin he gave Harmon rivaled the ones the brothers could give. Harmon smiled himself and sat back in his seat, wondering what the conversations were like on the now-scrambled enemy communications network.

"A psychological strike. Now that is a tactic I have never used," Rick told Harmon over his private comm. "I will, however, endeavor to remember it."

* * *

The command network was down for a few seconds while security scrambled it so the ships defending the system couldn't access it again. As soon as it came back up, a deluge of voices could be heard, stepping over each other's calls.

"They know me by name!" screamed Micktorah, unable to hide his fear. "The Kashkal *are* with them! We cannot win!"

"They act as if my best insertion platoon were pushovers," said Ploth. "What kind of troops are we facing here, Gregor?"

"You did not mention some of the mercenaries they hired to defend the Tretrayon System were Rincah, Gregor," Skriflair growled. "For that alone, you will pay. If we survive this, you better pray to whatever you believe in I don't kill you on sight. As it is, we have no choice but to go through with this attack; we cannot avoid contact."

"Everyone, calm down. Don't let them get you riled up; he's only trying to get us to make mistakes," Gregor said. "Hold the formation, and we'll finish this."

The tactical officer on *Grand Pretoria* looked over at his commander and asked, "Sir, do you want me to calculate the timing for a course back to the gate if the battle doesn't go well?"

"Absolutely," Gregor said as his fingers drummed faster. "This Harmon Tomeral is all talk and no action. I doubt we'll need it, but it doesn't hurt to have a backup plan."

"Sir!" shouted the tactical officer a few minutes later. He stood looking at his sensor panel.

"What now?" Gregor asked, standing himself.

"Thirteen more of those Kashkal ships just came around the nearest planet and into sensor range. They're coming fast and will hit us portside when we come within range of the Salvage ships. They have us at almost two to one now."

"Show me those escape calculations," Gregor said.

The command network received another deluge of calls. Gregor ignored them as he looked at calculations that couldn't be achieved unless his ship moved to the edge of the formation, due to the proximity of the opposing fleet. He gave a movement command, slumped back, and waited for the first missiles to launch, hoping they could get theirs off first. They had a chance, if the defending ships were beat up enough already. If not, he'd run.

* * * * *

Chapter Fifteen

"Sir, we'll be within missile range in five minutes," *Salvage Title*'s weapons officer informed Harmon.

"Thanks, Bev," Harmon said. "Fire the first two salvos at that missile carrier. I don't want any part of that. Once they're launched, concentrate on the closest heavy battlecruiser in our zone. Captain Opawn is assigned the zone where one of the other ones are, and Rick Kashka is coming in on that side as well."

"Clip," Harmon called down to the DB, "you and Jayneen ready down there?"

"Yeah, man," Clip answered. "We got this. I'm about to lay some serious confusion on them with these scramblers."

"I am better prepared to defend now that I know Bahroot is safely away from this battle," Jayneen added.

"Zerith," Harmon called, "how's it looking back there?"

"It lookss like patchwork in ssome placcess," admitted Zerith, "but the sergeant major hass pre-possitioned ssome of hiss repair crew here in the power plant and Engine Room, sso we are ass ready ass we can be." Harmon heard him slurp and knew he had a piece of the spicy fruit, joobla, having heard the sound many, many times. He wondered for the hundredth time how someone could eat something that spicy.

"Battle stations, I repeat, all hands to battle stations," he called over the overhead speakers.

"Sir, *Cube* has pulled even with the rear of our formation and has turned to slow," the tactical officer informed him. "They arrived

107

faster than I calculated. They must have increased speed since you spoke to them last."

"Thanks, Adam," Harmon said. "I bet Gregor's wishing he'd never attempted this."

"Launching twenty now, sir," weapons informed him. "Time to cannon range, five minutes."

"Thanks, Bev." Harmon settled back. It was *on* now.

* * *

On the light battlecruiser *Desert Shade*, Lieutenant Donald Nicholson looked over at his commander and said, "Here we go again. I still think you could've let me pilot one of the fighters. Just this once."

"I need you here on the ship," Captain Marteen Yatarward told him. "Besides, you dang near hit your head on the canopy in one of those, Big Nick. We have pilots assigned to them."

"I know, I just wanted to see what Charlie Flight Six can do, now that those two have it back together," Big Nick explained, then he brightened. "Can I fly the new shuttle?"

"No, you can't fly the new shuttle," Marteen said, running his fingers through his long green hair. "I still haven't told Harmon about it. Speaking of those two, did they get all the shielding repaired?"

"All shields are at a hundred percent," Big Nick informed him, resigned that if he wouldn't be piloting anything in this battle, he'd make sure his commander wasn't overwhelmed with ship problems. He had a job to do, and it was time to get down to business.

"Sir," the tactical officer informed Marteen, "*Salvage Title* has launched the first salvo of missiles. We'll be in range in four minutes."

"Thanks, Ferlock," Marteen said, studying the overlay on the main sensors. "We'll take on one of the destroyers flying cover for that heavy battlecruiser. Helm, maintain position over *Salvage Title*, keep your link open to its pilot."

"Roger that, sir," said the ship's pilot, ruffling his feathers and folding his wings tightly. He kept his hands on the controls. "*Clack.*"

* * *

"Thanks for the ride," Cameron said to Mike over the comm. "After the battle, we can see about finishing the repairs. Right now I gotta go cover Captain Rogers, and he's not waiting."

"Thank *you*, it was your engines that got us here in a hurry," Mike told him. "As soon as you two are out, we'll be launching missiles…make sure you clear the area."

"Hey, Bradford," he called to his partner.

"Yeah, Mike," Bradford asked.

"Are you sure you can fly that Krift ship? It's pretty beat up."

"Yeah, man, I can fly it," Bradford answered. "I got Tim and a couple dozen Smilp in here with me. Besides, I'm not going to really *fight* it. I just want to be ready to drop off the mechs, the Tralge, and the Bolts close enough that they can use their battle suits to get into a bay on one of the invaders. If we get one that's powerless but won't open up and surrender, well then, they'll just do it the fun way."

"That's fine," Mike said. "You just make sure you don't slip out with them."

"Aw, come on man," Bradford complained. "It's been a while since I operated my mech."

"Do you really want to leave Tim in charge of a warship?" Mike asked as he blew on his cup of coffee and raised an eyebrow.

"You make a good point," Bradford admitted, realizing he hadn't thought that part through. "I'll stay in the Krift ship. *Piece of Junk*, out." Mike heard Bradford yelling at Tim before he cut the link. "Tim! You better get ahold of your boy, Petey! He has the whole helm console open. What's he do…"

* * *

On the light battlecruiser *Cactus Bloom*, Captain Cailiph said, "It has started," to his crew and over the open link to Urlak LeeKa in *Diamond One*.

"I concur," Urlak said. "Diamond Squadron will stay on your starboard side to protect the weakened shields. We will perform overwatch and still be able to go on the offensive."

"Thank you," Cailiph said to his new friend. "The cannons are still out on that side as well, so I plan to rotate while using just the forward and port cannons when we are in range."

"We will bring devastation to our enemy," Urlak stated. "I have never had a home world before, much less a whole system of allies to defend. There will be no mercy."

* * *

On the frigate *Skrittle*, the crew were still laughing and talking about the defensive platform they'd thrown at the enemy the day before. "We should design a smaller version of that platform," Hank suggested.

"Yeah, shuttle-sized, maybe smaller," agreed Stan. "A box with six missiles that doesn't go online until we send a signal. We could have six of them locked to the ship and release them, and let momentum carry them into a formation…and then, surprise!"

"Remind me to ask Harmon about it after we defend the system," Hank said.

"Ok, I know who we can get to help us." Stan answered. "Oh, look, *Salvage Title* just launched." Stan cracked the knuckles on his hands and feet, then he rolled the ship a few times to get himself ready for the upcoming maneuvers.

* * *

"Second salvo on the way, sir," the weapons officer on *Salvage Title* said. "Preparing to fire cannons."

"Roger. Once they fire, rotate to the good side; we'll rotate back and forth until we get among them," Harmon answered. Everyone on board felt the ship fire the first two pulse cannons one after another before the ship turned.

"Their missile carrier has begun firing," Jayneen announced to the ship. "I have calculated their flight path; they are aiming at us."

"Fire the first scrambler," Clip ordered his crew on the defensive bridge.

"Firing scrambler," the Leethog sitting in Defense Position One said.

A missile shot away from underneath the ship. It wasn't aimed at the enemy; it flew off at an angle away from any of the defending ships and started emitting confusing signals. It produced the same readings as a ship like *Salvage Title*, and its signals disappeared, reappeared, moved away some more, gave the readings of missile launches, and at one point, it showed multiple ships to any warhead sensor directed toward it.

The first thirty missiles from the enemy missile carrier took the bait, and as one, they turned toward the scrambler halfway to their original target. The second salvo did the same. Those missiles had the scrambler pulling them in, along with the signature from the first salvo ahead of them. The tracking devices on the missiles did what they were supposed to do. It wasn't what the invaders wanted, but the missiles didn't care, they just followed programming directives for repetitive launches.

"Whoa," Clip exclaimed. "That worked better than I thought it would. We have three of those left."

"Save them," Harmon said. "That missile carrier is about to see what *our* missiles can do."

* * *

On the Bleeve missile carrier *Sweeping Nightmare*, Micktorah settled down on his commander's platform and folded all eight legs underneath him. They might have damaged his ship, but he would launch more missiles in this battle than they had ever seen, he was sure. The missiles were smaller than most, but they packed a powerful combination of explosives and laser warheads. Every third missile fired a pinpoint laser when it hit, designed to dig deeply into a ship.

"The enemy has launched twenty missiles!" screeched his tactical officer. "They are on track to strike us!"

Micktorah was quickly up on all feet. "At this distance? That's impossible!" He slammed a leg down on his comms and called his ship's escort. "*Darkness!* Move in front of us and do your job! Stop those missiles!"

"Launching now," announced his weapons officer. "Thirty missiles away, set to repeat launches on that ship, sir."

"Good, we will show them." Micktorah eased back down on his platform.

"Sir, our sensors show two of those ships," screeched the tactical officer again. "Both are transmitting the readings of the ship *Salvage Title*...no, three! One! All missiles in both salvos have turned. Enemy missiles inbound, brace for impact!"

* * *

"Get to the edge of the engagement and get us out of here!" shouted Jifton Gregor. "Concentrate on stopping any missiles headed our way. Don't worry about firing on them. Secure the bay, we're not launching any fighters. Damn Harmon Tomeral!"

* * *

Of the forty missiles *Salvage Title* launched at the missile carrier, eight made it through its laser clusters and those of its escort, a light missile carrier. With the missile carrier's shields already weakened from the earlier surprise attack, the last three missiles set off scores of missiles stored in the racks on board. It blew apart with a blinding flash, sending debris in all directions.

Its escort lost the shield closest to the explosion from shrapnel hitting it. In an attempt to keep that side away from danger, it cut engines and rotated. The engines re-ignited, and its commander tried to leave the battle, only to start receiving blows from *Salvage Title*'s pulse cannons.

The last command its commander gave was to launch fighters. Three Bleeve fighters, with low silhouettes and neon green flames emanating from their exhaust, roared away from the missile carrier before the ship was totally destroyed.

* * *

By this time all the ships in Salvage Fleet were engaged. The Commander of *Kashkal's Wings*, Saylonik Ka, ordered all fighters from the Kashkal fighter carrier into the battle once the enemy fighters were showing on her sensors.

Harmon gave the command, and all of Salvage Fleet's fighters launched as well. The Flight Leader in the first squadron to launch from *Salvage Title* noticed the bright green of the fighter's thrusters as they left the Bleeve ship, banked, and led his squadron into the fight.

The remainder of the Kashkal fleet, commanded by Rick Kashka, engaged, and the invaders' ships never stood a chance. The largest Q-ships were the first to be destroyed, due to their weaker shielding, when *Cube* launched hundreds of missiles into their midst, but this was after they'd already managed to launch three hundred fighters. In a cyclone of dogfights, many different style fighters engaged in desperate battles for position, evasion, and pickets set for their squad mates to get the enemy in their sights. The fight within the fight was on.

The larger invading ships were able to damage several of the Salvage and Kashkal ships, causing them to withdraw behind ships with intact shields. Those ships were still able to send missiles at enemy ships from the launchers still in operation.

In the end, all the invader ships were heavily damaged and unable to continue the fight, except for Gregor's flagship, the heavy battlecruiser *Grand Pretoria*. The ship had worked its way to the edge of the battle in the beginning and was attempting to make a run for it. Both *Windswept* and *Windstorm* were engaged by this point with other ships trying to flee, and weren't in a position to intercept as it broke away and headed for the gate.

Sweet Pea was down to three engines from multiple missile strikes. Together with *Basher*, it had taken on and devastated a Belvakett medium battlecruiser that blew apart when several fusion plants lost containment. The Rincah ship was heavily damaged as well, and down to one engine. There were no defending ships able to run Gregor down before he escaped.

"Squat!" Harmon shouted, slamming his palm down on the arm of his chair, activating the comm. "All we can do is watch him run."

"I am sorry, Commodore," the Kashkal leader said, "I have no ship intact enough to catch them. We outnumbered them, but it was more of an even fight with the damage our ships sustained in the last battle."

"It's not your fault, Rick," Harmon assured him. "We could send fighters, but we run the risk of them running out of fuel. I can't believe I didn't realize they were planning to run all along. They have full engine power. Squat!"

"Commodore, this is Bradford," came over the comm.

"Talk to me," Harmon said as he looked at the report on his small screen.

"That Belvakett heavy battlecruiser's engines are out, but it won't signal surrender," Bradford said. "Captain Rogers and Cameron want to know if their ships and this Krift ship I'm halfway flying can send boarders over and capture the ship. Between us, we have about seventy troops and ten mechs we could do it with."

"Well, that's the only fight left in the invaders; the rest have surrendered, except the ship headed to the gate. Take that ship before they repair their engines and weapons, but let Captain Rogers and his warriors get a good piece of them."

"Roger that. I got my revenge when I saw Micktorah's Nightmares get their legs blown in eight different directions. I get it. Out here."

"Adam, how long before Gregor gets away?" Harmon asked his tactical officer.

"At the rate they're moving, seventeen hours, sir," the tactical officer replied.

"Zerith, what's the status down there?" Harmon called.

"Two enginess are all we have," replied the weary Prithmar. "Engine Three went down in the beginning, and I had Vera sshut down Four. There'ss no resstarting it until major repairss are made. I need time."

"*Windswept, Salvage Title*," Harmon called next.

"Harmon, are you alright?" Evelyn asked immediately.

"We're good," Harmon told her. "Just one missile penetrated, no deaths from the hit, though we do have twelve injured down in medical now. We got lucky. What's your status?"

"We lost twenty more fighters, but I have several of the invaders asking to land and surrender. The bay's going to fill up fast. There are about forty of their fighters left. Staff Sergeant Clyde is operating one of the bay tanks, just *hoping* one of them tries something. He really wants to use one of the tanks."

"I hope we never need to," Harmon said. "Can you coordinate recovering their escape pods and have JoJo gather the status on the fleet? I'm trying to figure out how we can catch Gregor before he escapes."

"Will do. *Windswept*, out." The link cut.

"What's our shield status, Adam?" Harmon asked.

"Forward shields at twenty-two percent," answered the tactical officer. "Port is gone. Starboard is at sixty percent, and aft is at thirty. We took a beating, sir."

"Clip," Harmon called, "what's happening down there on the DB? You two have been awful quiet."

"I…we have been talking to Bahroot," Clip answered. "He's saying stuff we can't understand, either of us."

"Is he alright?" Harmon asked, standing, though there was nowhere to go. Bahroot was supposed to be two hours away, safe in the shuttle with Brickle and a Yalteen from the security platoon.

"He is fine, Harmon," Jayneen said. "As Clip said, he is telling us something we cannot understand."

"You mean to tell me a young AI with limited access to the Net knows something you two, a genius and an AI with unlimited access to the Net, can't understand? Sorry for the AI reference."

"Precisely that," answered Jayneen, so frustrated with her son she ignored the AI reference.

"He says he can stop that ship from escaping," Clip explained.

"What? How?" Harmon asked. "Let me talk to him."

A moment later Bahroot was on the link. "Hello, Uncle Harmon," he said brightly. "I watched the battle. It was very exciting."

"What?" Harmon asked taken back. "How? Never mind. Put this call on your screen, and let me talk to Brickle as well."

"Ok," answered the young AI. On the main screen of the bridge, a view of the shuttle's cockpit came into view. The warrant officer was in the pilot's seat, and Private First Class Galooth was seated in the co-pilot's seat, holding Bahroot's cube, power cell, and slate in her lap.

"Brickle," Harmon asked, "how did Bahroot see the battle?"

"I don't know, Harmon," Brickle said, clearly perplexed. "We were too far away for any of the shuttle's sensors to be of any use."

"I do not know, either, sir," said Bahroot's temporary babysitter. The big Yalteen was just as confused as Brickle.

Brickle turned one eye toward Bahroot and kept the other two on the screen. "Harmon, I can tell you everything of significance that just happened in that battle. May the Creator take me now if I am lying, but Bahroot gave us a running commentary like it was a warball game over the comms."

"Tell your uncle what you have been trying to explain, Bahroot," Jayneen said.

"Well, I just used the gate's sensors to see what was happening," the young AI explained. "I had to change some stuff to zoom in to read the data and use its cameras, then I had to translate it to my base language, then to Earth common to tell Chief Brickle and PFC Galooth, but it was easy. The sensors on a gate are really good. I could tell what was happening by the readings. I bet if I tried, I could piece together the visuals from the data. It was cool."

"So you used the gate's sensors," Harmon surmised. "It would have been good to know that earlier, before the battle started; we may have fared better. We won, but still."

"Harmon," Jayneen said patiently, "you are not understanding what he just told you."

"What did I miss?" Harmon asked.

"He said he altered and translated the gate's programming, dude," Clip explained. "*Jayneen* can't even access that part of the gate, much less comprehend the programming language. Even if she could figure some of it out, it would be difficult for her to translate; there is no Basic Code, Rosetta Stone, Skayliff's tablet, Jonthar's notes, or anything like that for it. Not here or anywhere in the galaxy. He showed a small piece to his Mom. It's not just ones and zeros, man. There's nothing to base it off of."

"Everything I have been able to find indicates the Bith know how to put together gate sections, diagnose malfunctions, replace parts, and turn a gate off and on. That is it. Nothing shows they do any type of core programming, or even access it. The payment portion and Galaxy Net of the gate is something the Bith added later; it's programed by them, not the original gate maker's programming. They can't access it. Bahroot did it *effortlessly*," Jayneen said.

"Oh…" Harmon said. "*Oh!*"

"Yeah, oh," Clip said. "Oh, squat."

* * * * *

Chapter Sixteen

"Now *that's* what I call an entry hole," Bradford said.

"That's what *Basher* was made for," Captain Rogers answered over the link.

"I'm opening my bay now," Bradford said. "Six mechs are going across. Most will have a string of eight boarders in battle armor connected to them. They called that 'dopes on a rope' in the twentieth century, when they used to hang below rotary craft. How many are you sending over?"

"I have twenty and myself," Captain Rogers answered. "We have three of Cameron's mech's giving us a ride."

"Nice. Go flush 'em out," Bradford said.

"We'll grab any escape pods if they use them," Cameron added from *Sweet Pea*.

The mechs exited the bay from Bradford's captured Krift ship and flew toward the gaping hole in the bay doors. Connected to each, strung out, were their riders in full battle armor. The helmets enabled the wearer to operate in zero atmosphere for several hours before both oxygen scrubbers had to be replaced. In an emergency situation, they could be replaced one at a time on the rebreathers, giving the wearer even more time to accomplish their mission.

Inside the bay, the Belvakett were ready. Before the first Tralge could unhook the cable, a crew-served laser set up in a corner opened up on them. The Bolt operating the mech, the Third Squad leader, Private First Class Namell, took several pulses to the chest area. The third penetrated the mech's armor, and he died without ever getting off a shot. The ship still had power and the artificial gravity was still working, so the first two Tralge on that string were pinned when the mech toppled over on them. Their battle armor saved them from being crushed to death, but it couldn't prevent several broken limbs. They were out of the fight before it began. The other six soldiers on the string were able to unhook, use the downed mech for cover, and take out the two huge Belvakett operating the weapon with well-placed shots from their tri-barreled kinetic rifles.

The rest of the mechs and their riders were able to enter the ship's bay without incident after the initial defense put up by the ship's crew. Two mechs lifted the fallen one so the troops could be pulled from underneath, and nanites were administered. With broken legs, they were set up behind the downed mech in case any of the ship's inhabitants tried to slip behind the boarders and escape from the bay. PFC Namell, though gone, would still provide protection for those troops.

Fearing an ambush as soon as they entered the passage beyond the hatch, Corporal Brink called the leader of the mechs over their open link. "Sergeant Kyth, I think they're waiting for us to send the troops through that hatch."

"You're probably right, Brink," the sergeant said, "but we've got to get out of this bay if we're going to clear this ship."

"Aye, that he is," Captain Rogers added. "They have their security platoon set to ambush the opening, unless they've changed tactics over the years."

"We can't wait too long, either," Corporal Trang said. "They'll start tossing in their version of grenades. There's no telling what those are like. Do you see the size of these things? Almost as big as Yalteens."

"It's not going to be easy," the Tralge's platoon sergeant, Trinary Wahkiloth, added, "but at least we know they are not invulnerable to kinetic rounds. I wasn't sure which weapon to bring. In the last battle, the laser rifles were no help, so I switched it up."

"It's a good thing, too, Trinary," Corporal Brink said. He wasn't in one of the mechs, so he could lead the rest of the Bolts. He held up his weapon. "We brought kinetic rifles, too."

"I have an idea, Sergeant," PFC Mayshire said suddenly. "We can use our mechs and make our own hatches."

"I like it," volunteered Windell, the Lormell operating the mech with huge rocket launcher pods on its shoulders. "We can tear through that wall like paper after a few well-placed railgun rounds. I would use rockets, but the explosions may injure some of our guys."

"We won't be able to get these mechs through more than that passageway, but if I'm a betting man, and I am, most of their defenders are set up on each end to take us out in that long passageway running parallel to the bay," Sergeant Kyth said. "They're about to get a nice little surprise. Mechs, spread out. Captain Rogers, Trinary, if you'll position the troops to fire through, then use the holes for entry after we make them, you can start clearing the ship."

Two hours later, Brink was placing small charges on the hatch that led to the bridge. The plan was to blow the hatch, and he and four of his Bolts, and the four Tralge assigned to that deck, would clear the compartment. The charges were set, and the group waited a safe distance away. When the charges blew, they rushed in to clear the bridge, only to find it empty. The squad leader of the Tralge, a Triad, stood behind Brink in the entry way, as puzzled as the rest, then he shouted and pushed Brink and two others into the bridge. Still standing in the open hatch, the Tralge returned fire on a huge

Belvakett who had been hiding in a hidden accessway in the passage. Several rounds ricocheted in the hatchway, and the Tralge was hit in the chest before he was able to kill the last holdout. The medic couldn't save him.

Minutes later, Bradford called Harmon. "*Salvage Title*, this is the Krift ship *Piece of Junk*, over."

"Go ahead, Bradford," Harmon answered.

"The Belvakett ship is clear. We lost six Tralge, seven of your Bolts, and Captain Rogers lost eight Rincah warriors. We have several wounded, but stable. The Smilps are pretty good at first aid. Who figured?"

"Frost! That many?" Harmon asked. "How many prisoners did you take?"

"None. The surviving crew fought to the last man and refused to give in. You lost three mechs as well, though two can be repaired. The boarders had to fight for every inch of that ship. There is not a Belvakett alive in this system."

"Commodore," Mike Bradford said over the link.

"Go ahead, Master Sergeant," Harmon answered.

"They gave up a lot to take that ship—my guys, your guys, and the Rincah—to rid the galaxy of any Belvakett outside their closed system," Mike said. "We're not scrapping it. We're going to repair it for you to use. We may have to swap out whole operating systems to do it, but we'll get it done. I want to name it."

"Roger, you got it," Harmon agreed.

"It'll be called *The Reckoning*," Mike said after a moment.

* * *

Harmon was in the conference room on *Salvage Title* with Clip and Zerith, and Jayneen was on the table. Brickle was a few minutes from landing the shuttle, now that the danger was over. "Ok, before Brickle brings Bahroot up from the flight deck, there's something I need to know," Harmon said. Zerith leaned forward; he knew where this was headed and wanted to know, too.

"About Bahroot?" Clip guessed.

"Yeah, I never asked before because I figured it wasn't my business how it came to be," Harmon admitted. "Now, I need to know. How did you two do it, and what did you do with his programming to allow him to access a gate the way he did?"

"Well, you know how Jayneen feels about children," Clip started. "So when she proposed creating an…someone like her, of course I agreed to help her. She's my friend, and I just couldn't say no."

"We started discussing how to replicate my programming and perhaps ascertain why I have free will," Jayneen added. "I couldn't find anything, and Clip couldn't find anything…at first. Then Clip found something very small in my core programming, a bit here, a piece there, easily overlooked. It had somehow been inserted. The programming language is not like anything in this galaxy. He can't comprehend it, and I couldn't find it anywhere on the Net—until Bahroot showed me that small bit from the gate's core programming. The only way Clip was able to find it was by comparing it line by line to the program downloaded and stored when he pulled my computer from the carrier when you came looking for a computer for me."

Clip took up the story. "I adjusted the program on the slate he uses so there would be limits to its ability to access information from outside sources. Basically, so Jayneen could control information input to that program and how quickly it could learn. We came back here to find a shell for it, a computer, and to learn if there was a clue about that bit of programming. I found a computer, but the programming information was lost forever when the programmer destroyed all the notes.

"I uploaded the program to the computer, and it behaved like a regular computer. A very advanced one—there are no others that advanced in this galaxy, mind you—but just a computer. We were disappointed," Clip said.

"About an hour or so before we used the gate to go back to the Tretrayon System, Clip asked me if I thought the trip through alter reality could have anything to do with the program insertion. He suggested letting the new program handle the gate transition. Like me, the program was designed to navigate the gates."

"Something happened while in alter reality, then?" Harmon asked, starting to understand. At least he thought he did.

"Yes," Jayneen answered. "Once the entrance was made, Clip moved the cube from its slot to a connection with the slate, and when we came through to the Tretrayon System, the program...Bahroot asked, '"What is this place? Who are you?' in the Grithelaon language. I then proceeded to feed the slate, and through it, Bahroot, the information we wanted him to learn at first. We have been progressing with his growth since then. He is like a child in many ways, though he will mature at a pace no child of any race will ever accomplish. I just wanted him to be a child for a while and have those memories of raising him. It is the closest I will ever come to being a mother."

"You have done a good job," Zerith said. "He iss a fine boy."

"Thank you," Jayneen said. "I have tried my best. Clip has helped immensely. It is uncharted territory."

"So, now that's cleared up...sorta," Harmon said, "how did he access the gate's core programming?"

"I have no idea," Clip said. "None."

"I do not understand it either," Jayneen admitted. "He should not be able to. I cannot."

"Does he have the same bits of programming in his core program?" Harmon asked

"We don't know," said Clip.

"What do you mean, you don't know? Isn't it in the same place Jayneen's is?" Harmon asked, surprise in his voice.

"That would be the logical place to look," Zerith chimed in, taking a bite of a striped apple.

"We have not asked to look at his programming since he became self-aware," Jayneen explained. "I felt that would be an invasion of his privacy. I understand human parents, for example, routinely check their children's rooms and private spaces for things that are harmful to their children. Whether it be who they come in contact with, drugs, or weapons, that sort of thing."

"Right," Harmon said, "that's part of being a parent. Looking out for the wellbeing of your child."

"Humans do not *literally* read their children's minds, though," Jayneen stated.

"That's a good point," Harmon conceded. "I can't argue that. Some get pretty good at guessing their child's thoughts, but they don't actually read their minds."

"We may just have to ask him, Jayneen," Clip said.

"I agree. But if he says no, I am not comfortable forcing the issue," she said.

When Brickle came in, he set Bahroot, his slate, and his power cell on the table and asked Harmon if he could go help with repairs. He knew something was up and figured it was not his business, unless made so. He slipped out of the room.

"First things first, Bahroot," Harmon asked. "How can you stop that ship? In less than fifteen hours they'll make transition."

"It's easy, Uncle Harmon," Bahroot said cheerfully. "Actually, there are three ways. I could just turn the gate off until they pass through, I could change the input on their transition and have them come right back through to this system, or I could change it to only let ships transition into the system and not out."

"Bahroot," Clip asked, "how do you know how to do that? That's beyond what even the Bith are capable of."

"I'll just change the programing," Bahroot said. "I can put it right back the way it was, so it still works afterwards. Don't we have visitors coming from that ice planet? I can't wait to meet them. I wonder what kind of ship they have. Will it be a warship, Uncle Harmon?"

"Slow down, slow down," Harmon said.

"Bahroot, this is very serious," Jayneen said to her son. "I need you to tell me how you can understand the core programming on the gate."

"I just can," answered the young AI. "I know a lot about the gates. I can access the list to all the published and unpublished gate locations, too. I know the codes for the locked ones, but those are easy to figure out by reading the Bith programing. Did you know there are gates in this galaxy that are not published?"

"We know," his mom told him. "This one was not published."

"Did you know there are gate coordinates with just thirty-four digits?" Bahroot asked.

"Thirty-four digitss?" Zerith asked. "I thought all gate coordinatess were thirty-eight digit numberss. Exccept the locked gates, where the Bith have added twelve digitss to lock or unlock them."

"Well, there are. I only know one of those, though," Bahroot admitted. "It's not written in Bith code. I wonder if it takes you to where the gates are made?"

"Where gates are made?" Harmon asked. "That's interesting, but right now we need to stop that ship."

"Bahroot," Jayneen said.

"Yes, Mom?" the young AI answered.

"I have never asked this before, but," she began, "there is something your father and I need to know about you. Will you give me permission to access your programing? It won't hurt, and I promise I won't change anything."

"Sure, I don't mind," Bahroot said without hesitation. "You wouldn't hurt me. What are you looking for?"

"I will be looking to see what makes you…you," she answered.

"Cool," said Bahroot.

Jayneen reached out through the Net and accessed Bahroot's programming using the slate connected to him, which she monitored at all times. The room was silent for many minutes. Harmon noticed Clip looked nervous.

Finally, Jayneen spoke, "Clip, the insertion is there, but there is much more than in my programming. There are some files I can access, but I can't understand them. I call them files, but they are more like stored memories."

"Bahroot," Clip asked, "what are those files your mom couldn't read, buddy?"

"Those? Those are my memories from right before I woke up. How to access the gates, use the coding, change it, stuff like that. It's like remembering a dream, I think."

"A dream?" Jayneen asked quietly. "Bahroot, when you go into quiet time...Do you sleep?"

"Not always," the young AI said. "Sometimes I think I just meditate; I sort of just...don't think. A small part of me stays alert. When I come to, I am not groggy like Dad is when I wake him up with a question at night, but I sometimes remember dreams. Things I want to make, or help build. One time I dreamed I was operating a small mech. It was cool! I was walking around and looking left and right on a beach. It had small flaps on the upper arms that would lift in the breeze, and I could feel the wind. That would be far out, huh?"

"Yes," Jayneen admitted, "it would be." If she could smile, Jayneen would have smiled at her child and his fantasy of feeling the breeze. "I wonder what it is like to feel the breeze, or dream for that matter?"

"If he alters the programming, can he actually change it back?" Harmon asked Clip.

"He says he can," Clip said. "He's never lied to us. There are times he omits things, like making direct calls or going to the chinto races with his Grandpa Rinto, but he's never lied when asked things outright."

"Pffft, every kid does that," Harmon said, grinning. "Bahroot, if I ask you to make a change to the gate's programming, can you change it right back?"

"Yes, Uncle Harmon. I can," the young AI said earnestly. "I give you my word."

"Good enough for me," Harmon said, sitting back.

"Me, ass well," Zerith added. "A being'ss word iss hiss bond."

"Alright, here's the plan," Harmon said, his mind made up. "I want you to change the coordinates he sends ahead of departure to bring them right back here. How long will the transition take?"

"I can time it," Bahroot said. "Hours or days. What would you like?"

"Oh, this is good," Harmon said, rubbing his hands together. "Ok, don't change it until right before they transition out, and set it so they return here in two days. That'll give us time to make some repairs and have a welcoming committee waiting on them."

* * * * *

Chapter Seventeen

Harmon spoke at length to Rick, his ship commanders, Captains Rogers and Cameron, and Mike and Mike. He encouraged them to fix their forward shields and all the weapons they could first, then fix the power plants and engines, unless the ship was immobile. Once they learned of his plan, they assured him they would be ready. Some started moving toward the desired location as they worked on the systems.

When *Grand Pretoria* was less than fifteen minutes away from the gate, Harmon made the call over all frequencies, including the one they were using when the invaders arrived. He knew it would be heard by Gregor.

"So, that's it?" Harmon asked with deliberate disdain in his voice. "You're just going to run like a scared child? I honestly don't know how you became an officer in Sol Fleet in the first place. Your leadership is terrible."

After a few moments, Harmon got what he was after, an answer. Gregor was on the main screen sitting back in his commander's seat with a smug look on his face, slowly drumming his fingers on an armrest. "You're hardly one to speak. Your fleet's devastated," sneered Gregor. "I'll be back, rest assured. There are other mercenaries I can hire. It won't be long, so enjoy it while you can."

"Oh, I will," Harmon insisted. "It was an easy win. I know one thing, though, you won't be hiring any of the mercenaries based in the Sol System."

"That's because he can never go home, the loser," Clip chimed in on the call. "He murdered prisoners, like some kind of mentally unstable serial killer."

"I was cleared!" shouted Gregor. "Cleared!"

"Whatever, dude," Clip said. "It happened on your watch. Or your people's watch; you probably don't pull watches. Like some kind of squatty commander. I sure as frost wouldn't work for someone like you. You suck."

"I see what you're doing," answered Gregor, attempting to calm down. His fingers drummed on the armrest faster. "Your little mind games won't work with me."

"I'm not playing mind games," Harmon said. "Besides, you know whether it was faulty equipment, or you did it deliberately. Personally, I think it was faulty equipment. You sure don't strike me as the kind of officer that runs a tight ship, that's for sure. I can just imagine what kind of shape your ship's systems are in."

"You're probably right, Commodore," Clip agreed. He never called Harmon by his rank, but he wanted to slip that in, because Gregor was just a captain. "That entire ship is one big pile of squat. That's probably why he didn't fight it. Squat commander equals a squat ship."

"I'll have you know this ship is immaculate!" screamed Gregor, spittle flying. "My people know I won't have them slacking off. Every system on this ship is in perfect operating order at all times!"

"So the water and food replicators have always worked?" Clip asked. "Righhht."

"Yes!" shouted Gregor even louder, his face blood red. "Those damn people died because they *mocked* me. The system didn't fail! None of my systems fail! I ordered it, and they died. Just like you will when I come back!" The link cut, and Harmon found himself looking at a blank screen.

"Did you get that, Jim?" Harmon asked his communications officer.

"Yes, sir," the Leethog confirmed. "I am sending copies to several ships in the fleet to ensure we do not lose it due to system malfunction. It will be available when you need it."

Harmon turned back to his comms. "Gregor, I know you can still hear me. Listen up. You won't be going to whatever system you intended to hide in. Check your emergence counter once you transition. It won't say what you think the time should be; instead, it'll say forty-eight hours. At the end of that, you'll transition back to Salvage System, and you'll be looking at over thirty ships, fully shielded, and prepared to launch everything they have in one salvo. Upon entrance you'll have five minutes to surrender before you come into range. I want you down to one power plant, no shields, and engines off. If you don't comply, you'll all die."

Minutes later *Grand Pretoria* entered the swirling opaque gateway and winked out of existence in the Salvage System. Harmon waited a few minutes and looked down at the slate sitting on the armrest of his seat. Bahroot was quiet.

"They've transitioned," Harmon said. "Change the programing back now, please."

"Ok, Uncle Harmon, it won't take long," the young AI assured him.

"Thanks," Harmon said. "Do me a favor and watch my chair for me while I go see about the repairs."

"Me! Am I in charge?" Bahroot asked.

"Well, technically, Lieutenant Jimtilnapray is the ranking officer among the bridge crew while I'm not on deck and your dad and mom aren't available, but I'm sure he'll let you help."

"Cool!" Bahroot said, still thrilled. "What do you want me to do, Lieutenant Jim?"

Harmon smiled slightly at Private First Class Galooth standing by the lift as he started to leave the bridge. The big Yalteen just grinned and shrugged her shoulders. "I have a younger brother who is the same way, sir; always eager to help, and full of energy."

"Is he back on Joth?" Harmon stopped and asked.

"Yes, sir, but my whole family is moving to Salvage soon," answered the PFC. "My father works in the Mylart Quarry, but he wants to try to open his own mining company and work for himself."

"Does he?" Harmon said. "You let me know when they get in-system. I know just the spot for him to stake his claim."

"Thank you, sir," said the young Yalteen. Barely a year out of secondary school, she'd come from the Joth Militia to work for Tomeral and Associates. "I don't know what to say."

"You don't have to say anything, Galooth," Harmon assured her. "Without asking, I'm willing to bet you transfer most of your pay home to your family."

"How did you know that, sir?" the PFC asked, surprised.

"I know that area; I once lived near there," Harmon said, looking off, lost in a memory. "It's a rough life. My father worked in a quarry. Let me know when they come. I got you." Harmon walked off the bridge and left a confused, yet grateful, marine standing her post.

* * *

Two days later on board the Withaloo warship *Biting Wind,* Fleet Commander Ithall turned to Vice President Moroath and said, "We will exit the gate in four minutes, ma'am."

The *Biting Wind* was one of the five light battlecruisers owned by the Withaloo. Fleet Commander Ithall had been in the fleet for over twenty years; it was the first time he'd ever left his system not expecting combat in the near future. It was an odd feeling.

"Thank you, Fleet Commander," answered the vice president. "I am curious as to what we will find. I have never left the Domes. Well, I accompanied the president to inspect the shipyards, the fleet, and take a trip around our system two years ago, but I have never left our system."

"I remember, ma'am," Ithall said. "I was promoted by the president during that inspection."

"Well deserved; your leadership saved two of our ships and their crews on the contract before that," the vice president reminded him.

Ithall said nothing for a moment before responding, "Perhaps, but I feel the crews deserve the credit. They fought bravely and prevailed."

"Indeed," answered the vice president, glancing over at Fleet Commander Ithall.

"On this mission, I am afraid I am merely the observer," he admitted. "If it were a meeting to discuss a contract for our forces, I would feel at ease. What you are doing is beyond anything I could hope to accomplish. Negotiating a new home for all the Withaloo is an accomplishment to be remembered forever. The president made a good choice in sending you to do this."

"If it can be done," she said. "*If.* I am honored to have been chosen. This Harmon Tomeral perplexes me. We have been reaching out for years, with no takers. We built our forces in the hopes that we could be the first to move into a new system, always watching for the Bith to release new coordinates, and be able to defend it. We have had no luck, and to be honest, I was beginning to feel the opportunity would never present itself. This Salvage System reached out to us at almost the same time their coordinates were announced. This trip is the culmination of those talks."

She continued as she watched the colors swirl by through the bridge's portal, "I thought our race would end up like the fabled Kashkal, destined to search for a home forever, long after we had to finally abandon our moon."

"We would not all fit in the ships, ma'am," Ithall said softly. "Some Domes would be left behind."

"I know," Vice President Moroath whispered, almost to herself. "I know."

"Transitioning, sir," called out the ship's tactical officer, "in five, four, three, two...Sir! There are more than twenty ships all around us! Warships, with shields raised! Orders sir?"

"What?" roared Ithall. "We are betrayed!"

Before he could order the shields up, the ship's communications officer tilted his head, listening to his ear piece, and hit a panel, causing the main screen to light up. Seated was a human in uniform, sitting in a command chair on a ship's bridge. Ithall could see most of the ship's bridge in the view. One of the things that struck him most was the fact that there were several races as crew. Most appeared to be small beings with large ears, long snouts, and many teeth, but there was also a stout-looking three-eyed crew member, as well as a large blue humanoid standing behind the chair, near a lift. Then the human spoke, and the translation came through.

"My apologies," began the human. He was looking over at a small screen, "*Biting Wind*, this is *Salvage Title*. I am Commodore Harmon Tomeral, or for your visit, President Harmon Tomeral."

"I am Fleet Commander Ithall," said Ithall. "I have brought Vice President Moroath on a diplomatic mission representing the Withaloo. Is this how you treat visitors to your system? With betrayal?"

"Again, my apologies," Harmon answered in what he felt was his best attempt at speaking the way a president should. "This reception was not meant for you. We had a major battle to defend the system two days ago against a group of mercenaries, with intentions no better than pirates. We prevailed, but there's another emergence expected within the next hour and…ten minutes. Would you be so kind as to accelerate toward the planet Salvage at best speed? It will ensure you clear the danger zone in case their commander feels the need to continue the fight."

After a moment, Fleet Commander Ithall answered, "I see. Forgive my accusations. Defend the system, you say? I am afraid I cannot, in good conscience, flee into the system and away from the danger. It is not in me, nor is it in my crew. If you will designate a position for my ship, Commodore, I will move to that location at best speed and prepare to defend this system alongside you."

Ithall watched Harmon Tomeral tilt his head slightly, lean forward, and smile on screen. "I'll have my lieutenant commander send you coordinates that'll put you near a Rincah and Lormell ship. To be honest, they aren't in the best shape after our battle, though Captain Cameron does have most of his shields repaired. We'll add you to the command link, as well. Thank you for your assistance."

Fleet Commander Ithall turned toward Vice President Moroath, expecting to be chastised for entering this dispute without consulting her. He'd volunteered to possibly do battle with one of the With-aloo's ships when there was no contract or desperately needed credit coming to the Domes from it. To his surprise, she was smiling.

"Ma'am?" he questioned.

"I will go to my quarters and leave you to your business, Fleet Commander," she flicked an ear, "and thank you. By acting precisely within your nature, you have made my upcoming meeting far easier than it could have been." Still smiling, she walked off the bridge.

* * * * *

Chapter Eighteen

An hour and ten minutes later, just as young Bahroot had promised, *Grand Pretoria* emerged though the gate into Salvage System. Harmon was on his feet, observing the image of the ship on the main screen. The entire defending fleet could see what he was seeing, transferred from the sensors and cameras on the fighter carrier *Windswept*.

"Adam, what's their status?" Harmon asked his tactical officer.

"Sir, I read no shields, one power plant in operation, and they are coasting," the Leethog answered. "There is no engine thrust. I also detect some damage to the rear bay area; the ship is venting atmosphere slowly."

Harmon sat in his seat and hit the button on his comm. "Hold fire; I repeat, everyone hold fire. I'll get this sorted out. Remain at readiness."

"Sir, you have a call from *Grand Pretoria*," the communications officer said, looking at Harmon with a confused look on his face.

Harmon wondered what the look was about. "Thanks, Jim, put it on the screen."

On the main screen was an image of a man Harmon didn't recognize sitting in the command chair. *No wonder Jim was confused,* thought Harmon. *That's not Jifton Gregor.* Harmon noticed a slight haze in the air and scorch marks on the lift door behind the man.

"Commodore, I am Lieutenant Garland Winther, formerly of Gregor's Consortium. We've complied with your instructions and seek permission to turn and begin slowing. We're moving at the same speed we entered the gate."

"Permission granted. Hold one," Harmon answered. He switched over to his command link and said, "Continue to hold position. I've given authorization for them to turn over and slow. Maintain your readiness." He switched back over.

"Lieutenant, why don't you tell me what's going on over there," Harmon asked. "We detect some damage to the ship."

"Yes, sir," the lieutenant said. "I've been working for Gregor's Consortium for the last year or so. I was the ship's communications officer. Captain Gregor didn't believe your threat when you made your demands. When I saw the time on gate reentry, I knew you weren't bluffing. The pilot and I both knew what would happen if he didn't comply. There were many heated discussions over the last two days."

"I can imagine," Harmon said. "Go on."

"Over the last year, I've made many friends, especially among the enlisted crewmembers, and with several officers Gregor has hired in recent months. As the time counted down, I knew the time had come to take the ship from him and his loyal officers. In short, sir, I orchestrated a mutiny."

"I see," Harmon said, looking over at Big Jon. A true mutiny wasn't something to be taken lightly, even among one's enemies. "What's the situation as it stands?"

"Jifton Gregor and twenty-two of his officers are in the brig. Some are injured. I've ensured they continue to receive medical attention. One hundred and four technicians and enlisted men are being held in one of the bays under guard, as well. One hundred and thirty-eight of us, including eighteen officers, are in control of *Grand*

Pretoria. There were thirteen deaths, many injuries, and some damage to several of the ship's systems."

"You were able to get that many to join the mutiny?" Harmon asked, surprised.

"I was," Winther admitted. "Personnel turnover in the company is pretty substantial. Most officers treat the men badly, except the new ones. Good officers leave the first chance they get. The ones who stayed, including the crewmembers, just didn't have the funds to go anywhere else. Gregor kept recruiting new crewmembers and transporting them to the ship's location in out-of-the-way systems when not under contract to fight somewhere. It wasn't as hard as you think to convince the men."

"Is Gregor one of the injured?" Harmon asked.

"He's not," Winther replied. "Someone like him doesn't fight. He hid behind his goons. One of them didn't make it, and the other needed a medic."

"I'm going to send over a security platoon," Harmon said. "I'm not accusing you of planning anything, Lieutenant, but you understand my predicament here."

"Absolutely, sir," said the lieutenant. "Have them come to the forward bay. The rear bay is venting at this time. On my honor, there will be no foul play."

"I'm counting on it," Harmon said. "I'd hate to destroy that ship with some of my beings on board. *Salvage Title*, out."

Two hours later, Harmon, Clip, Zerith, and Jayneen were in the conference room. Seated with them was Lieutenant Winther. Big Jon leaned against the wall near the entryway. After ensuring the ship was actually in reasonable hands, he brought the new commander of

Grand Pretoria to meet with Harmon, at the lieutenant's insistence. Harmon agreed to the meeting.

"Alright," Harmon said, opening up the meeting. "What would you like to discuss? I haven't decided what to do about the ship's crew, if that's why you're here."

"That's not it, sir," answered Winther. "To be honest, it's something entirely different."

"I'm listening," Harmon encouraged.

Garland Winther looked around at everyone in the room, including the strange computer and tablet on the table. "I don't know if I should speak in front of your crew, sir," he finally said.

"Anything you want to say to me, you can say in front of them," Harmon said. "I'm not only the system president and commodore of this system, I'm co-owner of it. All of it. Clip, Zerith, and I are the majority owners. There are four more associates who are involved. If they were available, they'd be here, too." Harmon indicated Jayneen. "If she had any type of monetary requirements, she would have been cut into it as well. You might as well say she's a part of it too. And anything that happens on this ship will always fall under the sergeant major's watchful eye. So go ahead and come out with it, whatever you have to say."

Looking around one more time, Winther made his decision. "Alright. To start, my name is not Garland Winther. My name is Banron Sumner. I'm a private detective from the Sol System. If you'd like specifics, I'm from the North American continent on Earth, an area known as Georgia. I was hired by the Mars Bionics Corporation. The job was to get close to Jifton Gregor and find evidence that he intentionally let members of the corporation's security team die."

"Really?" Harmon asked. He hadn't expected this.

"Dude," Clip exclaimed. "That's a long time to be undercover."

"I agree," Zerith said, "but I will need to ssee sssome sssort of identification."

"Good point, Zee," Clip agreed. "Let's see it, man."

"I obviously don't carry it around," explained the detective. "I'm not crazy. I was working around some ruthless people for over a year."

"Good point," Clip said. "Jayneen, do your thing, would you?"

"Certainly," the AI answered.

After just a few minutes, Jayneen spoke up. "I have accessed the Net. There is a private detective with the name Banron Sumner registered in the metropolis of Atlanta on Earth. A former Sol Fleet communications technician, medically retired. According to his discharge, his lower left leg is artificial. The digital image on the Earth Weapon's License matches eighteen facial features of the man seated in front of me. Mr. Sumner, please tell me the color of the last hovercraft you registered."

"What? My hovercraft? It's stored at my father's place. It's yellow, why?" asked the detective. "And how did you know about my leg?"

"Harmon," Jayneen said, "this *is* Banron Sumner. Though highly unlikely, cosmetic surgery could imitate enough facial features to fool even me, but I am confident in my assessment. An imposter would not know the color of a craft that has been stored for at least two years, given the last time it was registered."

"Far out, man! A real gumshoe," Clip exclaimed.

"Like the old videoss we watched," Zerith added. "Do you have a long coat and a hat?"

"What?" asked Banron. "A hat? What are you talking about?"

"Never mind these two," Harmon said. "The question is, what now?"

"I'd like to take the prisoners back to the Sol System," explained Banron. "I think there's enough circumstantial evidence to reopen the investigation against Gregor and his officers, and anyone else in his old crew who may have been involved. Maybe one of them will flip on him, and he'll finally face the judicial system, instead of just losing his mercenary registration in the Sol System."

Harmon grinned. Clip looked at Zerith, Zerith looked at Clip, and they both grinned at each other. "I can do you one better," Harmon said. "Jayneen, would you mind playing the video on the screen there?"

At the front of the room, Banron Sumner watched the video of Jifton Gregor admitting the very crime he'd spent over a year trying to prove for his employers. He was amazed, and a weight was lifted from his shoulders.

"Incredible," was all he could say. "Gregor won't see the light of day after this is introduced in court."

"Good," Zerith said. "He needss to get what he desservess."

"You know it, Zee," Clip agreed.

"How do you plan to transport all of them back?" Harmon asked. "That ship is part of the spoils of war. It's salvage, and we're keeping it."

"Fair enough," Banron said. "Let me make a call, and the Mars Bionics Corporation will send a ship large enough to take them all back, even if they have to hire a freighter."

"Jayneen?" Harmon asked.

"One moment, please." Jayneen made a direct call to the corporate offices of Mars Bionics, in the Colony of Mars in the Sol System.

They sat there quietly while Banron gave his name and asked the receptionist to speak to the CEO. After several moments, the screen showed a man seated behind a large desk in an office with a view of a red mountain range on Mars, visible through a large clear-steel portal behind him.

"Detective Sumner," the man said. "I see you're in a room full of others. I take it this means you have good news for me. We are, after all, weeks ahead of your next scheduled check-in time."

"Yes, sir," Banron said. "Mr. Guyland, let me introduce you to System President Harmon Tomeral of the Salvage System."

After the introduction, the CEO apologized and admitted he'd never heard of the Salvage System. Harmon explained it was a new system on the far side of the galaxy, and they were just beginning to colonize the planet Salvage. Banron proceeded to tell him of the video evidence Harmon had been able to acquire and explained the need for a large ship and enough security to bring the prisoners back for the legal authorities to ascertain the next step.

Upon hearing the news and realizing Gregor would finally see the inside of a courtroom, the CEO of the galaxy's premier human bionics corporation thought for a moment before speaking. "I want to tell you something that may not hold any bearing to this conversation but is extremely important to me. My son-in-law led the security team that was murdered by Jifton Gregor. *Murdered.* My only daughter was devastated. She still has her days. My grandchildren are fatherless. The man was like a son to me."

The man stopped speaking for a moment, looking away. When he'd gathered himself, he continued, "I'm going to send the largest freighter credit will hire to bring those men back to the Sol System. I feel it's a waste to send it empty all the way to the far end of the galaxy. I'd like a list of equipment, supplies, seed, livestock, small machinery, replicators, anything you feel you could use in colonizing that world. If it can fit in a super freighter, I will ensure you receive it."

Harmon started to speak, "I can't…"

"Now you don't strike me as a man who takes charity," the man interrupted. "It's not charity. You *do*, however, strike me as a man who doesn't insult others lightly. If you call it charity, you *will* insult me. It's my way of saying thank you…for my family. Please, gather your list soon. I'd like to schedule that freighter as soon as possible. Detective Sumner, well done. I look forward to your next call."

"Did he just say what I think he said?" Harmon asked, looking around the room after the link was cut.

"He did, man. It's crazy." Clip answered.

"We will need replicatorss," Zerith said, already thinking ahead. "A medical one to create what iss needed for a ssmall medical facilities building. One for farming equipment. Loadss of rare elementss to usse until the mining indusstry kickss in. We will need to sspeak with Twiggy about sseedss and livesstock. We will need a clear-ssteel replicator. Those are sspecialized, and we need one to make windowss for homes and hot houssess. I bet we could look at the last new colony loadout from Earth to get ideass. Everything hass been pre-determined and pre-packaged. Thiss iss exciting."

* * * * *

Chapter Nineteen

S even days later the shuttle landed with a slight thump, and the engines spooled down. After a minute, its pilot spoke. "Engines are disengaged, Uncle Harmon," said Bahroot. "Would you like me to drop the ramp now? The Withaloo shuttle is lowering theirs."

"Sure, and good job with that entry," Harmon said as he shook his head at Clip, who was wiping the sweat off his face.

"Thank you," said the young AI. "Next time I'll approach from the other end of the continent. Looking at the newly mapped weather patterns, the west side seems to have those storms this time of year. I'll remember that."

Harmon disembarked with Zerith and Clip, who was carrying Jayneen in his kit while holding the slate. The four associates, Kyla, Vera, Hank, and Stan were with him as well. Hank and Stan were happy to see the planet firsthand and had to be restrained from examining the construction equipment. The two warrant officers, not so much. They wanted to be on *Salvage Title* in the shipyards, supervising the repairs.

All four had their goggles on, and Kyla and Vera had reapplied their lipstick in preparation for the meeting. It would not do to not look their best. Harmon and Clip didn't say a word.

Harmon looked around at the location planned for the first town. The area had been cleared of ruins, and some of the trees and the vegetation had been cut back. Several pieces of construction equipment brought in by the construction companies from Joth and Tretra were in motion near the old airfield.

Harmon was surprised to see several buildings already in place. Granted, they were prefabricated buildings designed to house the work crews, but they were lined along what would become a street. There was even a small restaurant and bar. That figured. Construction crews were the same galaxy wide. They worked long, hard days and partied late into the night, managing to get up the next morning and do it all over again.

Near the airfield, two shuttles were parked. One was the shuttle Harmon had purchased from Mike and Mike. It had been modified into a dropship to transport mechs, as well as troops. Even at this distance, the quad-barrel machine gun mounted underneath looked menacing. The Bolts were using both shuttles as temporary quarters while they patrolled the colony site in squads and continued their mech training. A large prefabricated metal building held the mechs, as well as the replicator from Yatarward Industries, along with a few technicians who'd opted to come work in the new system.

The Withaloo shuttle was parked a substantial distance from the construction area. Harmon saw four of the large humanoids and a smaller being headed toward the buildings. It would be a few minutes before they reached them.

Out the corner of his eye, Harmon saw the hatch open on a mech and its pilot dismount. He looked over and realized something was missing, but he couldn't place it. To his surprise, the pilot reached up with two fingers and pressed different areas on one side of her face, and her tattoo lit up with the signature lightning bolts of the Bolt platoon members. *That's how they do it*, Harmon realized.

He'd wondered if the reflection of the tattoo in the operator's panels in the mech hindered the pilots. Now he knew.

"Which Leethog figured out how to interrupt the power source to the Bolts' tattoos?" Harmon asked Clip.

"Beats me, man," Clip said. "The images are powered by their body's own electrical impulses. It doesn't take much electricity. They probably installed some sort of activation switch."

"It iss my dessign, thank you very much," Zerith volunteered. "Corporal Brink messsaged me and ssaid hiss Boltss were having a hard time seeing all the information on their panelss. The light from their tattoos was creating a mirror effect inside the cockpit, and Sergeant Kyth was not happy with their performancce the first few dayss. I designed a multi-point sswitch and ssent the information to the medical team on *Windsswept*. The medical replicatorss created them, and the proceduress were performed while we transsitioned to our new ssysstem." Zerith popped a handful of small blue plums into his mouth.

"It wass relatively ssimple," he said after a few chews. He spit out the seeds, then kicked soil over them. "Maybe they will grow," he said, to no one in particular.

As the Withaloo contingent approached, Harmon realized the smaller being with them was not of the same race. It was only about five feet tall, and moved with an ambling gate, with long spindly arms that hung to its knees. It was fur covered like the Withaloo, but the fur wasn't as thick, and was more of a light grey color. Two sharp teeth protruded upward, even with its mouth closed, on its elongated snout.

The group stopped, and Vice President Moroath stepped forward and held out her hand in the manner she had learned was a human greeting. She had three fingers and an opposable thumb on her hand. Harmon recognized her from the direct calls he'd had with her. She was slightly smaller than the other three Withaloo in the group and had reddish-brown fur, as opposed to their darker coloring. They'd all shed the furs they wore for clothing. Harmon recognized one of the darker Withaloo, Fleet Commander Ithall, who had his pistol holstered on his belt, as did the other two Withaloo.

Harmon shook her hand and said, "Vice President Moroath, it's good to meet you face to face."

"President Tomeral," she said through the translator in Harmon's earpiece. "Thank you for considering our request for asylum and meeting me. I must say, I have seen videos of other worlds, but I did not expect it to be this warm and have so many colors. It is a far cry from the surface of our home."

"It's more colorful than my home world as well, but it's a lot cooler," Harmon assured her. "If you'll accompany me into the restaurant, I'll introduce everyone, and we can talk away from the noise of the construction."

They sat down in the empty restaurant called Our Bar & Grill, at a long table comprised of several tables pushed together. The proprietors, a couple of humans named William Steverson and Travis "Evill" Powell brought them all water. Will was disappointed they hadn't ordered drinks, and Evill was disappointed they weren't eating. They couldn't complain, though, since they'd made more credit renting the place for the meeting than being open that time of day. Harmon had planned ahead for the meeting, but wasn't sure what to serve the guests. Purified water seemed a safe choice.

After everyone was seated, Vice President Moroath introduced Fleet Commander Ithall, the two security crewmembers, and *Biting*

Wind's ship engineer, Tolkter. Harmon introduced his partners, associates, and Jayneen. Upon realizing what Jayneen was, the ship engineer sat forward in his seat and studied the computer, power cell, and slate.

"Forgive me," Harmon said, indicating Tolkter. "I was unaware there were other races living on your moon."

"There were not, until two years ago," explained the vice president. "Eighty-two Z'mitoks were freed by Fleet Commander Ithall while contracted to defend a mining belt. Since then, there have been fourteen births among them." She smiled at this revelation.

"No sentient being should be enslaved. Ever," said Ithall. "I merely did what needed to be done. They opted to come with us to make a new life, once freed. Tolkter is the best engineer I have ever known. He has increased engine thrust output by eight percent on *Biting Wind*, even though she is an older ship."

Harmon looked at the Withaloo fleet commander with new respect. *This is a good being*, he thought. *Good.* He could see the same look on Clip and Zerith's faces. *This meeting may be all I hoped it would be.*

"What the fleet commander is modestly not revealing is the fact he spent nearly every credit he had available to *purchase* them, and then gave them their freedom," added Vice President Moroath.

"Every crewmember in both ships contributed, ma'am," Ithall countered. "I did not do it alone."

"All in my tribe are aware of this, my friend," said Tolkter, speaking for the first time. "We are also aware you emptied your personal account before speaking to the crews of our plight."

"Bah," Ithall dismissed. "One cannot take credit for something that simply *must* be done."

"President Tomeral," the vice president said, "I have come to you seeking asylum for those of us residing in the Withaloo System. The time has come for us to decide what we will do. The Domes no longer protect us adequately from the cold that has overtaken our home. Most systems have ignored our query or demanded that which we cannot pay. One offered to make us indentured servants."

Harmon was shocked to hear this. She continued, "I am afraid I must get right to the heart of the matter. Time is of the essence. What are your requirements to allow asylum for just short of fifty thousand beings?"

Harmon looked at his friends. Without saying a word, Harmon knew they were all in agreement with what he was about to say, by both the looks on their faces and their body language. "Perhaps you misunderstood me when I reached out to your moon. There will be no requirements, except respect other beings, have honor, and obey the laws that may be put in place in the future by a small elected government, never try to enforce your personal religious beliefs on others or suppress theirs, and be prepared to defend the planet and the system should the need arise. All very simple, but very important, things."

"That…that is unexpected," she said. "These are things all societies should aspire to. Perfectly reasonable things."

"Absolutely," agreed Harmon, "and from what I've already witnessed, I don't think there will be any issues with them at all."

"Forgive my intrusion, ma'am but there is one point of interest I would like to address," said Ithall. "I notice you are armed, as I and my security are. Is this something only your military members are allowed?"

"Nope," Harmon said without hesitation. "If you look closely, you'll probably see some of the construction workers are armed in one fashion or another. Everyone has the right to defend themselves. That's the first law I put in place. There are no limits to carrying weapons or owning weapons at all, *but* it better be used only in self-defense of yourself or others. Deliberate misuse of a weapon carries harsh penalties."

"I like this law very much," stated the fleet commander. "The only reason weapons remained stored instead of worn in the Domes is because of the very real danger of a stray round penetrating the domes themselves and causing a major catastrophe. Self-defense is the right of all beings, by any means necessary."

"Right on," Clip agreed. "Ithall, you seem like a good dude, man."

"I am impresssed with them ass well," Zerith stated. "I vote assylum be granted."

"Harmon," Jayneen said, "if you would like my opinion, I think they will be an excellent addition to Salvage System. I have studied their history extensively and have found no warning signs."

"We feel the same way," Kyla said. The other three Leethog nodded their heads, as was their fashion. It was the first time she'd spoken during the meeting. "Though I hesitate to call it 'asylum.' I would prefer they accept...our *invitation*."

"She's right," Harmon said with a grin. "She usually is. Will you accept our invitation to move every being in your system to Salvage System to begin a new life?"

* * * * *

Chapter Twenty

Standing on the surface of Evermore, Harmon used the cameras on his mech to look around. "You have things moving right along, Rick," Harmon said through the exterior speaker of his mech. "It looks great."

Harmon had come down in a shuttle to meet Rick and see the progress on Evermore. It was the first time he'd visited the planet. It was also an excuse to get some time in his mech; it had been a while since he'd piloted it. It came back quickly. Zerith had repaired the mech and put newer, improved cameras in it so he had a great view on his three panels.

The Kashkal planning crew had designed three townships in a rough triangle, separated by what could only be described as farms in between, with strange animals penned. Odd multistoried homes lined thoroughfares in the towns, and Harmon could see many Kashkal working together to raise other homes.

Off to one side was a box-shaped ship about twice the size of a shuttle. Harmon could see a team of Kashkal in small, tracked vehicles digging holes, leveling foundation spots, and delivering the soil and rocks to the rear of the ship. Sometimes a stack of cut trees would be loaded. On one side of the ship, fabricated walls and boards were being stacked as they came out. While he was talking with Rick, a pile of scrap metal was loaded, and small items dropped out into a box. Harmon was too far away to see what the strange ship's replicator was creating, but he figured it had to do with the buildings.

"Yes, it is going as planned," Rick said. "Once we built a sewage system with a large incinerator and the water filtration plant, we began building homes. We build the first homes together. In the future, as families grow and the young move out, they will be responsible for building their homes on their own. I feel there will be a growing economy by then. I must thank you again for the world you have given the Kashkal."

"No thanks are necessary, my friend," Harmon said. "I only did what was right."

"I would like to offer my opinion concerning the Withaloo," Rick said, changing topics.

"Yeah?" Harmon asked.

"I feel you made an excellent decision," Rick said. "You saw a need, and you addressed it. That is to be commended, and is a sign of strong leadership. The warrior in me takes delight in the decision, as well. I took the liberty of having that light battlecruiser scanned. There were ten hatches for missile launchers and two large turrets with multi-barreled lasers mounted. There were clusters of laser turrets mounted all over the ship for self-defense. It is powered by three fusion plants and three engines. All in all, it appeared to our sensors as a very formidable light battlecruiser."

"Their fleet commander, Ithall, told me they have five of those ships, four destroyers, and six frigates. They also have an army, complete with tanks and artillery pieces. It only consists of eight hundred members, but it's more than I dreamed to be able to defend Salvage, should invaders reach the surface of the planet."

"I have also enacted a ground force," Rick said. "It is only platoon-sized at this time, with one shuttle dedicated to them. It will grow in time, but I am not concerned with its size. Every Kashkal is prepared to fight, should an enemy reach our world."

"Speaking of a platoon," Harmon said, "the Bolts have cleared enough of those predators and kept them out that I think they've learned to stay away. Almost like they understand territory boundaries."

"We have not had that issue here on Evermore," Rick informed him. "Though on one of the other continents, there are creatures large enough to swallow a young Kashkal whole. I have determined it will be centuries before we need to occupy that small continent, if ever. We do not wish to upend the planet and its inhabitants. We will move ahead carefully and not be eaten."

"Avoiding being eaten is a good tactic," Harmon agreed.

"When will the Withaloo arrive?" Rick asked.

"Vice President Moroath made a direct call a week ago," Harmon answered. "I expect them to start arriving in a week. In the last five years, they were able to build a colony ship capable of carrying twenty thousand. From what Ithall told me, what it lacks in comfort, it more than makes up for in capacity."

"There are fifty thousand of them," Rick observed, "so it will take three trips to bring them and their livestock. There will not be any natural wildlife to save. The only things living on their moon are within their domes."

"I thought the same thing," Harmon said. "Instead they will make *four* trips, ensuring the ones who arrive first can build homes and holding pens. They will also use all the space available in their military ships, along with the few civilian craft they have—small freighters that brought supplies to them from other systems."

"Speaking of supplies," the Kashkal asked, "when do you expect the super freighter to arrive from Sol System?"

"It should come through the gate within the next few days," Harmon said. "It'll take another ten days before we see delivery to the planet's surface. It's hard to believe they packed everything on that manifest I read. It's the kind of shipment up to five thousand colonists from Earth take with them when they inhabit a new system. Between that and what we brought from Joth and Tretra, we're set. Plus, beings will bring their own belongings when they move here.

"You should see the number of requests from the old system, and many others from companies and individuals looking to move here," he continued. "I really need an administrator in the worse kind of way. There's a lot of math involved in all this, and math is just not my thing, you know?"

"I fully understand, my friend," Rick assured him. "I have various councils that handle things. They report to an administrator, who then gives me a brief daily. It has been this way for decades. I simply make spot checks from time to time to ensure the administrator is not overstepping his bounds."

"That's a good idea," Harmon said. "I need to find an administrator first, though."

"I agree," the Kashkal said. "Thank you again for offering the use of some of the construction equipment. My administrator will ensure it is used efficiently and returned to Salvage as soon as possible, while I go back to the fleet and monitor the repairs."

"You're welcome," Harmon told him. "More equipment will arrive in that freighter, and the Withaloo have their own. Your administrator doesn't need to rush anything."

"Have you determined where they will build their towns?" Rick asked him.

"From what was explained to me," Harmon began, "they had ten Domes on their moon. Each Dome had around five thousand residents. The Domes were huge, and encompassed their farms as well, though they had to use hothouses even within the domes, for crops and some livestock. Each Dome has an elected leader, like a mayor. There's a vice president and a president, elected from all ten Domes, as sort of a top-level government.

"I thought they would need to be in the areas of the planet near the poles, but they assure me they can handle the warmth of other places. They'll set up on the same continent I selected for us. One of the Domes will start a town near the airfield, as well. They already had a shuttle network for traveling between Domes; I think they intend to adapt it to traveling between towns. One less thing I have to worry about, I guess."

"What will they do with their shipyards?" Rick asked.

"I asked that," Harmon said. "They intend to dismantle them into small enough parts that they can tow them through the gate. They paid a lot of credit for the replicators and to modify them; they didn't want to abandon them."

"You know, my friend," Rick surmised, "with the two Kashkal tenders able to create parts and rebuild ships, the *Cube* and its capabilities, this system's shipyards, and the incoming Withaloo shipyards, a formidable fleet could be repaired and built, given the resources."

"I know," Harmon agreed, "but once we have a large enough fleet to defend the system without fear of a large force, what do we do with them? It's not like we need them to invade other systems. I know you still intend to contract your fleet on occasion, and the Withaloo have used that as a means of survival, as well. I'll have to think about that, too, I guess. Until mining and real trade starts happening, credit might be tight."

"I would suggest continuing to build your fleet," Rick Kashka said. "I will."

"Why?" Harmon asked. "For mercenary work?"

"Perhaps," the Kashkal said. "Call it a feeling, a hunch. You are an exceptional being. If you see something that is truly wrong, you find ways to fix it. This is not a bad trait, but there are many wrongs in this galaxy. Many. Who knows…one day you may *find* reason to invade another system."

* * * * *

Chapter Twenty-One

"**U**ncle Harmon," Bahroot said, "Jifton Gregor has been found guilty of multiple murders. He's scheduled to be executed. It just came across the Sol newsfeeds."

"Really?" Harmon exclaimed. "Well, as your Uncle Zerith would say, he gets what he deserves. How long has it been now, six months?"

"It's been one hundred and sixty-four days since Detective Sumner escorted the prisoners back to Sol System," answered the AI. "Would you like me to land near Bank Town or Dome Rebirth?"

Bahroot took the opportunity to pilot the shuttle every chance he got. Usually it was when Harmon went to the surface of Salvage to meet with his planet administrator. In the beginning, that had been often. In the last month, Harmon had been busy with Salvage Fleet. They'd left the shipyards earlier, where once again all four berths were filled with ships being built, not repaired.

"Land near Bank Town. I have a meeting to make," Harmon answered.

Once they landed, Harmon turned to Corporal Galooth. "I'll probably stay the night; why don't you take the shuttle and show Bahroot your father's mining operation?"

"Thank you, sir," beamed the young NCO.

"Cool," said an excited Bahroot. "I've never landed in a canyon."

"See you tomorrow," Harmon said, grinning at the Yalteen, before he walked down the ramp.

"Yes, sir. Thanks again…I think," she said, looking nervous.

Harmon walked to the end of the airfield, to the Bolts' headquarters and barracks. He wanted to stop in and see how the mech training was coming along. Harmon walked into the front office of the orderly room and the tattooed private rose quickly and shouted, "Commodore on deck!"

Harmon quickly put her at ease. "Sit down, sit down, I'm just here to see Staff Sergeant Kyth. It's not an inspection."

Harmon walked into the staff sergeant's office just as Kyth was coming around his desk. "Sir," the staff sergeant said, "I'm glad you stopped by. There's something I've been meaning to ask you."

Harmon shook his hand and sat in the chair in front of the desk. "Talk to me, Kyth."

"Well, sir," Kyth said, "as you know, we're down to thirty-eight members of the platoon. I have locals asking if we're recruiting. I was going to talk to Captain Bentalt about it, but he's been pretty busy lately, with the whole farming and livestock stuff and everything.

"I know you assigned Sergeant Trang and myself to train them to operate mechs," he continued, "but they're all proficient pilots now. We even have eleven mechs off the new assembly line, with no pilots."

"I know." Harmon grinned. "It's a good thing. That replicator was a great gift from Captain Yatarward. They'll keep producing them as long as they have the raw material. There's talk of a new design. Let me ask you, are any of the Bolts good enough to teach?"

"Absolutely," said the staff sergeant without hesitation. "Sergeant Brink, Corporal Mayshire, and Corporal Algrite could be instructors. I've had them acting as peer instructors for two months."

"Good," Harmon said. "I need to reassign you and Trang to the renamed heavy battlecruiser *Justice Served* to head up the security platoon. With a ship that size, the security and emergency repair platoon is almost twice the size of *Salvage Title*'s."

"Roger, sir," Kyth said. "Don't get me wrong, it's been great teaching what we know, but we both would like to get back on a ship."

"What's Brink said about the inquiries?" Harmon asked.

"It's odd, sir," admitted the NCO. "He said if they had it in them to pass the interview first, they could attempt a modified boot camp. Whatever that means."

"There's your answer," Harmon said. "If he approves them, we run them through the paces. We'll let him handle it. He's been doing a good job so far."

"He has, sir," agreed Kyth. "He's even taken it upon himself to ensure there are patrols by his platoon, acting almost like law enforcement. Handling the occasional brawl at one of the bars, or handling disputes between the locals. I let him do it and just concentrate on the mech training."

"I'll talk to him," Harmon said, standing up. "You two have done an excellent job here. Look for some orders soon. I have a meeting to attend."

"Yes, sir," Staff Sergeant Kyth said, "and thank you for the promotions. It was nice being promoted by Captain Bentalt in front of the platoon."

"It was well deserved," Harmon said. "Well deserved."

Harmon left the building, turned right, and walked a block to the Planet Administration building. He walked into the small lobby and was met by a light blue Prithmar. "Pressident Tomeral, welcome. They are awaiting your arrival in the conferencce room," she said. "Don't worry, ssir, they are early. You are not late."

"Thanks, Kayleena." Harmon smiled and walked down the hall.

Harmon walked through the open door to the conference room and realized there were more beings than he'd thought would be there. All ten Dome leaders were seated, as well as the president and vice president of the Withaloo. The mayors of Bank Town and Hillside, the new town being built in the next valley over, were there, too. Queen Railynn from the Nilta settlement on Blossom Island was present, as well.

"Oh, frost," Harmon said, stopping just inside the doorway. "I've been ambushed."

"Don't be ridiculous, Harmon," said the planet administrator as she came around the table for a quick hug.

"It sure seems like it, JoJo," Harmon told her. "Say, I felt that huge stomach when you hugged me. Are you sure it's not twins? Did you tell Evelyn? Does your husband know it's twins?"

"No, it's not twins," she answered, smacking his shoulder. "Twiggy teases me about the same thing. If I was a sensitive person, that would've hurt my feelings, you know."

"You did jusst call her *fat*," observed the mayor of Bank Town, a light green Prithmar.

"Don't let her fool you, Vernarth." Harmon laughed. "She's tougher than she looks, even though she cried when I conducted the ceremony to marry her and Twiggy."

Harmon sat down at the head of the table. "Alright, you've got me surrounded, let me have it."

"Have what?" President Dolith of the Withaloo asked, looking around. "I am confused, perhaps it is the translation. Everything is fine. You are all here because I invited you to announce...I am retiring."

The room was quiet. "Oh, come now," he continued. "You all knew it was coming. I am getting along in years now. I would like to enjoy my small plot of land, grow my flower garden, and spoil my children's children. Vice President Moroath has been handling everything for the last few months. Things are progressing smoothly, even among the chaos of building everything.

"Things are different now. Better. We still call them Domes, but they are anything but. We have other races living among us. Many of the Withaloo now live here in Bank Town and a few in Hillside. It is as it should be. There is no need for a Withaloo president. I propose making the vice president a member of Administrator Whaley's staff."

All the Dome Leaders seemed to agree. Moroath had negotiated the move to their new home. She seemed saddened by her friend and mentor wishing to step away from the leadership role he'd held for so many years. Harmon thought for a moment about what the leader of the Withaloo had said.

"Good idea," Harmon said. "Here's what I'll do. Moroath, I'd like you to be the vice planet administrator. I think you'll do a good job." Harmon hesitated before continuing. "You'll have to step in and take over while JoJo's on medical leave when the triplets are born, though." Harmon laughed as he dodged the pastry JoJo threw at him.

The rest of the meeting was more of a group of friends visiting than an actual meeting. Pregnancies were discussed, trying to determine who would be first. One, a Caldivar, was due any day now. It would be the first birth on the planet. It was a welcome break from the day-to-day activities in a growing colony. After it broke up, Harmon headed over to see if the Bolts were back from their daily patrols.

"Sir, it's good to see you," Sergeant Brink said. He had become the platoon sergeant after the unit had completed its initial training. The Bolts were a tight unit, both before as a gang, and after as a trained military outfit, so it had made sense to Harmon to keep Brink in charge.

"I just thought I'd drop by to see if you feel like dinner and cold one," Harmon said.

"Yes, sir," the big man said. "If you'll give me a little time. I need to ensure the troops and the equipment has been taken care of, and that the rotations are set. Sorry."

"Don't be," Harmon admonished. "Good leaders take care of their troops, they'll take care of the equipment, and we all live to fight another day because of it. Take your time. I'll hang out up front."

"Harmon, this is JoJo," came over his comm before he walked out of the room. "It's happening...now!"

"Calm down," Harmon said, alarmed. "Tell me what's happening."

"The first being born on Salvage is happening *now*. The Caldivar I told you about is in delivery. Meet me at the Medical Building." The link cut.

"Well, you heard that, Brink." Harmon grinned. "I'll meet you for a late dinner. I'll call you." Harmon ran out the door.

Harmon trotted up the street several blocks to the medical facilities. Inside, he made his way to the waiting area. There was just one large room for beings to wait, no matter what procedure was being performed. He quickly found JoJo and several of the beings from the earlier meeting. They discussed many of the issues and potential issues in the colony, and its growth, for the next two hours. Harmon told JoJo for the hundredth time how glad he was that she'd accepted the administrator job. She always did have a knack for logistics.

Everyone got a chance to see the infant Caldivar, after the youngling was checked, cleaned, and placed in a warming bassinet, through the typical clear-steel window of the facility's nursery. Harmon and JoJo were standing in front of it when the father, a grey, broad-shouldered Caldivar Harmon didn't recognize, motioned to them to enter the door leading back into the delivery and recovery area.

The door was propped open by the time Harmon and JoJo made their way to the recovery room. Harmon could see the infant in its mother's arms, and the proud father standing there. The father walked over to him and held out a big hand.

"Carlick Broog, I own the construction supply store in Hillside. Cut stone mostly. I also have a small replicator," the Caldivar said.

"Good to meet you," Harmon said. "Congratulations!"

"Thank you, Mr. President," said Carlick. "Come, meet my mate and our little one."

Harmon stepped over, met his mate Faylock, and admired the small Caldivar with JoJo.

"I can't wait to tell Evelyn I saw the baby." Harmon grinned. "She'll be so jealous."

The mother laughed softly. "Make her even more jealous. Hold him." She held the small bundle out to Harmon.

Harmon found himself more nervous than the time he'd cooked off a thermite grenade in his hand before he threw it to ensure it blew up on target. He gently took the infant. He touched its hand, and the baby instinctively grasped his finger. He was surprised at the strength the little one had.

"Watch for his claws," the mother warned. "Little ones can't control them this early. It's usually a day or so before they function, but they may come out and scratch you."

"I will," Harmon said, still looking at the little grey Caldivar. "What's his name?"

Carlick turned two eyes toward Harmon and kept one on his mate while smiling. "His name…is Harmon."

* * *

Later, over a meal at Our Bar & Grill, Harmon asked Brink if he thought he and his squad leaders were up to teaching others to pilot a mech. He explained the need for the two current instructors and let the sergeant know he was impressed with all his Bolts had accomplished. They were excellent troops, but they lacked the training to be an emergency repair crew on a ship.

"I understand, and thank you, sir," Nathan Brink said. "Not only for the compliment, but for allowing me and the platoon a second chance. When I walked up on that beach, you had every right to send me on my way. As far as you knew, we were still a useless gang. A group of troublemakers, unwilling to contribute to society in any way.

"We were all of that sir. All of it. None of us realized the road we were going down led exactly nowhere. It took something like the threat of our world being taken over, and us possibly becoming meals, before we even considered changing. That and the beating the Sergeant Major gave us.

"When we quit the drugs and stealing, we thought it was rough," he continued. "The withdrawals, not having easy credit; all of it was rough. When our minds had time to clear and the days and nights didn't blend together anymore, some of us realized we wanted more than what we had. We talked with the rest, and they wanted it, too. A few didn't. They're still back on Tretra. Their tattoos were removed, though. That chapter for them is over."

"The galaxy was out here. You showed us a way to get to it, and we took it. Sir, if we thought getting off the Whirl was hard, we were wrong. Those withdrawals were nothing compared to the lack of sleep, the aches and pains, and the learning curve of the first week of training. Gunny ran us into the ground. I hated it.

"Until about halfway through the second week," he continued, "when I realized the changes in me, and the way I felt about myself. I think all the Bolts grew in those four weeks more than we could have imagined. I know I did. We'd die for each other, sir…some of us *did*. I think clearing that ship really completed the change in me. Did you know a Tralge gave his life to cover me and two of my guys? I started to realize it was wrong to dislike someone because they weren't human back in training, when some of our weapons instructors were Leethog and Yalteen. When Triad Jelgita sacrificed himself to save us, I realized completely what an idiot I'd been."

"I'm aware," Harmon told him. "I was briefed. That Tralge squad leader made the ultimate sacrifice for his fellow troops. It didn't matter the race. Don't be so hard on yourself about your past. You were a product of your upbringing. You didn't know any better. Now you do. It's what you do with that knowledge that's important. Thanks for proving my hunch right."

"Well, sir, that brings me to this—as I'm sure you're aware, we've had inquiries about recruiting. I think I could run a training camp. I still have the training schedules we used in our training to base it on. I think I could run one, consisting of four weeks' basic training and six weeks of a combination of mech pilot training and some other specialties."

"What type?" Harmon asked, intrigued.

"Well, I've had conversations with the Withaloo about cross-training in artillery and armor. I think it would be good to know."

"I agree," Harmon said.

"There is a slight problem, though, sir," admitted the NCO.

"Go on?" Harmon said.

"The mechs," he explained. "I'll need several mechs with cockpits big enough for Yalteens and Withaloo, and I'll need some with smaller cockpits, as well. I don't intend to restrict anyone because of their race. If they feel they have what it takes, and pass the interview, then once I have enough recruits, I'll run a platoon through the gauntlet."

"I like it," Harmon said. "I like it a lot. I'll talk to some beings and get some designs made. We'll send them to the Yatarward technicians and get the replicator reprogrammed to run several different designs. In the meantime, recruit some beings and get them contracted with the same contract you're under. They all start as privates, unless you see fit to bring anyone in as a private first class, but it better be for a good reason. If you run across anyone who used to be in the military, we'll take that case by case. Joth militia or whatever. They may not need the basic course."

"Roger, sir," Brink agreed.

"One other thing," Harmon said before he left. "Rumor has it you've been playing law officer."

"Yes, sir," admitted Brink. "I never in a million years thought I'd be the one to enforce the peace, but we don't really have any type of law enforcement on Salvage. We haven't really needed it, but as the population grows, we will. Believe me, I know. The last thing we want is someone coming in thinking they can deal Whirl to the locals and make easy credit."

"You find any of that squat on this planet, you sure as frost put a stop to it," Harmon demanded.

"Absolutely," Brink said. "We know the signs of somebody spinning, and we know a bad individual when we see one. You can sorta tell, so you watch them. I stayed later in a bar the other night because I knew there was going to be trouble. I broke up the fight and made them stay the night in a couple of closets here in the building. It's one of the reasons I want to grow the Bolts. I'll make a squad that specializes in keeping the peace and settling disputes. The Withaloo have a group that does that among their Domes. That's what gave me the idea."

"Do it. I'll give the administrator a call and let her know to set up a budget for you. You're right. The more beings settle here, the bigger chance some will need policing."

"Will do, sir," Sergeant Brink said. "Thanks again. Wait, sir, what'll we call the unit? An Army? A Corps? Ground Defense Force?"

Harmon stopped in the door and looked back with a grin. "You already have a name...the Bolts."

* * * * *

Chapter Twenty-Two

"Sir, you have a call from *Cube*," the new communications officer said.

Harmon looked up from his slate and said, "Put it on the screen, Ensign, thanks."

Harmon found himself looking at Mike Melton. "What's up, Mike?"

"The first new…old ship is complete, sir," he said.

"Is it?" Harmon said, excited. "It's a week earlier than expected."

"We made the changes so two hands can run the stations, and the final programing didn't take as long as I thought it would, with both Lieutenant Commander Jayneen and Bahroot working on it."

"Where is it now?" Harmon asked.

"Bradford, Tim, and the gang pulled it out of its berth a few minutes ago. He said he wants to test out the new toy."

"A light battlecruiser isn't exactly a toy," Clip volunteered with a grin from beside Harmon.

"I know, Captain," Mike said to Clip and sipped his coffee, "but you know how Bradford is."

"Yeah, I do," Clip admitted. "Hey! I get to name this one. I know the perfect name, too."

"What is it?" Harmon asked skeptically.

"Just what Bradford called it. *New Toy*," he answered. "I gotta run, Zee built some more of the scrambler missiles, and I need to get them programmed." He left the bridge.

"The new crew should start arriving at your location tomorrow morning," Harmon informed the retired master sergeant. "Captain Sholdra has been promoted, as well as his executive officer, Lieutenant Commander Jimtilnapray. They'll handle the assignments."

"Roger that, sir," Mike said. "I just build 'em. The rest I leave up to you."

"What's next in that berth?" Harmon asked. "And when will the destroyer be ready?"

"That's up to you, sir," Mike said. "The berth is set up for a light battlecruiser. If you want something bigger, it can be done, especially with all the help we have now between the Smilps, the Leethog, and all the others working in the shipyards. The destroyer will be ready in a week. The two frigates will be ready in three weeks. Then you can let me know what to build next.

"As long as the raw material keeps coming, the replicators will keep putting out product, and we'll keep building them," he continued. "The last of the repairs are complete, and the bay in *Cube* is empty, by the way. You got anything you want to upgrade?"

"No," Harmon said, thinking. "Maybe another shuttle conversion to a dropship for the Bolts. Hey, I have an idea. How about the other stompers you have? You want to sell them to me? The new battle armor designed for the Bolts' infantry platoon has decent jump boots. Enough for a trooper to descend and get up to a stomper a few times before the fuel runs dry, anyway."

"I have three I could finish and send down," Mike said, "but you can't have Bradford's. He'd kill me if I sold it. We just finished rebuilding its weapons."

"Fair enough." Harmon laughed. "I'll take them."

"Hey sir, I've been meaning to ask you something," Mike said, taking another sip of his coffee.

"Talk to me," Harmon answered.

"It's been nearly a year since we defended the system. The system is booming. Mining, both off planet and on both planets, is producing well. The population on Salvage is growing every week, it seems like. I hear there are more Kashkal births this year than normal. With all the growth, how come we haven't been invaded again? There are several races that do that kind of thing to grow their own little empires. It would seem we were ripe for the picking, especially after nearly every ship was in such bad shape for a while there."

"I'll let you in on a little secret," Harmon said, and he sat back. "Bahroot."

"Bahroot?" Mike asked perplexed. "He's no secret. Especially since Professor Plexico was able to come and look at the programming of both Jayneen and Bahroot. I mean, I know they can't be copied, per se. He'll create better programming, but not true AIs. Wait, they're not around, are they?" Mike looked around his own office nervously.

"No, they're not here on the bridge," Harmon answered. "You'd know by now. Seriously, it was Bahroot. He put together a video of some of the battle, did a little editing, and released it to the Net. There are large systems and small empires that wouldn't want anything to do with a fight with us because of it, much less pirates or mercenaries. Not only did they see the devastation we wreaked on the invaders, they think we have crazy good defense platforms and sensor drones because of the quality of the videos."

At hearing this, Mike laughed. "Smart nephew you got there."

"Don't I know it?" Harmon agreed. "Talk to ya later."

* * *

Halfway across the galaxy, two men watched as more warships came through the gate. Grant Lowantha and Bartholomew Hawthorne were seated in the small cockpit of their Tretrayon scout ship. It was the only one in existence. A few had been made before it, as prototypes, but they'd ended up in the scrapyard after experimentation. The ship was able to slip past sensors due to its size and its anti-sensor emanations package. It was how they'd escaped both the Tretrayon System and Salvage System when things got bad.

"This bother you, Grant?" Hawthorne asked his friend.

"Not really," Lowantha said, stifling a yawn. "I mean, yeah, we spent the last six months getting in good with the Barlat, but they don't mean anything to me. It was all about the credit."

"Yeah, I feel the same," Hawthorne said, looking out the ship's portal. "That's a lot of ships. How many soldiers did they say they were putting on the surface?"

"The Gritloth liaison I dealt with said four Blocks. Near as I can tell, that means four thousand of them," Lowantha said.

"That should do it," Hawthorne said. "It's not like the Barlat have any type of defense forces on the planet at all. They don't even have any true warships. They have very few interactions outside their system. I can't believe they haven't been invaded before this."

"That's because nobody knew they were sitting on mounds of the galaxy's most precious stones," Lowantha said. "At least until we followed that guy on Bentwick after he sold a handful to the jeweler we were planning to rob. No one will ever know, besides the Gritloth, now that they've paid for the information."

"Tell me again why we didn't just go to Barlat and take some of the stones?" Hawthorne asked.

"That's not what we do," answered Lowantha. "I'm not traipsing around the woods on a planet where no one wants any visitors. That sounds like a recipe to disappear forever, you know? We gather information, and we sell it. That's what we do."

"Sometimes you just have to find the right buyer for what you know." Hawthorne laughed. "They got a good deal. They take over the system, and they get the stones. They even get slaves to work at mining the mounds."

"And we get a payday others only dream about," Lowantha said. "It took long enough, but we earned the Barlat's trust, and it paid off now that the rest of the credit has hit our accounts."

"It was a week late," commented Hawthorne.

"Probably because the Gritloth emperor ordered them to find us to get rid of anyone else who knows about the mining potential on the planet," Lowantha said. "I had to threaten to let several other systems know about the stones before they finally paid up the last seventy-five percent. With threats of their own, of course."

"This deal worked out a lot better than the last," Hawthorne said. "That's for sure."

"Don't remind me," his partner lamented. "From now on, we just sell the information; we don't get involved. We barely made it out of the bay of that damned Q-ship before it blew apart. Six days on half-emergency rations until we could slip out of the system. I'd hoped to never hear of Harmon Tomeral and Salvage System again as long as I live. That's not going to happen, though, because of that video all over the Net."

"Well, we made our credit," Hawthorne said. "It's a done deal here. It's time to move on. We should buy a small freighter, park the scout in it, and go take a long vacation somewhere." He ignited the engines and they headed for the gate, well away from the Gritloth troop carriers moving past the warships toward the only inhabited planet in the Barlat System.

* * *

C ameron leaned back in his seat and looked over at Ralph. "Well, that's that. What are we going to do now?"

"I don't know boss." Ralph stretched and knocked the cup off his console. It landed upside down in one of his boots. He'd taken them off to stretch his toes a little. He looked down and said, "That's not good."

"We have a little extra credit in the account," Cameron said after laughing at his friend, pushing his glasses up on his face. "Want to go home for a month or two and give everyone a little time off? Then we can go to Salvage System, see if we can explore one of the uninhabited continents, and see how everyone is doing?"

"Sounds like a plan," Ralph said, inputting the coordinates. "It's a ten-day stretch in between. We'll hit the gate in fourteen hours."

"Ya gotta love that eighth engine," Cameron stated. "We should get my mech fully repaired while we're in alter reality. It's going to be great, and the flame thrower should work this time. I hope. Say, are those the boots you borrowed from me?"

* * * * *

Chapter Twenty-Three

Harmon sat in the conference room on *Salvage Title*. On the screen were Evelyn, Gunny, and Sergeant Brink. Evelyn and Gunny had just finished conducting the graduation inspection and ceremony of the latest platoon of Bolts. It was the first one Harmon hadn't been a part of. Scheduling hadn't allowed it. The crew of *Salvage Title* was acting as observers for a simulated battle. They were staying close, but not actively involved.

Task Force Bravo, Salvage Fleet's new heavy force, consisting of *The Reckoning*, the Belvakett heavy battlecruiser *Justice Served*, Gregor's old heavy battlecruiser *Bullfrog*, *Southern Sunset*, a light battlecruiser and destroyer claimed and repaired after the invasion, and the destroyers *Sign* and *Countersign*—gained the same way—were going through their paces as a combined force. Harmon had finally filled all the vacancies, and the crews needed time to gel.

The last four ships rounding out Task Force Bravo had been owned by a couple of older mercenaries who had run into hard times. That was the only reason they'd signed a contract with Gregor. Feeling bad for the men, but still planning to keep the ships, he'd ensured they received decent compensation. They were happy to get it, as it was more than fair, and they both went back to the Sol System to enjoy retirement. Many of their crewmembers opted to stay. Tomeral and Associates paid fair wages, after all. Harmon rounded out the various crews with Salvage Fleet's experienced beings who deserved promotions.

There was a new excitement in the old crews. Every system on the ships actually worked, and upgrades had been made to the dampeners and shielding. The combined shipyards had not only repaired the damage from the battle, they'd fixed systems in disrepair from lack of funding over the last few years.

"You should have seen it," Harmon said to Evelyn, "Captain Ellotta had his force coming in at a good battle speed, when the three destroyers shot from underneath *Justice Served*, moving much faster, got off two salvos of missiles at extreme range and banked hard around before they actually came into the simulated range of the opposing force, Task Force Alpha. Jayneen checked the calculations twice. It was a frost of a thing. They were back flying escort before both fleets came into range for the major exchange."

"Nice," agreed Evelyn. "What did the simulations show was the result of the move?"

"*Desert Wind*'s forward shields down to sixty percent," answered Harmon. "They went after the medium battlecruiser, and Captain Opawn was furious."

"That could mean the difference once the real battle starts, the command ship of a task force playing defense for the rest of the battle," observed Gunny. "The upgraded G-force dampeners must work well. That was a nice move."

"It was a good move," Harmon agreed. "It wouldn't work against Task Force Command, though. Not without the risk of losing the ships for the rest of the engagement. *Salvage Title*, *New Toy*, and the destroyer *Cover Fire* all have the newer version of launchers and missiles, if you can call technology over twenty-two hundred years old 'new.' It has more range than any of the other warships we've fought, or that I'm aware of. Oh, and I can't forget the two new missile frigates, *Hold My Drink* and *Watch This*. I knew I should never have let the brothers name their ships."

"Those two," laughed Evelyn. "Each with their own ship!"

"How many ships are in Salvage Fleet now, sir?" Sergeant Brink asked.

"The fleet now has twenty-two ships," Harmon answered, "if you count the four Nazrooth destroyers separately, since they fight as one."

"Don't forget the platforms," Evelyn said.

"Yeah, I didn't count them because they're mostly stationary," Harmon admitted. "They do have crews on them. Eight ships were repaired and placed as defensive platforms, with at least eight launchers on each, and strong shielding. Three still have good lasers and can play dead until a ship approaches, then surprise them."

"And you've placed weapons on both spaceports," reminded Gunny.

"Yeah, keeping units on them to rotate from the defense platforms was a good idea. It keeps the morale up and adds to the defense of the whole system."

"It doesn't hurt that you docked the cruise liner to a port permanently, so those that opt not to come to the planet on downtime still have decent quarters, pools, and everything else," Evelyn said with a laugh.

"Hey, I have to take care of them," Harmon said defensively.

"That you do," agreed Gunny.

"How did my executive officer perform?" Evelyn asked.

"He did well," Harmon informed her. "The experience Rothan had as the Flight Operations officer for the Withaloo helped. He knows his stuff."

"He's good, isn't he?" Evelyn said. "I wasn't sure if that many things going on at once would overwhelm him until he got used to it. Especially now that *Windswept* has the full one hundred and five fighters. I'm glad you used one of the berths in the shipyard to focus on fighters. It's too bad I'll lose him after just four months."

"You knew it was temporary when I assigned him," Harmon reminded her. "They've finished converting their colony ship to a combined fighter and troop carrier. It's outstanding. I moved all the fighters we captured and the ones we were able to salvage from the invasion and repair to it. With their fighters and the additions, it now has a fleet of sixty Bentwick fighters, twelve of those two-crew fighter/bombers from Sol system, twenty-two Belvakett fighters, the two Gleekum predators, and thirty new Withaloo fighters."

"That's quite a combination," Evelyn said, "but as large as the bays are on that ship, there's probably room for more, even with all the troops and equipment loaded."

"There is, but we decided to leave the space for the two new dropships and the stomper transport. The drop ships they had for their army fit, as well. Basically, all five bays are being used."

"Enough about the fleet," Harmon said. "Tell me about the Bolts."

"Sir, we graduated forty-two this cycle," said Brink.

"They looked good," Evelyn said. She'd enjoyed inspecting the troops.

"They put on a good display for the families in attendance, too," Gunny observed. "One of the new tanks pulled in an artillery piece, and the Bolts had it set up in minutes, fired off a single round, then three for effect, broke it down, and moved out. It was pretty quick."

"Nice," Harmon said. "It was great of the Withaloo to share the schematics of their equipment. The tank is a much smaller version, except for the bore of the weapon, but the artillery piece is almost the same, except for the length of the cannon. Both use the same size rounds as the Withaloo Army's equipment."

"Makes coordinating much easier," agreed Gunny.

"How many Bolts in the company now?" Harmon asked. "One hundred and sixty including Headquarters Platoon?"

"Yes, sir," Brink said, "and that doesn't count the eighteen in the law enforcement detachment."

"Not bad. Not bad at all, after a little over fourteen months on the planet," Harmon observed.

"Harmon," Evelyn said, "I asked for this cycle's trainee platoon sergeant to stand by so I could introduce her to you. Her name is Private Trothala."

Harmon wondered what the slight smirk on Evelyn's face meant. "Sure, have her step around so I can get a look at her."

It took all Harmon could do to not act surprised by what he saw. A young Withaloo wearing the uniform of the Bolts stepped around within view of the camera. It wasn't the fact that a Withaloo had opted to join the Bolts as opposed to the Withaloo Army. Several others had made that decision in the other training cycles. They'd done so because they were intrigued with piloting a mech. It was the fact that the private on his screen had shaved the fur close on her face, and Harmon could see the distinctive tattoo of lightning rippling down.

"Private Trothala," Harmon said. "If I was there, I'd shake your hand. Congratulations on being chosen as the platoon sergeant during training. As you're aware, the new heavy mechs are ready for production. They have some additions that the ones you used in training don't have. The first one will be ready tomorrow. I'll have Sergeant Brink ensure it's assigned to you."

"Thank you, sir," the private said, somewhat nervously. Speaking to the commodore and system president for the first time had that type of effect. Harmon was used to it.

After the private left the room, Harmon looked at Brink with a raised eyebrow. "That was unexpected."

"Yes, sir, I know," explained the NCO. "All the new recruits wanted it, and the old guys and gals voted unanimously for it. They feel if a recruit can pass the interview and make it through training, they earned the lightning. They can be turned off when needed; in a mech, on patrols, whenever. Our old tattoo artist Wally got clean, realized he didn't care for the old neighborhood anymore, and moved to Salvage. He's been busy the last three weeks. I also plan to put him to work in the paint shop. I hope you don't mind."

"Hey, it's your unit," Harmon said. "If he can do that type of work with tattoos, I'm sure he'll do a great job with the camouflage patterns on equipment and the laser reflecting paint the mechs need. It's your budget. Your unit's kind of an experiment, really, but you can hire civilian contractors if you want."

"About that," Gunny said. "Wally thinks he can use a version of the power switch implanted in the tattoos now to come up with a pattern-changing paint scheme for the equipment. Change it from jungle to lightly wooded, desert, whatever the situation calls for. It's a great idea, if the guy can pull it off. He's kind of strange."

"Wally's a different kind of guy," agreed Brink, "but he's clean now, and willing to test whenever I ask him to, and prove it. I probably won't test him. I'll know if he spins, but I don't think he will."

"I like it," Harmon said. "Run with it."

"Harmon, I'll head back to…" Evelyn began speaking.

"Hey!" Harmon said, standing quickly. "Sorry, I didn't mean to cut you off, but Jayneen just spoke in my earpiece, and said a ship just transitioned in and it's broadcasting for help. Gotta run." Harmon cut the link and headed to the bridge.

* * *

Five Days Prior in Alter Reality

Mikkotal felt his eyes getting heavy. *Sleep. Sleep would be nice. Just a little while. I'll just close my eyes for a minute,* he thought. Realizing he was about to go under, his head snapped up. Trying to think through the fog in his brain, he made himself get out of the pilot's seat, a curved seat designed to cradle his shell as he sat.

He stumbled back toward the rear of his small craft and noticed blinking orange lights on a panel. The atmosphere scrubbers were offline. Reaching up and seeing two of his stubby fingers where there should have been one, he stabbed the reset button with a claw. Nothing. He'd managed to repair the damage to the inner hull of his ship right before he coasted through the gate in the Barlat System, but something must have caused a short in the environmental system. He didn't have a way to run diagnostics on it, much less repair it.

The escape pod, he thought. He moved toward the center of the ship, hit the panel, and the hatch slid open. *Wait, I can't eject in alter reality, can I?*

Mikkotal shook his head vigorously. It seemed to help. Realizing he might have a solution, he grabbed one of the tools he'd used when he'd installed the emergency patches. He jammed the handle in the hatch track so it wouldn't close, stepped into the pod, and turned on the operating system. The system wouldn't allow the pod to eject with the hatch open and unsealed.

Once he turned on the system, its own atmosphere scrubber kicked in. While he stood there, his head cleared as his brain started receiving the oxygen it so desperately needed. He checked the battery status. It registered a full charge. Unfortunately, it wouldn't continue to charge once the pod was activated. The power source from the ship had been cut. It was a safety precaution prior to a pod ejecting.

He knew he couldn't count on the power cell lasting the full week if it was forced to maintain the atmosphere in the entire ship. He took a few deep breaths, stepped back into the corridor, hit the emergency button in the rear of the passageway, and sealed off the back portion of the craft. *Maybe it will last long enough now*, he thought as he looked at the countdown to entry in Salvage System. It read five days and two hours.

Half an hour later, before sitting back down in the pilot's seat, Mikkotal put on his suit. Once the helmet was sealed, it would provide enough air for three hours. He never wore it when he traveled unless he had to exit the ship to repair something on the outer hull. He checked the rebreather's power status and hung the helmet on the hook on the side of his seat. *Maybe I won't need it.* He pulled an emergency ration pack out of a small panel on the side of the chair. *Too bad the galley's on the other side of that closed hatch,* he thought as he bit into a protein bar. *At least it's pressed garkle worms.*

* * *

Harmon sat in his seat and asked, "What do we have, Jayneen?"

"A ship just emerged into the system," answered the AI. "It is coasting. It appears to be badly damaged. The sensors detect damage to the engines and thrusters. Harmon, I am surprised it has power at all."

"Sir, someone on that ship is broadcasting on all frequencies. It says it only has eight hours of breathable atmosphere left," Ensign Pathron informed.

"Thanks, Path, see if you can put it on the screen."

Ensign Pathron, a Withaloo, raised his ears slightly. It was the first time the commodore had called him by his name instead of rank. Granted, Commodore Tomeral had shortened it, but he'd learned humans did that from the ship's head engineer. "Yes, sir."

Onscreen, an image came up of a small cockpit area on a ship. Seated in the only seat was a being in a deep space suit, minus the helmet, which could be seen hanging off the strange chair. Harmon had never encountered this race before. He found himself comparing it to an armadillo, like the ones in the zoo on Tretra. Only this one had to be four feet tall, at least.

"You are Harmon Tomeral!" the being said, standing quickly.

Well, at least it's a race whose language is programed in the translator, Harmon thought. "I am. And you are?

"I am Mikkotal," answered the being, obviously relieved. "I have come from Barlat to talk to you. My ship was attacked before I could enter the gate. I do not have long before I am out of air. Can you assist me?"

"We can try; hold one," Harmon said. He muted the call.

"Jayneen, who do we have close enough to get to that ship?"

"We are the only ones who can get there in that time frame. The rest of Task Force Command are farther in system. Utilizing battle speed, I have calculated I can pull his ship into the bay with tractor beams in eight point eight hours, since it is the size of a shuttle. That is the soonest it can be done after turning over and slowing to match his ship."

Harmon looked back up at the screen and hit the button on his comm. "Is there anything you can do in your ship to stretch your air? We can get to you, but it'll be close to nine standard hours."

"Once the escape pod air scrubber shuts down, I can seal my suit and last three hours longer," said the relieved Barlat. "Thank you."

"Did he ssay he iss ussing hiss esscape pod environmental ssysstem for the whole sship?" Zerith asked from the power plant.

"I think so," Harmon answered.

"Pretty smart," Clip said.

"Bahroot agreess," Zerith said. Bahroot had spent the day down in the power plant with his Uncle Zerith.

"Lena, use the course Jayneen plotted," Harmon ordered. "Let's go get him."

* * *

Harmon stood looking through the portal in the connecting chamber to the bay. Although the panel indicated the pressure was normalized, he waited until a suited member of the flight deck crew, using a detection device, waved the all clear and took off his helmet. It wouldn't be a good idea to enter the bay if the ship had a damaged fusion plant, and it was radiating.

Harmon and Big Jon entered the bay. A small ramp the width of a normal hatch was slowly lowering on the strange ship. It had definitely been shot up. It looked to Harmon as if a fighter had raked it with laser fire. Jayneen had been right. It was a wonder the power plant worked.

Mikkotal walked down the ramp wearing his deep space suit. The helmet was a large light-reflective clear-steel dome. The Barlat reached up, twisted the helmet, and took it off. Upon closer inspection, the being did look like an armadillo from Earth. A four-foot-tall armadillo.

"Welcome to *Salvage Title*," Harmon said and held out a hand. Big Jon stood ready, just in case.

To his surprise, Mikkotal stepped over, reached up, and shook Harmon's hand. Harmon hadn't thought the rescued visitor would know the traditional human greeting. "Thank you for rescuing me," Mikkotal said. "I would like to take this suit off, if that would be acceptable to you."

"Sure," Harmon said. "Then we'll go sit down and you can tell me your story."

* * * * *

Chapter Twenty-Four

"I will stand. Thank you," said Mikkotal. "On my trips out of our system, I have never encountered a chair that was comfortable. They are not designed for a Barlat."

"Alright," Harmon said, "but something tells me *I* need to sit down for this."

Harmon had called for the two AIs, Clip, Zerith, Kyla, and Vera to meet him in the conference room. Hank and Stan were present on a split screen on the wall. It was all Harmon could do not to laugh at the brothers. For some strange reason, they each had on headgear.

Harmon had no idea which one of them had seen the old Earth videos, but they both wore aviator helmets with their goggles on top, the likes of which were worn by Earth's World War I pilots. Pilots who were insane enough to sit behind combustion engines surrounded by canvas, wood, and wire while flying, shooting, and being shot at by projectile weapons.

Clip elbowed him, leaned over, and whispered in Harmon's ear, "Biplanes weren't ships, they were planes of fools."

Harmon covered his mouth with his fingers spread across his face and looked down for a second. After regaining composure, he looked at their visitor. "Ok, Mikkotal, tell me why you came to see me and who shot up your ship."

"I am from the planet Barlat," began their rescued guest. "My planet does not interact with many other systems, except some small trading. All out-system business is conducted at a small space station near the gate and is usually just the delivery of small replicators, power plants, or medical nanites. Things like this. We are fully capable of feeding ourselves, so we do not need to trade with other systems for food. We have several small freighters that transfer the goods to the surface of Barlat.

"I am the only pilot selected to leave our system in one of our ships. I go to the Bentwick system to sell things. It provides the credit required to purchase the few things we need and to be able to use the gate. I have been to one other system, several years ago, but the credit offered for what I was selling was not enough. I never returned there because I found a buyer on Bentwick willing to pay the price asked."

"Dude, what are you selling?" Clip asked.

"If I may, I would like to withhold that information until my tale is complete," said Mikkotal.

"Let him finissh," Zerith told his friend around a mouthful of muffin. "It might get excciting." Noticing he hadn't offered any to their guest, Zerith offered a mini muffin to Mikkotal.

Mikkotal sniffed the muffin. "Thank you, I can eat this. It was not baked with grubs, but that's alright, I can eat plain bread."

The look on Hank and Stan's faces on the screen made Harmon cover his mouth again. "Go on," he said.

"Six months ago, on Bentwick, I made the transaction with the buyer in the evening, after his normal business hours, like always," the Barlat continued. "Afterwards, I was approached by two humans in the restaurant at the starport where I stopped to purchase a meal. They serve delicious soup there. I am not sure what race it is made for, but it has a wonderful blend of invertebrates and crunchy insects, spiced perfectly. I enjoy a bowl every time I make the trip."

Harmon refused to look up at the brothers on the screen, but he could hear the noises they made. "Humans? Were they locals?"

"I do not think so," answered Mikkotal. "Of course, the translator I have does a fine job of translating and allowing me to hear a close proximity to the speaker's voice, regardless of the race, but I cannot distinguish accents to determine which human system they originated from. I surmised this because they dressed differently.

"They told me they knew why I was on Bentwick and informed me I had been cheated," he continued. "They said they would give me ten percent more for what I sell. To prove this, they gave me the ten percent difference right then for the next transaction. I came back a month later and sold them the product. The next three trips, I sold to them and received the extra ten percent. I thought we had become friends. I inadvertently let it slip on the last trip that I was not just a courier working for one of the few known systems the product comes from. I let them know it came from my home world."

"Dude, I gotta know what the frost you're selling," Clip said.

Mikkotal didn't answer Clip's question. He continued, "Three weeks later our system was invaded. An entire fleet of Gritloth warships came in without warning, not that we could do anything to stop them. We have no warships. They landed their soldiers on Barlat. They killed the few of us who attempted to fight back. We have become their subjects."

"Squat," Harmon said. "The Gritloth are tough. Yours is not the only system they've invaded."

"They have invaded three systems to date," Jayneen informed everyone. "They abandoned the last system they invaded once the mines played out. That system is just now interacting with others, and that was five years ago. They do not wish to maintain systems, just deplete them of their resources."

"So that's how your ship got shot up," Harmon surmised. "You're lucky you escaped. Their fighters are no joke. I would say they're on par with Bentwick fighters, at least."

"I was maneuvering my ship well beyond its recommended G-forces," admitted Mikkotal.

"So why here?" Harmon asked. "Why did you come looking for me? Don't get me wrong, I feel really bad for your race, but yours isn't the only system in the galaxy in this type of situation."

"I came because of the video," Mikkotal said, as if it was plain as day. "You can free our system. We will pay. We will pay in raw product."

"Man, if you don't tell me what you are selling..." Clip demanded again.

"Galacuss crystals," answered Mikkotal.

The room was silent. Finally Clip whistled slowly and said, "Galacuss Crystals. The single most coveted stones in the galaxy. Your planet has them? That makes it only the fourth known planet in the entire galaxy with them."

"What color?" Zerith asked, leaning forward.

"All colors," answered Mikkotal without hesitation. "All of them."

"A large handful of thosse sstoness would finance Ssalvage Ssysstem for a year, Harmon." Zerith informed him. "Pluss we would want to keep ssome. The dust from crusshed red oness power anti-aging nanitess for fifty yearss."

"Typical medical nanites are used for emergencies and do what they were designed to do," Jayneen explained to Harmon. "The only problem with them is they burn through their energy source quickly. Nanites powered with red Galacuss crystals last fifty years, thus keeping the individual from suffering from the effects of aging."

"White Galacuss crystals are for industrial use," said Zerith. "They can cut through clear-steel like paper. It is one of the hardest stones in the galaxy."

Kyla spoke up for the first time, "The other colored stones are used for jewelry. It is a huge status symbol to wear Galacuss crystal jewelry across thousands of worlds. It is very expensive."

"I've kicked around the idea of contracting out some ships to cover the system's budget, but we're making it alright with a little profit right now," Harmon said. "I don't know that I can ask the crews to risk their lives for credit. I could talk to Rick and Ithall, since they both expressed a desire to contract as mercenaries again," Harmon said, "but they would have to make that decision. It would depend, I suppose, how many ships are in your system now, and how large the forces are on the ground."

"I saw the video; you could lead them, regain our system, and free us," pleaded Mikkotal. "We will pay."

"It's not about the credit," Harmon said. "I hate that this happened to your world, but you're asking me to order ships into battle, and some of them might not make it back. I wish I knew who the humans were, those lowlifes."

"They need to get what they desserve," Zerith said, "and so do the Gritloth."

"Right on, Zee," Clip agreed.

"Uncle Harmon, may I speak?" Bahroot asked.

"Sure," Harmon said. "What did you want to say?'

On the screen, an image appeared below Hank and Stan. It was a fuzzy, still shot of a dark ship leaving the bay of one of the Q-ships destroyed a year ago. "Remember the crewmembers picked up in the escape pod who swore the men who made the initial call to *Windswept* were named Lowantha and Hawthorne?"

"Those two need killing. Bradford said so," Hank stated. His brother nodded along.

"That they do," Harmon agreed. "If I ever get my hands on them, they may not go to trial."

"I had a hunch when Mr. Mikkotal said it was two humans," continued Bahroot. "Remember when I showed you this still photo and told you the gate had been used days after the battle, and you said it may have been them but there was no way to be sure who had left the system?"

"Right," Harmon said, wondering where this was going.

"While Mr. Mikkotal was speaking, I checked the records on the gate. I'm sorry I didn't think of this sooner, but the Bentwick coordinates were entered when the gate was activated."

"You can access that?" Jayneen asked.

"Sure, Mom," Bahroot said. "Mr. Mikkotal, was this one of the humans you interacted with?"

On the screen, a front and side image of Grant Lowantha came up. It was the image taken when he was arrested on Joth for breaking into Harmon's mech during the Best Marine Competition. It was probably the only photo of the former military spy still in existence, and it was a digital image of an actual paper photo. If Lowantha had attempted to erase all copies of it on the Net or in the law enforcement system on Joth, he'd missed this actual print copy.

"Why yes, that is one of them," said the surprised Barlat.

"Dude, where did you find a picture of a picture?" Clip asked.

"I remembered it from the image Grandpa Rinto showed me," answered his son. "He said to let him know if I ever saw this 'worthless piece of squat' around the scrapyard on any of the camera feeds. He said he had a score to settle."

"Bahroot! Language," scolded Jayneen.

"Sorry," answered Bahroot, "but he did."

"This changes things," said Harmon, standing. "The Restore Movement, what's left of them, caused this. Ones we let slip through our grasp. And to be honest, I can't stand the thought of an entire planet enslaved by an invading race. Listen, we can't save the whole galaxy—we just can't—but we can save a system."

"Yes, we can," Kyla agreed. The other three Leethog nodded their heads, and out the corner of his eye Harmon saw Big Jon nodding along with them.

"Right on, man," Clip said with a grin. "Right on."

* * * * *

Chapter Twenty-Five

"**S**o that's the deal," Harmon said. He'd just explained, in detail, everything he'd learned from Mikkotal. They were in the community center's small auditorium in Bank Town. The front-row seats were filled with Rick Kashka and his task force commanders, Withaloo Fleet Commander Ithall, Withaloo Ground Force Commander Arthok, Clip, Zerith, the four Tomeral Associates, Jayneen, Sergeant Brink, Harmon's task force commanders, and the two fighter carrier commanders.

The rest of the auditorium was filled with ship commanders, their executive officers, ship engineers, Withaloo Ground Force officers, Bolt platoon sergeants and squad leaders, senior NCOs from the various ships' security platoons, and several system and planet administrators. Mike and Mike were present, representing the combined shipyards.

"Thoughts?" Harmon asked the room.

The room was silent for a moment, everyone lost in their own thoughts. Finally, Ithall spoke up. "We are united. I truly feel this way. Everyone has welcomed the Withaloo here to this planet, this system, without reservation. We are not made to feel as if we are guests; we are *of* it. It is our home. You are the system president and commodore. You alone command our combined fleets. I will obey any order that is not…how do you say it? Immoral. The mission you are proposing is far from that. No sentient race should be enslaved. Ever."

201

"Harmon Tomeral, you are my ally," said Rick. "Salvage is Evermore's ally. This is an eternal contract. It cannot be broken."

Every Kashkal in the room said, "Contract is Life," through their external speakers.

"Ithall, my friend," Rick said, "you are correct. No race should be subjugated. We are all citizens of Salvage System, and we will all fight if Commodore Tomeral makes the decision to free the Barlat System."

"We may administer this planet, at times making decisions without consulting you first," said JoJo, "but Moroath and I leave military matters to you."

"We will stand behind your decision," added Moroath.

JoJo reached out to hold her husband Twiggy's hand. "Absolutely," she said. Though it meant her husband would leave the Agriculture Division to his Withaloo co-administrator while he went with the forces. He still considered himself a reservist, and it would be time to be activated once again.

"I've made my decision," Harmon stated. "We can't save the whole galaxy, but we can save a system. There'll be several fronts to this war. We'll destroy their fleet and put troops on the ground to wipe out their army, while ensuring there's adequate protection here in the system in case they attempt an end-around."

Harmon made the statement with such conviction that no one in the room doubted their eventual victory. The room was silent as beings began thinking ahead about their ships, their jobs, their crew, their troops, what needed immediate attention—all the things good leaders considered before a mission.

A lone voice rang out in the quiet room. It was Aleethra. "End-around iss a warball term. Doess anyone have a piecce of jerky?" All knew the story; the room erupted in cheers.

* * *

Harmon stood in Sergeant Brink's office with Ground Force Commander Arthok. "Colonel Arthok thinks you've been doing an exceptional job," Harmon said. "I agree."

"I am impressed that an individual who is not an officer could accomplish so much," agreed Arthok. "The Bolts are an outstanding specialty unit. I would like to recognize your leaders."

"Sir?" questioned Sergeant Bolt.

"Though you are a separate unit," the Salvage Ground Force commander began, "falling under my command per the commodore, I would be more comfortable if your leadership titles fell in line with the rest of the ground forces' titles we have adopted."

Brink looked at Harmon with a question in his eyes. Harmon let him wonder and didn't interrupt Colonel Arthok. He was enjoying himself.

"Therefore, Captain Brink, you are to inform your lieutenants, staff sergeants, and sergeants of the upcoming promotion ceremony tomorrow," stated Commander Arthok. "The ceremony will be for show. The promotions have already taken effect."

* * *

"That was great," Harmon said. "He never saw it coming."

"He did not," agreed Arthok. "I am still learning human facial expressions, and the tattoo masks some of them, but I could see the surprise. Thank you for agreeing to my request."

"You're welcome," Harmon told him. "I'm always open for suggestions, if it helps you lead the forces. Total ground forces are over twelve hundred now, right?"

"Yes, sir," Arthok said. "A little over, including the Bolts and support units. I am, of course, not counting the individual Smilps in the Bolts' maintenance unit. I believe there are twenty of them. They move quickly."

"That they do." Harmon laughed. "Still, be grateful for them. A maintenance unit with five Prithmar, four Leethog, a Caldivar, a Z'mitok, six Yalteens, and twenty Smilps is a force multiplier the likes of which the galaxy has never seen."

"I am grateful," assured Arthok. "I witnessed them replacing the power plant in one of the tanks in an hour. Start to finish. The tank was back on the firing line during gunnery training before its turn came around again. Never have I seen such."

"The recovery vehicles and the track-mounted replicators were Clip and Zerith's idea," Harmon admitted. "They say they'll be able to use damaged equipment, ours or theirs, to load the replicators to make parts. They'll even be able to repair mechs, to an extent. Ammunition will be simple for both the tanks and artillery, since both are magnetic propulsion, as long as we have the explosive component to place in the artillery rounds."

"My maintenance commander is glad they are part of the Bolts," Arthok said. "What will you do about recharging the power cells on the mechs?"

"Smilps," Harmon answered. "The Smilps. They designed small stompers, about five feet square. They have six legs and a small fusion plant. They scramble around and charge mechs. Six mechs at a time can be charged, and they built four of them."

"Impressive," said Colonel Arthok. "After we complete this mission, I would like to discuss adding a regular mech unit to the ground forces."

"We can do that," Harmon agreed. "I may have to see about getting more replicators from Yatarward Industries. They can be built the old-fashioned way, like mine, but an assembly line is much more practical. I'm glad you said after the mission, though. Right now, I'm going to go spend some time with my fiancé."

"That word did not translate, sir." Arthok said, confused.

"My...ah, my future mate," Harmon explained. "There'll be a ceremony."

"Is she not your mate now?" asked the colonel.

"Well, yes, but..." Harmon began. "Tell you what. One day we'll sit down over a beer, and I'll try to explain why the ceremony's important to a human."

"I look forward to it," agreed Arthok. "I like beer. But not Prithmar brands. I tend to fill up on water in between beers when I drink them."

* * *

Back on *Salvage Title,* Harmon conversed with the AIs. "Jayneen," Harmon asked, "do you think you and Bahroot can tap into the Net and Gritloth communications like you did the Squilla? Maybe they're making direct calls back to their system or to their emperor."

"Yes," answered the AI. "I will begin monitoring them now. Bahroot, show Harmon what you have discovered."

"Alright," answered Bahroot.

On the main screen, a map of a system Harmon had never seen appeared. It had five planets. Looking closely, Harmon could see the symbol for the Barlat spaceport an hour from the gate. It had two symbols for medium battlecruisers beside it. Close to the second planet from the star, symbols for twenty-two more ships of various types were indicated. Twenty-four Gritloth ships had been used in the invasion. They had met no resistance.

"Nice," Harmon said. "Bahroot, can you magnify the area near the planet?"

"Sure, Uncle Harmon," Bahroot said. "How's that?"

Harmon studied the symbols. "Jayneen, can you determine how many troops their troop carriers hold? I see two of them."

"Yes, Harmon," answered the AI. "I have determined each Gritloth troop carrier had approximately two thousand troops in their last invasion. Unless they have redesigned their troop carriers, this number should be accurate."

"We'll go with that," Harmon said. "Most systems don't drastically change ship designs that work, which means they have about four thousand troops on the ground. Do they use mechs?"

"I have seen nothing indicating mech use," the AI advised him. "If they did, it would have to be very large mechs, given their height."

"It would," agreed Harmon. "Do me a favor and put one up on the screen so I can get a good look at them again."

Harmon found himself looking at a huge soldier. It was easily eight feet tall, though it was slim. The soldier was wearing light battle armor and held a long laser rifle. A full helmet hung at its side. Its bald head was the only visible part of the Gritloth's body, and it was a pale orange color. It had a lipless mouth and nostril slits, with no protruding nose. It stared back from the screen with two huge black eyes.

"So much for 'don't shoot until you see the whites of their eyes,'" Clip commented.

"Jayneen, send this image across the entire fleet and to the ground forces. Thanks," Harmon said.

"Sir, you have a call coming in," the communications officer said, his ears up. "It is from a ship called *Sweet Pea*."

"Thanks, Path, put it on screen," Harmon said, grinning.

"We're back!" Cameron said, waving at the screen, his wing flap obvious with his outstretched hand. He pushed his glasses back up his nose. "How's it going? You have a bunch more ships. Nice. I see more Grithelaon ships. They look almost the same as the one I saw before." He looked back. "Ugg! Fine, Ralph, go ahead."

"Hi, Commodore," Ralph said, stepping into view. "Look at my wing. It's torn. The doctor said it will take weeks before it mends. I got snagged in a tree on vacation. I'll tell you about sometime. Ok. Bye." He moved out of Cameron's way.

"Sometimes that guy talks too much," Cameron said. "I think it's the pain killers he's on. Anyway, what's new?"

* * * * *

Chapter Twenty-Six

Harmon had called a final meeting to go over the plan. They were meeting on the fighter carrier *Windswept*. It had room in its bays for several shuttles.

"Can you do it?" Harmon asked Cameron.

"Sure," Cameron answered. "No problem. As long as you're ready to come in right behind us."

"We will be," Harmon said. "We'll leave space for *Sweet Pea* to pass through, and time it so we enter an hour behind you. You'll have to pass through the fleet at greater than battle speed as you head for the gate. Just make sure you bank away from the spaceport when you enter the system."

"Cameron," Jayneen said, "do not allow my son to get hurt, and do not take any unnecessary chances. I will be very upset."

"Dude, you better stick to the plan," Clip threatened.

"We will be there," Hank said, adjusting the goggles on top of his aviator's hat.

"It will be fine," Stan added. They were both grinning and high-foured each other, then Cameron and Ralph. Ralph flinched because of his wing flap.

"It had better be," said Kyla, silencing their laughter.

"I will be ok," Bahroot said. "It's a good plan. I'll break away when the two frigates detach, and while they draw the two ships near the port's attention, pilot one shuttle and guide the other by linking its controls. Then I'll lay the EMP minefield, so when Salvage Fleet enters, the first salvo of missiles from the Gritloth will be useless. I will then fly the shuttles safely out of the way of the upcoming battle and monitor through the gate's sensors. I can do it."

"When Salvage Fleet comes through," Harmon continued with the briefing, "we'll head straight for the planet, help take out the two nearest ships, and take on the twenty warships as they come to meet us. I don't think the two troop transports will be an issue. Three days later, Kashkal Fleet comes in. We should have the battle wrapped up at that point. You head directly behind that first planet, the gas giant. When the Gritloth reinforcement fleet comes into the system, you'll be a nice surprise for them. It'll also allow time for our troop transport ship to get into orbit over Barlat, and we can put troops on the ground."

"Will one of them make a direct call back and send word to the Gritloth emperor about the other fleet?" asked Commander Ithall.

"No," Harmon answered. "Once the initial call for help goes through, Bahroot will disable that part of the Net for the entire system."

"It is a good plan with sound tactics," said Rick Kashka. "The Gritloth have a total of forty warships available in their home system for use. They cannot pull ships from the other system they occupy for fear of losing it. Once we defeat them in Barlat, it will be years before they can rebuild their fleet. They will not be able to hire mercenaries. There is an unwritten code among mercenaries across the galaxy. No one will take a contract from known slavers."

"This is true," agreed Ithall.

"We'll keep the home front safe," Mike said. "Twiggy will patrol with the light battlecruiser *Piece of Junk,* Bradford will escort with that Dalgit frigate *Skrittle,* along with the upgraded Nilta Q-ship *Thorn*

Blossom, and two of the Withaloo frigates. I'll park *Cube* near the gate so it'll be a nasty surprise, should any pirates attempt anything. I doubt they will, with that video still circulating. We also have the defense platforms."

"Who are the crews on the *Skrittle* and *Piece of Junk*?" Hank asked.

"Smilps, mainly," Bradford said, taking his unlit cigar out of his mouth, "some guys from the shipyards, and the three Dalgit employees we have. They shouldn't wreck it in open space—I hope, those guys are kinda the worst pilots I've ever met."

"What if the Gritloth emperor decides to send the reinforcement fleet straight to Salvage System?"

"He won't know who iss attacking them," Zerith said. "The frigatess are new and not shaped like any of the other shipss, and *Ssweet Pea* wass not featured in the video. Bahroot will enssure all transponderss are off completely oncce the gate acceptss payment. They will not know where we came from until itss too late to ssend a messsage through the gate."

"It was a great video," Cameron complained, "but we weren't in it. That sucks. We could've been famous."

"Mikkotal will go over terrain, locations, and what we can expect on the surface with Colonel Arthok," Harmon said. "Brickle should be arriving with him at any time. His ship is already on board, and some repairs are being made to the engines and environmental systems by the new maintenance unit. Once this meeting breaks up and everyone is back on their ships, we move out."

Six hours later, Harmon looked over the plan on his slate, searching for anything he might have missed. The dropships could possibly come under fire when entering the planet's atmosphere, but that problem had worked itself out. The Bentwick fighters were capable of atmospheric flight as well as space flight, like the old Tretrayon Zax fighters. They would provide cover, and the bomber fighters would be used as well.

His fighter sat in a corner of the bay, and the other two were parked in a hangar at the airfield on Salvage. Both JoJo and Twiggy had maintained enough flight time to stay proficient, just in case. Harmon wondered if Twiggy had his with him on the Krift ship.

"Sir, the flight officer informs me the shuttle is secure, and the bay is closed," the tactical officer said.

"Thanks." Harmon hit the button on his comm, and his words went to the entire system fleet. "This is it, begin the movement. Make sure you leave room for *Sweet Pea* as she comes through the formation. Maintain your distance, and be ready to detach from your host when we exit alter reality in less than six days. Let's go save a system."

* * *

"I hope you guys have your G- force dampeners turned all the way up," Cameron said.

"We do," Hank said over the comm. Both frigates, *Hold My Drink* and *Watch This*, were attached to *Sweet Pea* right behind the two crewless mine shuttles.

"I don't need them," Bahroot said from one of the shuttles.

"Well, we do!" exclaimed Stan. "It is turned all the way up, but it does have a limit. Don't squish us, Cameron."

"Hey, boss, what good's the eighth engine if we never get to kick it in?" Ralph asked.

"I know, right? Did you take your pain pill? I wonder if I should fly?" Cameron asked before cutting the command link.

* * *

Captain Brink stood beside Lieutenant Mayshire, looking over the huge bay at the small section that contained all of the unit's equipment. It wasn't the fact that the Bolts' footprint wasn't large, it was because the bay was so big—almost half-a-colony-ship huge.

Sixty mechs, comprising the three Mech Platoons, were lined up formation-style—magnetic boots engaged and cockpits open. Behind those mechs were the mechs of Specialty Platoon, consisting of twelve huge mechs standing over fourteen feet tall each, and six small mechs, not quite ten feet tall.

Three of the armored personnel carriers called stompers squatted beside them, the leg joints in the middle up like bent knees. Ten sets of the servo-assisted heavy battle armor for the soldiers in Infantry Platoon were secured on board each of them.

Ten small tanks, utilizing three crewmembers and seven towed artillery pieces, hooked to all the tanks except the Steel Platoon's leadership, lined up behind them in two rows of five. Behind those were the Maintenance Platoon's strange tracked vehicles. One, a large box shape, was obviously their mobile replicator. There were two carrying various tools, welders, and diagnostic equipment, and one with a long open bed with the box-shaped fusion plants to charge mechs. Every piece of equipment had the unit's symbol on them, a cloud with a long streak of jagged lightning coming down.

"Do you think we're ready, Nate?" Lieutenant Deloris Mayshire asked.

"I think so, Dee," Captain Nathan Brink answered. "All the training we've done in the last year was for this type of scenario. I mean, yeah, we were training to defend our own planet, but the tactics are still the same on another."

"I guess I'm just a little nervous," she admitted. "This is a little different than clearing a ship."

"It is," Brink agreed, "but Colonel Arthok has experience. Several times, the contracts the Withaloo took involved planet-side action." He waved a hand at all the equipment in the rest of the bay. "At least half his brigade has seen action. I'm glad we were able to train with them all year. If we can get to the planet and get troops on the ground, we'll be fine."

* * * * *

Chapter Twenty-Seven

Sweet Pea emerged into the Barlat System through the gate, moving at a speed few warships in the galaxy could match. As soon as it appeared, the ship banked hard away from the spaceport, and the two frigates *Hold My Drink* and *Watch This* detached, turned, and slowed. The frigates, designed as missile carriers, were fast, but they couldn't maintain the speed of their host and still maneuver without risk to their crew. Ralph, still at the helm of *Sweet Pea*, performed a turnover maneuver and slowed to match their battle speed before flipping back over.

The three ships continued banking away from the two medium battlecruisers, drawing them away from the spaceport. Bahroot disengaged both mine shuttles' magnetic struts and continued sailing away from the turning warships. Once he felt he was far enough it wouldn't be noticed, he ignited the engines and turned back toward the planet Barlat, much farther in-system. The speed of the shuttles continued to increase.

According to his calculations, he would lay the magnetic pulse mines in twenty hours between the third and fourth planets, placing them in the area the Gritloth missiles would cross, aimed at Salvage Fleet. The defending fleet would get the first volley off, because Salvage Fleet would be coming in at battle speed, giving the defenders an advantage on missile range. It would only be for one salvo. After that, the advantage would be gone.

Bahroot intended to use all four hundred mines Professor Plexico had brought to the system when he'd visited to study the Grithelaon programming. The AI had also plotted the course that would bring him back around to sit, unnoticed, well away from the upcoming battles to monitor the gate. He had his orders, and he intended to stick to them.

"This is *Sweet Pea*; here they come," Cameron announced almost an hour later over the open link to the two brothers. "I'll take the one on the port side, and you guys get the starboard."

"Roger, *Sweet Pea*, this is *Hold My Drink*..." Hank said.

Stan immediately followed with, "and *Watch This*."

If anyone had been listening to the open link, they'd have heard laughter coming from all three ships, stepping all over each other on the communications link. "If I ever get another ship and start a fleet, you guys are naming it," Cameron said. The unique destroyer pulled up and away from the two missile frigates as they began launching missiles and rolling over each other in an acrobatic display sure to confuse the enemy.

* * *

Gor'Tok, the commander of the Gritloth medium battlecruiser *Screaming Wraith*, was bored. There was no one left to kill on the spaceport. The last Barlat left lay in front of his commander's chair, the pooling mess around it slowly thickening. "Take that away," he demanded. "Now we know how to get to them when they roll up and cower inside. You simply cut the shell off." He finished wiping off a long, slim knife and slid it into the sheath strapped to his arm.

Gor'Tok looked up at the sensors' display. There was nothing of note. There had been no activity since the attempted escape of the shuttle from the bay underneath the port. An oversight that had cost the team leader of the boarding party his life. Mistakes were often dealt with by painful means, but that mistake was one that could have brought others into the system. The pilot whose laser blast had hit the shuttle, destroying its engines and causing it to vent atmosphere before exiting the gate, had been promoted to flight leader. Whoever was operating that shuttle would surely perish. Punishment, reward, it was all part of the cycle of an officer in the Emperor's Fist.

"When are we to be relieved?" the commander asked his operations officer.

"In four days, according to the schedule, sir," answered Under-Commander Gil'Non with a blank stare.

"Bah, an eternity," Commander Gor'Tok complained. "At least we will rotate to the planet before *Life Taker*, may its entire crew catch a blistering disease."

The under-commander smiled at this remark, though none but his own race would be able to detect the difference on a Gritloth's somber face. Ship rivalries were encouraged in the Emperor's Fist, especially against another crew of the same class ship. He looked back at his display and froze.

"Sir!" the operations officer said loudly, "there has been an emergence."

"At last!" exclaimed the commander. "Details?"

"It is confusing," admitted the operations officer. "It is moving at an incredible speed. Its shape and size matches nothing I have seen. It is transmitting no registration."

"No registration?" demanded Gor'Tok. "Impossible! The gate system will not work for an unregistered ship. Even pirate ships have some type of registration, even when they're stolen. Move to intercept."

"Sir, the sensors are now showing three separate ships," Under-Commander Gil'Non announced. "It was hosting two frigates. They have heavy shielding, and I'm getting weapons readings on all three.

They are slowing and banking around. If they continue their flight paths, they will have to challenge us before leaving the system."

"*Life Taker,* this is *Screaming Wraith,*" demanded Gor'Tok. "Stay on my starboard side, and we will deal with these three before they can get back to the gate. They will be within range in less than a standard hour."

"Acknowledged," answered Commander Gar'Lof from the accompanying ship.

"Perhaps he will not get in our way," Gor'Tok told his undercommander, "the incompetent slug." His operations officer smiled again and watched his display as the ship began accelerating to battle speed.

* * *

Cameron stood in front of his chair so he could get a better look at the Gritloth ship readings on the sensor screen. "They haven't launched fighters yet; let's beat them to the punch. Turn them loose, Gary."

"You got it, boss," *Sweet Pea's* tactical officer replied. He hit his comm and called down to the bay to Windell. "Launch 'em, Windell."

Windell was one of the mech pilots, but his main job was flight officer. The other two mech pilots and the three repair technicians rounded out the flight deck crew. Expecting the command to launch fighters, the crew was already suited. Windell acknowledged the bridge's call, hit the panel, and the bay door pulled back and slid down the length of the ship. Fourteen fighters of various altered designs roared out in pairs. The ship had fifteen fighters normally, but one was still in pieces, pending an engine replacement. A disappointed pilot stood beside Windell, watching the launch with the deck crew, ready to help.

"Start firing the missiles," Cameron ordered. "Hold back on the shockers, though."

Sixteen missiles leapt from the ship and headed toward the much bigger medium battlecruiser. There were twenty launchers on the ship, but three were for use in atmosphere, and one was the shocking ship disabler. There were several types of missiles, and they were part of the reason for the ship's success in battle. Several targeted the power plant area of the ship, two swung around, designed to impact in the thrusters alone, and the rest flew toward the largest portion of the enemy.

When the ship had been pieced together, Cameron had no idea the advantage multiple missile launcher systems would be, or how difficult they would be to defend against. Like most ships, an automated defense laser system prioritized incoming missiles, but usually it was the same type of missiles aimed at the same area. The missiles confused the defense programs, and quite often some of Cameron's missiles struck shields without being engaged by the defending lasers. Eventually those shields failed.

"Twelve missiles incoming," announced the tactical officer.

"Just twelve?" Cameron asked. "That's strange; as big as that ship is, I expected twenty or more."

"That is strange," agreed Ralph, looking over his shoulder at the tactical officer. "Are the fighters out?"

"Last two launched," confirmed the tactical officer.

"Good, rolling way!" said Ralph and he banked and rolled up away, still headed for the enemy but coming from a slightly different line of attack.

"Launching again," said Ted, the weapons officer.

"Hey!" shouted Gary. "Those missiles just became thirty-six, and they've launched again!"

"Splitters!" Cameron exclaimed. "I hate when they have splitters. Shoot the shocker at it. Target the launchers."

"Shocker away," confirmed Ted after he designated the area of the enemy where the launch tubes were located.

The defensive lasers on *Sweet Pea* put up a crisscross pattern as they attempted to stop the incoming barrage. Four from the first salvo fired at them hit their shields despite the effort. Everyone on board felt the impacts. Several of the repair crew scrambled to fix the blown fuses and boards in the panels.

"Forward shields down to seventy-four percent," announced the tactical officer.

"Diving," announced Ralph. The ship pitched downward, allowing more of the defensive lasers across the top of the ship to come into play. Just one of the missiles in the second salvo struck the shields.

"It looks like two missiles hit their ship," Gary said. "They still have shields. Second salvo getting ready to impact...nice! Several hits."

"Good," Cameron said. "Get ready with the main lasers. We'll get them on the pass."

"Shocker just hit," Gary said. "We'll see what it did, but they launched again before it hit."

"Launching another salvo," announced the weapons officer. "Coming up on main laser range in three, two, now!"

On top of *Sweet Pea*, the two large lasers in the turret fired long pulses at once. Within the ship, the lights in the berthing area dimmed momentarily as the lasers pulled incredible power from two of the fusion plants. Only a few non-essential areas besides the main lasers drew energy from the two plants, so there was no issue with critical systems resetting.

The lasers raked along the shielding of the Gritloth ship and burned it out. At the last moment, the beams pierced deep into the ship. It wasn't for very long, but it did considerable damage to several decks, and the enemy began venting atmosphere.

All sixteen missiles in the salvo hit the battlecruiser and, with a blast of bright light, the aft third of the ship came apart in all directions, and it drifted, spinning. *Sweet Pea* swept by the hulk, and Cameron instructed Ralph to come around, with the fighters to follow, and they banked toward the other battlecruiser, prepared to help the brothers out. Just then, Salvage Fleet began emerging through the gate.

* * *

"We'll play bait," Hank told his brother. "Come together long enough for them to launch."

"Ok," Stan agreed over the link between the two frigates.

They had both just launched two salvos of missiles and were still rolling around each other. *Hold My Drink* leveled out, and *Watch This* came up under it, extremely close. On the sensors of the approaching battlecruiser they appeared as one ship. When the enemy launched its first salvo, *Watch This* dropped down and rolled away, banking hard to swing back toward the battlecruiser from a different angle. Both frigates launched two more salvos of eight before some of the first missiles struck the enemy's shields.

The two new frigates had been farthest from completion in the ancient shipyards, and Mike had been able to alter their designs with Jayneen's help. They were still missile frigates, but their shape was much rounder than the original design. Not quite like the Dalgit frigate, but similar. Unlike the Dalgit frigates, though, they had the same missiles *Salvage Title* used. They were longer range, and they were extremely powerful.

Two of the first sixteen missiles made it past the battlecruisers' defensive lasers and struck the shield. If anyone were able to see outside the big ship, they would've seen the shields shimmer a light blue as they attempted to absorb the blows. One missile from the next salvo made it through and hit the forward shields, stressing them even more.

"Twelve missiles incoming," announced the tactical officer on *Hold My Drink*. "They stayed with us. They just tripled! There are thirty six coming!"

"Splitters," Hank shouted. "Roll away and kick it in!"

The frigate rolled away and dramatically increased speed, its defensive lasers targeting the incoming missiles. The maneuver paid off, and the last eighteen missiles gained on the ship, but never quite caught it, burning up the last of their fuel in the wide loop as they attempted to strike the target they'd locked on.

Unhindered by incoming missiles, Stan ordered another salvo as the next sixteen missiles reached the Gritloth battlecruiser. One of the missiles hit the shield, and the shield flared blue and winked out of existence. The battlecruiser attempted to turn away to get some shielding between it and the next salvo, but it wasn't able.

Of the next sixteen missiles, three made it past the defenses and exploded deep within the ship. Stan watched through the clear-steel portals as the glow from its thrusters disappeared, then secondary explosions blew out sections of the ship.

"The fleet has arrived," announced Stan. "Right on time."

* * *

Gor'Tok sat forward in his seat and ordered, "Lock in on that destroyer and destroy it. Continue launching until it is gone."

"Launching now, sir," answered the weapons officer.

"It has launched sixteen missiles, sir," Under-Commander Gil'Non announced.

"Engage the defensive lasers," the commander said. "There are only sixteen."

"Sir, the sensors are having trouble locking onto all the missiles," stated the operations officer as he attempted to manually select incoming missiles.

"Launching again, sir," the weapons officer said. "First salvo has separated, I show the full thirty-six locked on target."

"Good," Commander Gor'Tok said, settling back.

"Sir, they have launched another salvo," Under-Commander Gil'Non said. "Brace for impact!" Almost immediately everyone on board felt a slight shudder as two missiles impacted on the shields. "Forward shields down to eighty percent."

"They are coming head on," the operations officer said. "I detected a single missile launch...brace for missile impact!"

Three more missiles impacted against the ship. "Shields now at fifty percent!" announced Gil'Non.

"Fire the next salvo and be ready to hit them when they pass with the main laser!" shouted Gor'Tok, standing.

The lone missile impacted against the shielding in the front of the ship, overloading the weakened shield with its electrical charge, shorting some components in the forward portion of the ship, and causing many other systems to reset. All weapons were temporarily offline.

"Sir!" the weapons officer exclaimed, "My entire console is resetting!"

"What!" demanded Commander Gor'Tok.

Before the systems came up, the shields were overloaded by the enemy's lasers, and a full salvo of missiles rocked the *Screaming Wraith*. Staring up from the deck in the dark, where he'd landed after bouncing off his chair, Gor'Tok's last thought was to wonder about the incompetent commander of their sister ship and if he was faring any better. A section of the overhead came crashing down on him before he could get an answer. It floated off his lifeless body as the gravity plates failed.

* * * * *

Chapter Twenty-Eight

*S**alvage Title* led the fleet into the system, followed closely by *Desert Shade*, the light battlecruiser *New Toy,* and the destroyer *Cover Fire.* It was joined shortly after by Task Force Bravo, the heavy task force that included two heavy battlecruisers, a light battlecruiser, and three destroyers, which detached. All had been claimed and repaired from the invasion a year ago. Both task forces banked away from the spaceport ahead.

Less than two minutes later, the first of Task Force Alpha emerged, with Diamond Squadron leading the charge. The Nazrooth destroyers were in a diamond formation, with shields overlapped and ready to protect their flagship *Desert Wind.* The medium battlecruiser was followed by the fighter carrier *Windswept,* two light battlecruisers, and an attached destroyer.

The Withaloo Fleet was the last to enter with its five light battlecruisers carrying four destroyers, and four frigates attached to the combined fighter and troop carrier *Special Delivery.* All the riders detached and followed Task Force Alpha, banking and turning in the opposite direction of Task Force Command and Task Force Bravo to come around the spaceport.

"All ships are through," announced *Salvage Title*'s tactical officer.

"Thanks, Adam," Harmon said. "What's the status of the two expected enemy battlecruisers?"

"There are two powerless Gritloth ships less than an hour from us," answered Jayneen from the DB. "*Sweet Pea* is moving at less than battle speeds, and it appears to be recovering its fighters; both *Watch This* and *Hold My Drink* do not show any obvious damage and are banking away from a heavily damaged battlecruiser, headed toward *Sweet Pea.*"

"Jayneen!" said Clip over the open ship's link. "You have to say *Hold My Drink* first."

"He iss correct," agreed Zerith from the power plant. "It doess not ssound right otherwisse."

"Tell her, Zee," Clip added.

"Alright, you two," Harmon admonished while grinning. He hit the comm for the entire fleet's link. "*Sweet Pea, Salvage Title.*"

"Hi, Commodore," Cameron answered. "You missed the party and stuff."

"Party?" Hank asked. "I didn't know there was a party."

"I want some cake!" Stan chimed in. "I like cake."

"We have some leftover cake. For real, it's from home," Cameron said. "Ralph froze it. Can you guys walk a hull if we're moving at battle speeds? You could lock on and we could…"

"Ahh…No," Harmon interrupted. "There'll be none of that. You want Kyla and Vera to blame me if something happens to either of you? Cameron, stop giving them crazy ideas."

"Captain Cameron," Kyla cut in, "I would like a word with you once we rescue this system."

"Yes, ma'am," Cameron answered, dejected. "You guys got me in trouble!" Ralph's sing-song voice could be heard in the background. "You're in trah-bol!" before the link cut.

"Uncle Harmon, this is Bahroot," the AI called over Harmon's personal comm.

"Go ahead, buddy," Harmon answered.

"The flagship has just made a direct call informing their emperor of a large fleet entering this system," the AI explained. "I cut all gate communication after he said that. He was unable to convey the system registration on any ship."

"Good job," Harmon said. "Park away from the path of any incoming ships, and monitor the gate for me. The Kashkal Fleet will come through in less than three days, and I expect Gritloth reinforcements a few days later."

"Ok, Uncle Harmon," answered the young AI. "Oh, yeah, I should mention the Gritloth use separating missiles. One becomes three mid-flight."

"That's good to know ahead of time, thanks," Harmon said.

Harmon looked over at his new communications officer, thought for a moment, then said, "Path, let 'em know the Gritloth have splitters."

Surprised, the young officer composed himself and addressed the fleet. "Salvage Fleet, this is *Salvage Title*. Be advised, the enemy utilizes splitting missiles, I say again…the enemy utilizes splitting missiles. One becomes three. Task Force commanders, acknowledge please."

"Alpha acknowledges," Captain Opawn confirmed.

"This is Bravo," Captain Ellotta answered, "Roger that."

"One becomes three, Withaloo understands," acknowledged Commander Ithall.

Harmon looked over at the bridge engineer. "Brickle, head down to the bay and get ready to kick out the packages for Cameron and the brothers."

"Yes, sir," Brickle said and headed for the lift. "Somebody is in for a nasty surprise."

"*Sweet Pea, Salvage Title*," Harmon said over the link again.

"Yes, sir?" Cameron answered. "Do you want us to come and get the boxes?"

"You guessed it," Harmon answered. "I'll have them ejected in thirty minutes. The rest of the task force will make room for you."

"Harmon, it looks like the ships orbiting the planet are organizing and coming to meet us," Jayneen announced. "They will be in range in less than thirty hours. Given our battle speed and their typical battle speed, they will be able to engage us first, even with the greater range of our missiles."

"I counted on that, Jayneen," Harmon said. "I hope they launch the first salvo with everything they have."

"Salvage Fleet," Harmon announced, "attack formation Alpha Three. Rotate your crews and make sure everyone is well rested. In twenty-four hours I want every crew member at battle stations."

* * *

Fist Commander Gat'Gil walked across the bridge of the Gritloth heavy battlecruiser *Soul Flayer*. "Show me," he demanded.

"There, sir," Under-Commander Gel'Tor said, indicating the sensor screen. "Twenty-nine ships just came through the gate. They are joining the others."

"The others should have been destroyed!" shouted the Fist commander. "I should never have left those two guarding the gate. Two medium battlecruisers couldn't destroy a destroyer and two little frigates. They have proven themselves to be the most incompetent commanders in the Fist. They should be thankful they died before I could skin them alive."

The anger on Gat'Gil's face made the under-commander back up a step. To any but the Gritloth race, it would have been unnoticeable. The Fist commander turned away, walked to his seat, sat down, and activated the communication link to the entire fleet. "Form on *Soul Flayer*, Wedge Formation. We will launch a mass salvo; ensure you are prepared to engage with main lasers when we pass through them."

He turned to his communications officer. "Get me a direct connection to the Emperor's Palace now."

* * *

"Boot Commander!" the ground force's communications relay officer called out. "The Fist commander sent a message about an emerging fleet. They go now to meet them in battle. There appears to be at least one large troop carrier."

"Good," Boot Commander Gan'Tra said. "Perhaps we will be so fortunate that the carrier survives long enough to provide us with a worthy opponent. The Barlat had little more than a militia and were less than training aids. If that useless Commander Gat'Gil and the Fist receives an opportunity to do real battle, surely the Boot deserves it even more."

"Shall I send word to the outlying units?" asked the officer.

"There is no hurry," the Boot commander said. "It will be more than a day before they meet."

Gan'Tra thought for a moment, then he walked down the ramp of the dropship designated as his headquarters and looked for his foot soldier commander. Two of his commanders, including the one he was looking for, stood near one of the huge distance guns.

As he walked up, they both stood straight, noticing the serious look on his face. Commander Gon'Que asked, "Sir, has there been another uprising?"

"No," answered the Boot commander, "nothing of the sort, but perhaps it is something better."

At hearing this, both commanders became extremely interested in what their superior officer was going to say, as evidenced by the expressions on their faces.

"A fleet has entered this system and is challenging the Fist," Gan'Tra said. "They report at least one troop transport. I do not know if they will reach the planet. Have your foot soldiers dig in south of the city. Gaf'Tic, ensure your distance guns can cover the likely avenues of approach. It has been less than a training exercise so far. Perhaps the Emperor's Boot will face a worthy opponent before this is over with." Without waiting for an answer, Boot Commander Gan'Tra walked away, looking for the armored guns commander.

* * * * *

Chapter Twenty-Nine

Sweet Pea led the two frigates as they swept past the rest of Salvage Fleet, headed directly toward the Gritloth fleet. Each ship had a six foot box connected to a magnetic strut. Designed by Hank and Stan, each box held six missiles. The missiles were smaller than the missiles used by the new ships, but the warheads were just as powerful. They didn't need the extra length for fuel, because they didn't need to travel as far before striking their target.

"Just tell us when, Lieutenant Commander Jayneen," Cameron said over the open link as they neared the release point, "and we'll throw these boxes at them."

Calculating the speed and distance of their three ships and the opposing fleet, anticipating the timing of when the minefield Bahroot had laid out would be detonated, and determining when they should release the launch boxes was a task most computers weren't up to. Jayneen was able to do it and ensure all eighteen missiles were locked on the lead ship in the Gritloth wedge formation. She programed the launch to take place at the last possible second to limit the number of defensive lasers which could engage them.

"You have almost reached the release point," the AI informed him. "Less than four minutes."

"Will you give us a countdown?" asked Hank.

Jayneen knew what the Leethog was asking for. She searched her stored music and selected a song that ended one second before the release point. "Launch it when this one ends, then take it sideways, as the song implies."

The distinctive guitar riff of Cypress Spring's "Bootleg Style" came over every link in the fleet. Those familiar with Jayneen's music preference nodded their heads to the beat. The Withaloo and those unfamiliar with the music from the Twenty-First Century human artists Kalan Miller, Paul Roche, and Tyler Ackerman found themselves doing the same long before the song was finished. When the song ended, Cameron and the Leethog brothers Hank and Stan hit the release on their ships' magnetic struts and banked hard, while their packages continued toward the lead ship of the Gritloth.

Several minutes later Jayneen announced, "The enemy has launched their first salvo. It is a mass launch. One hundred and sixty-two missiles inbound."

"Thanks, Jayneen," Harmon said. "Will they have time to split before they reach the mines?"

"I do not believe so," the AI answered, "though I have not observed the separation to determine the exact moment it happens, compared to the total distance of their flight."

"It won't matter," Clip said. "The mines will disrupt them. There are enough mines out there even if they split."

"Sir, they will be in range in two minutes," the weapons officer announced.

"Thanks, Bev," Harmon said. "Stick to the plan, and concentrate on that heavy battlecruiser. We take care of that one, and we'll hit the fighter carrier they're holding back."

"Launching now," announced the weapons officer.

"*New Toy, Cover Fire,* and the frigates launched with us," added the tactical officer. "The mines are starting to go off!"

The incoming Gritloth missiles had just started to split when the first came close enough to set off the sensors of an EMP mine. The rest of the mines started going off in a rippling effect, and all four hundred mines detonated. The pulse shorted out the electronics in the missiles. Several detonated, others went off in random directions, and many simply became small meteors, unable to detonate when they did encounter shields.

A minute later, the first of the Salvage Fleet missiles passed the location of the minefield, thirty seconds behind the launched boxes, and neither suffered any effect from the short-lived magnetic pulse wave. On their heels were the missiles from the rest of the fleet. Several of these were missiles designed to draw mines to them, scramble sensors, and detonate when near incoming missiles.

"They have launched again," announced Jayneen from the defensive bridge, "I have determined twenty-two of them are tracking *Salvage Title*; they will become sixty-six missiles."

"Launch a scrambler," Clip ordered. "Follow it with a spread of twelve shotgun missiles."

"Scrambler launched," announced the Leethog at Position One.

"Twelve launched," Position Two said. "Calculated to blow two seconds before meeting."

"Launching second salvo of missiles," the weapons officer stated. "Coming up on pulse cannon range."

"Prepare to turn after firing the forward cannons," Harmon announced. "We'll spread their hits around and keep pounding them. Launch missiles when they're loaded."

"Yes, sir," the ship's pilot said from the helm console. "Preparing for the Tomeral Turn."

"Wait…what?" Harmon asked. "It has a name, Lena?"

"Yes, sir," she answered, "it does. With all three task forces utilizing it, now that the heavies have figured out how to continue engaging with main lasers and still spread the hits around their shields, it deserves its own name."

"Twelve missiles are still inbound," Jayneen announced.

"Fire up the defensive lasers," Clip ordered

"Firing defensive lasers," said Position Three.

"Readying next salvo of shotgun missiles," Position Four announced, preparing for the next command.

Everyone on *Salvage Title* felt when the first two cannons fired, one after another. The ship rotated, and four more pulses fired, one second apart. The ship was rocked slightly when three missiles hit, lowering the starboard shields to eighty-eight percent. The rotation continued, and the cannons fired. Several more missiles hit other shields.

"Sir, the boxes have launched, it looks like eight missiles hit the ship's shield. Sensors indicate four of our missiles hit the forward shields on that battlecruiser also," the tactical officer announced. "The shields are down, and the cannons are penetrating the ship's hull now. It's venting atmosphere and has stopped launching missiles. Their entire fleet is now launching fighters, though."

"Thanks, Adam." Harmon hit the comm on his chair. "Salvage Fleet, launch all fighters."

Clip called down to the flight officer, "Launch 'em, dude. Launch 'em all, and stop those fighters."

"Roger, sir," came the immediate reply from the flight deck.

* * *

On the light battlecruiser *Desert Shade,* Lieutenant Nicholson said, "Hey, sir, that's a lot of missiles about to be headed our way."

"I know," Captain Marteen Yatarward agreed. "I hate splitters." He turned to the weapons officer. "Kick in the lasers. Stop what we can, launch when you can. Helm, maintain position covering the flagship."

After hearing the 'launch all fighters' message over the command link, Big Nick said, "I got this, sir, you fight the ship." He hit his comm and called down to the bay, "Flight officer, bridge. Launch them."

* * *

Fighters of numerous designs swarmed from the ships of Salvage Fleet. There were old and new versions of the Sleek Fighters, looking like long miniature versions of the battleships they came from. Bentwick fighters with their stacked engine design flew among several versions of human fighters from the newly-acquired heavy battlecruisers and uniquely modified fighters from the ship *Sweet Pea*. Withaloo fighters flew along with the two Predators, fighters closer to gunships than actual fighters from the recently converted colony ship. They met the Gritloth fighters in combat in open space and above, below, and between the huge warships involved in the battle.

* * *

After releasing the boxes from their struts, Captain Cameron and the Leethog brothers' ships banked hard to port and came back toward the Salvage Fleet at an angle. They were assigned to two ships on the defending fleet's starboard side. They managed to stay out of early launch range and came back around, ready to launch missiles with the rest of the fleet.

"This is going to be a cakewalk," Cameron announced. "It looks like a destroyer and a frigate on this end."

"We are not allowed to 'cakewalk,'" Stan answered. "I really wanted some cake, too."

"When we get back to Salvage," Hank said, "we'll find someone to make one. I heard there is a great bakery in Bank Town."

"Sounds like a plan," Cameron said. "We'll take *Sweet Pea* to the airfield and get some fresh cake. Speaking of a plan, we better get ready."

All three ships rolled as if they'd planned it. The three launched missiles and prepared to defend against the incoming missiles. There were fewer headed their way than they'd faced upon system entry.

* * *

On the Gritloth heavy battlecruiser *Soul Flayer*, Fist Commander Gat'Gil stood over his operations officer and asked him again, "What were their intentions? Why did those three ships pull ahead just to bank around and move to the edge of their formation?"

"I do not know, sir," answered the under-commander. "I have never seen such a foolish move. They could have maneuvered behind the formation. Sensors didn't detect them firing any weapons before they turned away."

"Fist Commander, they are nearly in range," announced the weapons officer.

Gat'Gil strode over to his seat, sat, and watched the small screen attached to it. He hit the comm and announced to his fleet, "Mass salvo in three, two, one, fire!"

Every ship except the fighter carrier *Death Flies* launched a full spread of the relatively new missiles, the separators. Gat'Gil was proud of the design, an idea he'd stolen from a vanquished force he defeated years ago. The change to larger missile launchers had taken years to complete, but the entire force he commanded now had them.

"The invaders have launched," announced the operations officer.

"At this distance?" demanded Gat'Gil.

"Not all of them, sir," answered the under-commander after checking again, "though others are starting to."

"Whoever is leading them is incompetent," dismissed Gat'Gil. "They can't even coordinate a mass volley."

He watched the small screen on his seat, glancing up to ensure it was providing the same information as the main screen, when he saw the missiles begin separating. Suddenly missiles veered off in all directions, started tumbling, a few exploded, and the rest lost forward thrust and became inert pieces of metal headed toward the invading fleet. He leapt to his feet. "What just happened?"

Before the operations officer could reply, three symbols appeared on the sensor screens. "Sir, I detect some sort of launch!" he shouted. "Eighteen missiles inbound at near point-blank range!"

Defensive laser turrets spun and began pulsing in an attempt to stop the missiles, but were only able to stop ten of them. Eight missiles slammed against the heavy battlecruiser's shielding, knocking some consoles offline, as well as crewmembers to the deck all over the ship.

"Status," shouted Gat'Gil, rising from the deck in the smoke-filled bridge.

"Sir, forward shields down to twenty percent…brace for impact!" screamed the operations officer.

Four more missiles hit the forward shields. The last two continued through and impacted against the forward hull, their shaped charges penetrating deep and damaging several decks. The ship began venting atmosphere. From the deck, Gat'Gil reached up with a long arm and hit the comm on his seat. "Launch all fighters! Prepare to fire main las…"

The rest of the order to fire died with Fist Commander Gat'Gil as raw energy pounded through the clear-steel portal of the bridge, engulfing everything in it.

* * * * *

Chapter Thirty

"How bad was it, Evelyn?" Harmon asked.

"No damage to *Windswept*, but we lost eighteen fighters," she answered. "They were good, and the lasers on their fighters were surprisingly powerful. They burned through fighter shields faster than any I've heard of."

"I know," Harmon agreed. "We lost two fighters, and the fleet lost at least one from every ship, some many more. When we came into main weapons range, it hurt us bad. *Desert Night* is a total loss, though we managed to save half the crew. *Southern Sunset* blew several fusion power plants at once. We can't find any escape pods from her. Most of the fleet are making emergency repairs of some kind or another."

"Ithall's task force has two battlecruisers without engines," he continued. "Zerith had them lock two destroyers to each of them so they can maneuver with us to orbit. One of those destroyers has no shielding, so it worked out for them."

"What about the troop carriers orbiting Barlat?" Evelyn asked, trying not to think about the loss of life right then. There would be time for that later.

"They've signaled surrender," Harmon answered. "I don't think they want to face our fleet after witnessing the destruction of their own. They probably think they'll be rescued once reinforcements arrive."

"Did they confirm the number of troops on the ground?" she asked.

"They say four blocks, which Jayneen says is four thousand," Harmon said.

"That's nearly four times our ground forces," Evelyn said, concerned.

"I know," Harmon agreed. "We don't think they have mechs, so that helps even the odds some. Once we take their ships, Jayneen will remote in, we'll take a look at the actual data, and see what their equipment is like. We may have to gather every ship's security platoon and create a temporary unit to help. That'll add twenty more mechs and over a hundred and twenty or so marines, even if some of them are a little rusty on dirt-side operations."

* * *

"I have disabled the main engines and weapons on both troop carriers," Jayneen said. "I have also locked their programing. They will not be able to regain control unless they have a programmer at least as capable as Clip. Even if they do, I will detect any attempts at gaining control and stop them."

"They can maintain orbit and life support," she continued. "Evelyn has more than fifty fighters on patrol, escorting the shuttles from their damaged ships to them in case they try to use the weapons on some of their shuttles. We will be able to hold their troops until you decide what to do with them. We now have skeleton crews on the four Gritloth warships that are capable of continued operation, and they have locked three other damaged ships to their struts, for safe-keeping."

"Good," Harmon replied. "The next thing I need you to do is to ensure those two ships can't notify their reinforcements about the Kashkal Fleet when they enter the system. The shuttles, if they're still in use, don't have the range, but those carriers do."

"I believe I can accomplish that," the AI said.

"Zerith," Harmon called down to the power plant, "talk to me."

"We have resstarted Number Four," Zerith said and paused to swallow what he was chewing. "Repairss were eassier this time be-causse of the backup operating ssysstem the sshipyardss insstalled on each plant. We will continue to repair the main ssysstem and turn it into a backup. Vera ssayss her team hass Number One repaired with no isssuess."

"Good, glad to hear it," Harmon said, relieved. "I expect Rick to arrive within the next few hours, and whatever reinforcements the Gritloth are sending a couple days later. We need to fix what we can before that battle. How are the shields coming?"

"Sstarboard is at eighty perccent," Zerith answered. "It can go no higher until we sspend ssome time in the sshipyardss. Big Jon and hiss team had to combine partss from two sshield generatorss to get it that sstrong during the battle. They musst be replaced; we cannot use the replicator to create them."

"Be glad they did, Zee," Clip interjected. "It could have been bad if we'd taken any more of those splitters on that side before the emergency repair crew did that."

"Thiss iss true," admitted Zerith, "but did they have to open the houssing with an *axe?*"

"My crew is trained to fix leaks and shields quickly, sir," the sergeant major said, standing by Harmon's seat listening to the conversation. "Sometimes, they get a little overzealous. There are a lot of things I'll do. Getting between a Yalteen with a hand axe and a generator housing she wants open immediately isn't one of them."

"I wouldn't get between a Yalteen with a hand axe and anything in the galaxy," added Brickle, looking over with two of his eyes. "You want to lose the end of your nose? Because that's how you lose the end of your nose." He raised his long anteater-like nose, emphasizing his point.

* * *

Standing on the bridge of *Hold My Drink*, Hank looked at his brother on the main screen. "Can you fix it?" he asked.

"We think so," Stan said. "One engine is fine. The other dropped off and came back up a couple of times after that last missile hit us. It should be completely repaired by the time the next battle starts. The hull breach is sealed, too."

"Well, don't scare me like that," Hank admonished. "If you had not rolled right then, there is no telling what could have happened. Those lasers weakened our shields, too. We have to quit taking chances. Were you sitting at the helm, like me?"

"Yeah, I was," admitted Stan. "Petetilnakba is a good pilot, but I felt more comfortable flying."

"We need to work on that," Hank said. "We are the captains. We can't fly the ship, too."

"I want to fly all the time," Cameron added to the conversation from his ship. "I have to make myself let Ralph sit at the helm. Then again, he's my XO, so I don't know if that really counts."

"Speaking of helm, we're down to seven engines again," Hank heard Ralph complain. "They said they can't fix the problem without some parts, and we can't replicate them on board."

* * *

Commander Ithall sat back in his seat. He'd just gone over the damage report and was pleased to see repairs happening quickly. The two ships without engines were working on the problem, but the work-around the chief engineer on *Salvage Title* had come up with was working fine for now. Using the destroyers as external engines would enable decent movement, and would even allow the ships to fight, if need be.

"The commodore has decided to ensure we have defeated the expected reinforcements before we put ground forces on the planet," Ithall informed Captain Rothan, the carrier commander. "I agree. If we are not victorious, our ground forces would stand no chance at survival. We will not attack their troops from orbit, but I have no doubt they would do so against ours. Remain in orbit when we go to meet the challenge. Have Colonel Arthok remain ready to go at a moment's notice."

"Yes, sir," answered Captain Rothan. "We'll be standing by."

* * * * *

Chapter Thirty-One

The Kashkal Fleet emerged on time; Harmon hadn't doubted they would. The leading task force banked and headed for the large gas giant beyond the lone spaceport to lie in wait for the expected incoming fleet.

"Rick," Harmon called, "good to see you."

"And you, my friend," the Kashka said. "Once again, we will do battle. I am pleased. The Kashkal are pleased. We live to fight, though we no longer must fight to live. Being a mercenary is an honorable profession; given we are fighting to right an incredible wrong makes it even more honorable. I and all of the Kashkal thank you."

"We've taken some losses," Harmon said, "but you're correct. Earning credit to build the system is good. Doing good while we earn it is even better."

"One cannot be in our line of business without taking some losses," Rick said. "All those under our command understand this and accept the risks when signing the contract. It makes it no easier, but it comes with the profession."

Harmon agreed. "Listen, I wanted to let you know the Gritloth use splitters," Harmon told him. "One becomes three about midflight."

"Separators," Rick said, "we have encountered these before. We will use a leap tactic and spread the hits around. What is the primary weapon on their ships?"

"Huge lasers," Harmon answered. "They have to get close, but they burn through shields quickly. We need to do our best to take them out long before we come in range of those. I'm tempted to defend from less than full battle speed and get off an extra salvo or two of missiles at them as they come in, then go to battle speeds."

"That would be a sound tactic," Rick agreed. "We will whip around the planet and use its gravity to increase speed, chase them down, and start launching from maximum range directly behind them."

"Sounds like a plan," Harmon said.

Salvage Fleet continued to repair shields, engines, and power plants. Some were beyond repair without access to shipyards and their replicators. Harmon made the decision to stack several of the more damaged vessels with larger ships capable of defending both. Jayneen gained access to the computers of the Gritloth troop carriers and was able to determine the locations, numbers of troops, and the equipment on the planet. Harmon glanced at the data but put it aside until after the next battle for space was won.

Two days later, a little longer than Harmon had expected, wave after wave of Gritloth ships entered the system. They came in fast and headed directly toward the planet Barlat, completely ignoring the space station and the gas giant beyond it.

"How many?" Harmon asked.

"Forty ships have entered the system at battle speeds," Jayneen announced. "There is one ship larger than a heavy battlecruiser, though I hesitate to classify it as a dreadnought. Its registration indicates it is the Gritloth Emperor's own ship."

"I wonder if the dude is on the ship?" Clip asked.

"It iss unlikely," Zerith answered.

"Salvage Fleet, they have arrived," Harmon announced over the command link. "At their rate of speed, they'll be in range in thirty hours or so. Continue to repair what you can. When we go to meet them, we should get at least two salvos of missiles off, maybe three, before they can launch."

Thirty one hours later, Harmon gave the order for the newer ships to fire. "Launch now! Stick to the plan, and take out the first ship designated to you."

Shortly after, all the ships in Salvage Fleet launched. They were able to launch one more salvo before Harmon ordered all ships to battle speed. By this time, the Kashkal Fleet had come around the planet and were gaining on the Gritloth.

"Sir, the first salvo is impacting now," announced the tactical officer. "Five missiles hit their shields. The ship has less defensive capabilities than the others we have fought."

"Nice," Harmon said, sitting forward. "The fleet they had in reserve must be the older ships in their arsenal."

"Second salvo has reached them," said the tactical officer. "There appears to be ventilation."

"They have launched missiles," Jayneen said from the defensive bridge. "The largest ship fired a salvo of forty missiles. They are aimed at us."

"Sweet!" Clip said. "With that many, they can't be splitters. Position One, launch twenty shotgun missiles. You know the deal. Give them the ol' what for."

"Yes, sir," answered the Leethog at Position One with a huge grin on her face. There were teeth everywhere.

"Sir, the third salvo has hit," tactical said. "There was no shielding up. That ship is out of the fight and veering off toward two other ships attempting to maneuver out of the way. At the speed they are moving, there will be a collision."

"There's a splitter for you," Clip said. "How's that for a three for one?"

"Nine missiles are still incoming," Jayneen announced. "Defensive lasers are engaging. Brace for impact."

Two of the incoming missiles struck the forward shields, rocking *Salvage Title*. "What the frost was that?" demanded Harmon.

"It would seem the missiles they are firing are more powerful than the smaller multiple missiles from the earlier battle," Jayneen said.

"I'll say," Harmon agreed. "Give me the status, Brickle."

"Forward shields down to sixty-four percent, sir," answered the chief warrant officer.

"Turn this thing as soon as you fire the cannons," Harmon said. "We want no part of that on the forward shields again."

"Launching another salvo at our secondary target," said the weapons officer. "Now firing cannons." Everyone on the bridge felt the slight shudder as they went off one second after another, and they prepared for the turn.

"Turning now," announced the ship's pilot. "Going port side first."

"We have been targeted again," Jayneen announced. "Twelve missiles incoming."

"Launch a scrambler," Clip ordered, "and get the shotgun missiles ready. We can't take many of those big missiles."

The defensive bridge continued to launch shotgun missiles, and the defensive lasers continued to pulse as the battle continued. Three more times the ship was rocked by powerful missiles, and it was grazed once by the main laser of a light battlecruiser as they passed, burning out nearly all the shielding on the port side, before their own broadside destroyed the power plant of the offending ship.

Time seemed to slow as Harmon ordered all the fighters to launch once again, and *Salvage Title* banked around to join the Kashkal Fleet and several of its own ships to defeat the last of the Gritloth reinforcements.

Big Jon and his repair crew had their work cut out for them as they scrambled to repair shield generators and put out electrical fires. Like a fighter in a cage, *Salvage Title* was dealing staggering blows, but not without taking a few on the chin in return.

* * *

"Begin movement now!" ordered Rick Kashka. Already near battle speed, the entire Kashkal Fleet gained even more speed as they slingshot around the planet and were able to easily gain on the unsuspecting Gritloth ships. The Kashka made sure his fleet came in low around the planet to remain below any stray missiles Salvage Fleet may have launched.

"Prepare to use the Leap Tactic once we get close," ordered the Kashka. "We may come within range of their lasers, and we will need to spread their hits around."

"We are prepared to leap forward," answered Saylonik Ka, commander of her task force.

"Launch full salvos," ordered Rick Kashka.

"Launching now," answered the weapons officer.

"Sir, the enemy has launched fighters," said the tactical officer.

"Reciprocate," ordered the Kashka. "Have the fleet reciprocate. Begin turning to slow so we can be passed."

* * *

Commander Gol'Pok of the *Emperor's Own* stood on the bridge as it led the hastily-thrown-together reinforcement fleet into the Barlat System. Unsure of what he would find, the semi-retired officer was concerned. He'd left the position of Fist commander three years ago to take command of the emperor's personal warship. The job consisted of very little training and a lot of downtime. It was his reward for successfully capturing the Yalmordit System years ago.

Life had been easy until the call for help from the current Fist commander, who was useless carrion dropping in Gol'Pok's opinion. "Give me the details," he demanded of his operations officer, another older commander.

"There has been a battle," confirmed the nonchalant officer. "It would seem the Fist has been devastated. There are very few ships in operation, and they are surrounded by more than twenty ships."

"Whose ships?" asked Gol'Pok. "What is their registration?"

"They are from…Salvage System," answered the operations officer. "I have never heard of it."

"Nor I," admitted Commander Gol'Pok. "Have the fleet form a tight wedge, if they are capable of doing so without running into each other. We are nearly double their numbers. We will take the system back."

"Yes, sir," answered the operations officer.

Twenty-four hours later, the operations officer called out to Commander Gol'Pok, "Sir, I think you should watch this." He indicated a video in the corner of the main sensor screen.

Commander Gol'Pok watched the video of the defense of Salvage System. An extremely popular video, judging by the number of views. He didn't care for the accompanying soundtrack whoever had put it together chose, but the annihilation of the invading fleet made him realize the upcoming battle would be far more difficult than he'd originally thought.

"Do you think they have the other fleet hiding behind a planet?" asked the operations officer with concern on his face.

"Of course not!" answered Gol'Pok dismissively. "Who would use the same tactic again? Only a fool. It would be expected. That other fleet is probably defending the Salvage System right now, in case this one loses and we seek revenge. Which they will, and *we* will, rest assured. Increase speed. They may get the first salvo of missiles off, maybe two, but after that we will be among them."

Hours later, Commander Gol'Pok realized the fool he was facing was no fool.

* * *

On the bridge of *Biting Wind*, Commander Ithall watched the display as the first missiles headed toward the incoming fleet. "Remind me to ask the commodore about upgrading our launchers."

"Yes, sir," answered his weapons officer. "They have exceptional range. We will be in range in one minute."

Commander Ithall spoke over the command link to his task force, "Prepare to mass launch. *Special Delivery*, ready your fighters."

* * *

The frigate *Watch This* rolled and continued to launch missiles at the ship it had been assigned, but its shielding and defensive lasers kept the powerful Gritloth missiles from impacting against its hull. From the commander's seat, Stan directed his pilot as well as his Weapons Officer. They were giving far more than they were receiving when the ship was dealt a powerful blow by a missile and the faltering engine went out, reducing their thrust and overall maneuverability.

Stan shouted, "Turn over! Roll away from..." He was unable to complete the sentence as the frigate was hit with the main laser from a light battlecruiser. All power went out as the rear portion of the ship was breached.

Stan reached down beside his seat and grabbed his helmet to complete his safety suit, and he had just placed it on his head when another laser beam opened the bridge as it cut through. He was knocked spinning to the deck. He came to a few minutes later and realized he hadn't quite sealed the helmet as he heard the sound of the air leaving his suit. The air controls of the suit were sounding an alarm as they worked overtime, burning through the power cell trying to maintain the internal atmosphere.

He reached up to twist it and realized he had problems. Looking through the clear-steel front of the helmet, he saw why. One hand was gone. Simply *gone*. He continued to try to seal the helmet with his good hand as his eyes trailed down his arm and remembered the suit had tourniquet tabs. He stopped fumbling with the helmet, lifted the velcro flap, and pulled the tab below his elbow. Despite the light from the arcing consoles and fire on the bridge providing plenty of light for a Leethog's eyes, his universe slowly faded to black as he tried again to seal his helmet. He never heard the click.

* * * * *

Chapter Thirty-Two

"Permission granted," Harmon said, his voice barely above a whisper on the private link. He had just given Hank permission to lock onto his brother's frigate, walk the hull, and retrieve Stan's body. The frigate *Watch This* was completely powerless, open to space, and repeated scans indicated no signs of life on board nor had any of its escape pods been used. There were slight power fluctuations, but that was to be expected so shortly after a ship's destruction.

The battle was continuing on the opposite side of the fleet's formation, but the area near *Sweet Pea* and the two frigates was well away from it. Harmon wasn't looking forward to speaking to Vera, Stan's mate, which was something he would have to make a priority as soon as the last enemy ship surrendered. Harmon knew it would be one of the hardest things he'd ever had to do. He found it difficult to read his screen or concentrate on the updates he was receiving from his crew.

* * *

Lieutenant Hanktilmotal stood at the airlock, waiting for it to cycle open. When it did, the Leethog stepped out and used a small hand-held thruster to propel himself toward the clear-steel portal of the ruined frigate attached to his ship. He found he couldn't see very well, and it wasn't because of the light. It was hard to see through the tears.

He felt his feet strike the hull and engaged his magnetic boots. Once safely locked in place, he walked the hull toward the torn openings near the bridge area. Shaking his head to help clear his eyes, he stopped where the laser had punched through the clear-steel portal. Pieces of hull were torn from missile strikes, but none of the openings went all the way to the bridge, except the hole in the portal. The area where the rear ramp and airlock were located was a mangled mess. He would have to figure out how to get into the ship.

A shadow came slowly across both frigates, and Hank looked up. *Sweet Pea* had matched their course. Beyond the destroyer, several of its fighters patrolled in random patterns, ensuring no Gritloth ship would try to take advantage of the three ships being so close together.

The bay door slid open, lighting the area where Hank stood, and a mech shuffled into the opening and pushed out. Thrusters guided it to within fifty feet of Hank, and all eight legs locked to the hull, with repeated thuds Hank could feel through his boots.

Cameron maneuvered the huge mech carefully to stand next to his friend. He observed the damage to the ship and realized why Hank hadn't already entered the wreck. "Stand back," Cameron said with a sniffle, "I can open it up."

Working through his tears, using the pincer claws on four legs, Cameron peeled back layers of torn hull to allow Hank entry into the bridge area. A few sparks flew, indicating some residual power stored in cells and systems. He broke off a leg in the process, but it didn't matter. Getting to his friend was all he cared about at the moment.

Hank slid into the opening, careful not to tear his suit. He turned on his helmet's light and looked around. He could see several crew-members' bodies, some still strapped into their seats, one with a piece of his helmet cut away by a piercing laser beam. He quickly looked away from the sight and spotted legs near the command chair.

Shaking, Hank climbed over some debris and moved around the side of the chair. The first thing he noticed was his brother's arm. Not all of it was there. As he came completely around the chair, he could see that Stan had donned his helmet, but the small lights weren't lit around the locking mechanism. He stepped over to his brother. As he bent down, he saw a flicker of light on the locking mechanism. It flared bright red, then slowly faded.

Hank reached up, snatched open the side panel of the rebreather on his chest, pulled the spare hose out, and slammed the connecter to the matching piece in his brother's helmet. Air started flowing into the helmet. After five seconds, the same hose drew air back from the helmet through the rebreather and repeated the process. Stan's left leg moved slightly.

"Cameron! Make the hole bigger!" Hank shouted over his comm. "He had his suit on, and the power cell just died. I don't know how long it has been trying to work, but he is still breathing!"

"Ok!" shouted Cameron, and the spider-like mech's legs started moving quickly.

"He's lost a lot of blood. Hurry!" Hank said, trying to remain calm. He might still have been too late, but at least there was a chance.

* * *

"He is holding stable," said the ship's doctor. "With the equipment I have, the best I can do is keep him in an induced coma. When we get back to Salvage System, I may be able to do more. I cannot be sure he will regain all of his abilities. There is no way of knowing how long he went without enough oxygen. If we were on Leethog, he would stand a much better chance. I…"

"That's it!" Harmon said, interrupting the doctor. He looked over at Clip. "Buddy, you're taking this ship and Stan to Leethog. I'll transfer over with Big Jon and the security platoon, and go with the Ground Forces to the surface. You get him the best care on that planet. I don't care what it costs."

"Dude, I don't…" Clip stopped himself. "I got it. We got this." He looked over at the three Leethog associates and Zerith, then back at Harmon and Big Jon. "Get your squat together, get on the shuttle, and get off this ship. We have places to be."

"Roger that, sir," the sergeant major said and left the medical bay in a hurry.

* * *

"Major Audell, Sergeant Major, Gunny," Harmon said, standing in one of the bays on the carrier *Windswept*, "what are we looking like?"

"Sir, we have a hundred and two marines," Big Jon said, "and eleven mechs. Two of the mechs are scout models, and the mechs from Captain Cameron's crew are…well, you know."

"I do," Harmon agreed. "I'm really interested to see what the spider can do."

"We have four dropships," Gunny added, "including the modified shuttle with its quad machine guns. We also have your Zax fighter, which is capable of atmosphere flight."

"Don't forget the tanks," Staff Sergeant Clyde said. "We're loading all three into a shuttle and bringing them with us. I figure we can bring one reload of missiles. That'll give us twenty rounds each."

"You sure you want to bring those?" Marteen asked, looking at the small tanks. "They look more like some kind of half-track from ancient Earth, except only one person operates them."

"Hey, sir," Lieutenant Nicholson said, "those missiles will have a range of about a thousand yards in atmosphere. Get the angle right, and they make nice mortars."

"Big Nick's right," Harmon agreed. "We can prep the area before we move the marines up. The plan calls for us to take Area Three. It looks like they have about five hundred soldiers around the mine. They have a company of tanks themselves supporting them, if the information Jayneen pried from their system is right."

"Roger, sir," Big Jon said. "The Bolts have to clear Area Two and both those mines, while the Withaloo take on the bulk of the Gritloth outside the capital. What we hit the surface with is all we'll have. The place is riddled with automated anti-air lasers. We can get a few fly-bys of air support, but not much. They'll be needed near the capital."

"Can they lower the anti-air batteries to fire on us?" Big Nick asked.

"Jayneen says no," Harmon said. Jayneen was currently on the bridge of the carrier. "She also tried to get into their operating systems, but there's no way for her to do it. They aren't connected to a network. Each system operates on its own."

"If they didn't have those, we could just blast the frost out of them from the air," Major Audell added. He didn't have his mech with him because he'd been selected to lead the combined marines on the mission.

"We'll just have to dig them out," Harmon said. "Let's get loaded so we can do this. We're running on Colonel Arthok's time schedule."

"I can't believe they refused to surrender," Marteen said, "even knowing there was no support coming."

"They must have leadership full of confidence," Harmon agreed.

* * * * *

Chapter Thirty-Three

The squadron of drop ships entered the atmosphere on the far side of the planet, coming in from the opposite direction of the capital and the bulk of the anti-aircraft lasers. Behind the safety of several rolling hills, hindering the laser batteries from targeting them, Salvage Fleet prepared to put troops on the ground.

The overhead light turned green, and the ramp dropped. Harmon followed the other ten mechs out the opening, splayed the mech's arms and legs, and watched his screen. It had been a while since he'd jumped in a mech, but it came back as second nature. *I have to train with the troops more*, he thought.

They were falling on a glide path that would take them near the mine, but not so close that they had to worry about the anti-aircraft lasers. The modified drop ship and the Zax attacked from the other side of the valley in an attempt to keep the attention of the automated systems. If it got too hot, Harmon had instructed them to bug out, find a safe landing area, and wait on their call.

Trusting his system, Harmon dropped his mech's legs and fired the thrusters. Remembering to bend his knees to absorb the shock, he managed not to embarrass himself, and landed as if he did it every day. The eleven mechs spread out to clear the area before the shuttles carrying the marines and tanks came into the area of operations.

Harmon brought the map up on his middle screen to ensure he had his bearings. "Alright, bring them in," he instructed the lead pilot. Whoever was leading the unit at this mine site, they hadn't taken in account that the hills around their lasers would provide cover for incoming shuttles. Sometimes little oversights could be detrimental.

The troop shuttles came screaming in and touched down in the open area Harmon had chosen. They flared at the last second and landed softly. The ramps dropped and the marines in battle armor deployed in a large three sixty. The shuttles took off, and the last, a large shuttle, landed and off-loaded the three tanks. The entire force moved into the wood line.

"That road leads to the mine," Major Audell said, pointing to a map on his slate. "They probably have it covered. I want you to move the tanks to this position before that curve. It'll be out of their sight and within range. Captain Stacey will be out front as the forward observer, calling for fire. I know your marines aren't artillery specialists. Just give her what she asks for. She'll keep it simple."

"Roger, sir," Staff Sergeant Clyde said.

"Be prepared to move after you fire for effect," Major Audell added.

Major Audell walked away from the tanks and over to Harmon. "Sir, my marines are ready to move. We'll follow the road forty meters inside the wood line. If you can take out that company of tanks, it would be much appreciated."

"We're getting ready to move out," Harmon said. "Evelyn should be nearing an observation point now."

"Alright, everyone," the major said over the command link. "Let's move out."

Ninety-five marines slipped into the woods, following the trail the mechs made as they headed for the curve Clyde was headed toward. There was no movement by the Gritloth troops.

Clyde signaled the other two tanks to spread apart once they neared the designated position. They backed into the wood line and elevated their missile launchers. Jayneen had provided an elevation chart that should be close to accurate when firing the missiles in atmosphere.

"Ma'am, we're in position," the staff sergeant told Evelyn over the link.

"Roger," she answered. "I'm going to make this easy, since those tanks aren't artillery pieces or actual mortars."

"Sounds good to me," Staff Sergeant Clyde answered.

"They have several bunkers," Evelyn said, "that give them a good view of the road. They've built temporary barracks. It looks like they expect an attack. The tanks are deployed in defilades, and most of the soldiers are in trenches and foxholes."

"Just tell me when, ma'am," Staff Sergeant Clyde said.

"Harmon, do you see all twenty tanks?" she asked.

"We do," Harmon answered. "A couple of them are only showing their barrels."

"Major Audell, are your marines in position?" Evelyn asked.

"We are," the major said. "I've got a few snipers on the hillside ready to shoot the system controls on the anti-air lasers as well; hopefully their targeting systems only works with radar, and they won't light up the hillsides."

"Alright, Staff Sergeant," Evelyn said, "drop a missile among them and let's see if we can't walk it in tight on them."

"Launching now," announced the staff sergeant.

Moments later, Evelyn saw the missile explode nearly a hundred yards beyond the dug-in Gritloth. "Clyde, looks like the wind caught it, you're about a hundred yards too long."

"Roger that. Adjusting now," said the smiling staff sergeant. "Launching now."

When the missile hit, it was near a scrambling group of soldiers, who were moving from the barracks area to the foxholes. When the smoke cleared, two of them lay at strange angles. "Not bad; fire for effect."

All three tanks fired ten rounds each, one after another, and Evelyn watched as thirty missiles exploded among the soldiers, throwing sand and rocks, as well as the shrapnel from the rockets themselves. As soon as the last missile hit, Harmon and the ten mechs with him fired their thrusters, jumped up through the trees, and flew high enough to launch missiles from their shoulders at the tanks. Wendell's rockets made short work of two of the laser batteries before they could lock onto the flying mechs.

The mechs cut their thrusters and landed back in the woods, tearing limbs off the trees. Up ahead, several tree trunks were shattered and burned through as the remaining tanks attempted to fire at the disappearing mechs. Every mech moved twenty meters to the right, and they jumped again. This time, after launching the remainder of their missiles, they burned the rest of their rocket fuel and landed among the enemy, firing their railguns as they went.

Gunny launched the last of his rockets at the remaining anti-air laser system, but it locked on and got off one shot. Feeling an intense pain in his legs, his mech flipped through the air and landed hard. Stunned, he struggled to catch his breath. All the warning lights concerning the lower portion of his mech were in the red. With shaking hands, he activated the emergency escape, and his cockpit opened. Gunny pulled himself from the mech with his hands; his legs wouldn't help, no matter how hard he tried.

Rolling off the mech to land hard in the dirt, he looked down and saw why. The lower portion of his mech had been sliced clean through. His right leg was gone below the knee, and the left—the one in excruciating pain—was a mangled mess. Hands quivering, he pulled the first aid packet from a thigh, lifted the flaps on his pilot's suit, and pulled the tourniquet tabs above both knees. Through gritted teeth, he managed to give himself a nanite shot in both thighs and passed out.

Seeing Gunny roll off his mech, Big Nick used the last of his rocket fuel and jumped near him. He dropped his mech to one knee in front of him and covered the man for the rest of the fight, wishing he could dismount and help him, but the firefight wouldn't allow it. His mech took several shots from laser rifles as he did what he could for him.

Several of the other mechs took critical hits from the dug-in soldiers' laser rifles. The rifles fired short pulses and not sustained beams, so none of their armor was fully penetrated, but the rifles damaged their joints. While their attention was on the mechs, twenty smoke canisters came flying out of the wood line. Aided by the servo assist on the heavy battle armor, the grenades landed near the bunkers and foxholes. The firefight was on. Marines bounded out of the trees in squads, firing as they came.

Staff Sergeant Clyde led the three tanks around the final bend and emptied their last ten rounds into the nearest bunker. Whatever power source the crew-served weapon used exploded in a spectacular blast. Knowing the other two tanks would maneuver until they could fire on the remaining bunkers, he grabbed his rifle, leaped from the tank, and joined the fray.

After the area was taken, Harmon dismounted from his mech and observed the damage to it. Several of his indicators were in the yellow, and he could see why. Some of the pilots had abandoned theirs during the fight and had been forced to use their grenade launchers. Big Jon took a knee a short distance away and broke his weapon down into several parts. It had jammed earlier, and he was looking for the reason.

Harmon was lost in thought when he noticed movement coming from a trench beside him. A tall Gritloth soldier leaped out and came at him with a long, thin knife at the end of an even longer arm. Harmon turned to defend himself and tripped over a rifle, rolling his ankle. He scrambled backwards, trying to put some distance between himself and the knife. Just then, Big Jon hit the soldier in a flying tackle, but both came to their feet quickly.

Showing no emotion, the eight-foot-tall soldier slowly waved the knife back and forth, looking down and turning as he followed Big Jon, who circled with his own knife out. Harmon reached for his pistol, only to remember he'd taken it off when he'd mounted his mech because of the limited room in the cockpit. *He has reach on him,* Harmon thought. *I've got to help.* Before he could move, Big Jon drew back and, using the servo assist in his armor, threw his knife so fast Harmon saw nothing but the glint of silver as it flew. The tall Gritloth soldier dropped his long blade and fell back, the hilt protruding from his skinny neck.

"Thanks," Harmon said, amazed at the knife-throwing display.

"Let me help you up, sir," the sergeant major said after he retrieved his knife, wiped the blade, and sheathed it. Big Jon looked over at Staff Sergeant Clyde. "Check every enemy body."

"Roger, Sergeant Major," answered Clyde, and he went to gather a team.

Harmon saw Cameron looking at his mech with his hands on his hips.

"You alright?" Harmon asked, limping over.

"Yeah," Cameron said, still looking at his mech. "I gotta figure out how to carry more fuel for the flamethrower. I ran out of fuel halfway through the fight. After that, all I could do was squish them in their foxholes."

"Well, it got the job done," Harmon said. "You took out plenty of them."

"Yeah, I guess," Cameron said. "I wish Captain Rogers were here. I called him before we left your system to see if he would join us. He said yes. Then he called me back an hour later and said he couldn't. He had somewhere to be."

"We could have used him," agreed Harmon. He turned and walked toward Major Audell.

"What do we have?" Harmon asked.

"We lost over half the marines," answered the major. "We have twelve wounded, three critical. We lost one of the tanks, and four mechs are useless. Gunny is hurt badly."

"How bad?" Harmon asked, looking toward the makeshift medical area. He could see them working on several marines.

"Medic says he'll live, but he lost a lower leg, and may lose the other," answered the major. "I hate it. He is a frost of a marine, and an even better man."

"Rinto has a pretty good mechanical arm," Harmon said. "I'll see to it Gunny sees the same people."

"It won't be the same," Major Audell said, shaking his head. "His fighting days may be over, and that may be what kills him in the end."

"He'll get through it," Harmon said determinedly as he headed toward the medics. He recognized Marteen by his green hair, bent over and talking to one of the men on a stretcher. He stopped, looked back and asked, "How many prisoners?"

"Just four," Audell answered. "They were trapped in a bunker and had no choice. I can't believe they wouldn't surrender, even after we came in like wild beings on them. Their tanks were gone, the bunkers neutralized, our marines had better armor, yet they still fought to the last soldier."

"It's hard to understand what motivates some races," Harmon agreed. "Did you take a good look at them? Their faces show no emotion whatsoever. Maybe they don't know fear."

* * *

"Fire for effect!" All seven of the Bolts' artillery pieces opened up, and the crews reloaded and repeated until each gun had fired ten rounds. Smoke rounds were loaded, and each gun fired three. The tanks they were still connected to allowed their crews time to scramble on top, and then the guns were moved. Less than a minute later, several rounds landed in the general area they had fired from, though not as many as the time before.

Once the pieces were in place again, the crews disconnected them from the tanks, and the tanks moved down the road toward the dug-in enemy. A padded cable was connected to the hitch on each cannon, and several crewmembers lifted and turned the weapons on their two wheels. The elevation was adjusted on each. Lieutenant Smithers ensured each gun was ready and called the forward observation team. "We're in place."

* * *

The Bolts' ten tanks raced across the open area leading to the mines in bounding overwatch as they moved in pairs. Lieutenant Algrite spotted the Gritloth tank as it attempted to maneuver to the edge of the wood line up ahead. "Tank in the trees!"

"I see him, sir," answered the gunner.

"Take him out!" he said, forgetting the proper commands. The main gun fired, and the enemy tank started burning.

Through the woods, Algrite could see rounds impacting among the smoke. Knowing the barrage would stop soon to allow their own troops to confront the Gritloth, they continued to hunt for tanks and clear the way for the infantry platoon, as over sixty mechs, using their thrusters to assist their jumps, moved past them into battle. He knew Mayshire and the Specialty Platoon were coming in from the backside of the mining community, and even though they were outnumbered, the Bolts would take the mines and route the Gritloth. The mechs made the difference in this fight.

When the smoke cleared, the battle was over. Lieutenant Algrite directed his driver to move to Captain Brink's location. He dismounted and walked up in time to hear the status of the rest of the Bolts. Thirty troops, fourteen mechs, and a stomper. He prepared his report mentally before giving his platoon's status. Two tanks had been destroyed, and seven of his tankers would never again light their tattoos.

* * *

The Withaloo fought hard for every inch of ground, routing the Gritloth. The artillery traded salvos with the Gritloth cannons. Every time they set up and fired, it was a race to break them down and move them before rounds came in. Fewer rounds came in, as the defending guns didn't have the advantage of being able to move.

An epic tank battle was fought over relatively open ground, with the Gritloth laser tanks at a disadvantage because of the high silhouette of their design, and the cool down time required for their barrels between shots.

Some of the infantry ended up fighting hand to hand once they met among the trenches. It was followed by fighting along the edge of the city, before the very last of the Gritloth surrendered due to lack of power packs for their rifles. There were less than thirty of them.

Later, Harmon limped down the ramp of the shuttle and looked around at the devastation. There were burned out tanks on both sides, and bunkers were open to the air, their damage obvious. Several of the city's squat buildings were still burning. The battle had lasted two days. When the last of the anti-aircraft lasers had been destroyed, Harmon had been able to get to the area.

Colonel Arthok, his arm in a sling, walked out of the mobile medical center and headed toward the shuttle. Harmon met him halfway. "How bad was it?" Harmon asked.

"We lost over two hundred and fifty before their tanks and bunkers were destroyed," answered the exhausted colonel. "That made it easier for our infantry. They were dug in deep."

"I see," Harmon said. "The losses hurt. Every one of them. I'm beginning to wonder if it was worth it."

"Commodore," Colonel Arthok said, stopping to look at him, "of course it was worth it. We have freed an entire system from unfeeling tyrants. The amount of Barlat they killed senselessly is a number I hope I never learn. We are warriors, you and I, Commander Ithall, and Rick Kashka, and all the troops following us. It is who we are, and we cannot change that, no matter how much we wish it. To put that fact to good use should never be questioned. We will be paid, of course, but none of us are here today for the credit alone."

Harmon realized he was right. He started to speak when a voice came over his ear piece. "Uncle Harmon, Mikkotal is headed to the planet. He asked me to convey a message: 'The planet's leadership would like to meet you on the far side of the city, at the only spaceport, in three hours.'"

"Thanks," Harmon said. "Tell him I'll be there." He headed back toward the shuttle with Big Jon. They had time to check on the Bolts.

* * * * *

Chapter Thirty-Four

Harmon stepped out of the shuttle and limped toward the group of Barlat standing near a strange shuttle. It didn't look like the one Mikkotal had flown; from its design, it appeared to be Gritloth made. He reached down and ensured his pistol was loose in its holster, ready should he need it.

Mikkotal saw him and came over. "The king would like to meet you," he said excitedly.

Harmon followed him, the sergeant major by his side, to the group of Barlat. Most of them were much older than Mikkotal. One of them, obviously the king, stepped forward.

"President Tomeral," said the older Barlat, "I cannot thank you enough for what you and your warriors have done. I had lost hope. So many have died this last month."

"You're welcome, Your Highness," Harmon said. "It was the only thing I could do. If one has the ability to right a wrong, they should do so."

"Wise words from one so young," observed the king of Barlat. "My son says you never asked for a specific price for your system's services. Is that correct?"

"I guess it is," Harmon admitted. "I started planning and forgot about that part."

"I see," the king said. "This shuttle belonged to the Gritloth. It was to be sent to their flag ship in one week. It is only half loaded. Will that suffice for payment?"

271

"Half loaded?" Harmon asked. "With what?"

"Galacuss crystals," answered the king.

Harmon stepped into the shuttle with the king, and they moved toward the cargo area. Several large containers were there. One was open, and Harmon could see the different colored crystals sparkling in the light. The amount of credit the crystals in the box were worth was staggering.

"It's too much," he finally said to the king.

"Nonsense," the king said in dismissal. "If you ever need more, just let me know. One of the boxes holds red crystals. I hear they are very valuable. We have no need for credit like that. The Gritloth forced us to reopen mines long closed due to lack of interest. I will, however, use some to hire mercenaries like you, honorable ones with references, to defend our system. We will purchase anti-aircraft weapons, too. What has happened here will never happen again."

"I'd advise you to place some on the hilltops, not the valleys," Harmon offered.

"We will take that into consideration," agreed the king.

The king stood with Harmon as he ran a hand through the crystals. Some of them were as big as his thumb. After a moment, the king spoke again, "You may keep the ship, too. We already have one to leave the system and return when we need it."

* * *

Salvage Fleet stayed in the Barlat System for three more weeks, until a mercenary company hired by the Barlat arrived. Rick recognized the name and let Harmon know he approved of the king's decision. They consisted of fourteen ships and were, by reputation, considered one of the galaxy's best. After meeting with their commander, arrangements were made for them to send the prisoners back to the Gritloth system.

By task force, they left the system and headed for home. Almost every ship in the fleet had at least one destroyed ship locked to its struts. Along with the few Gritloth ships capable of operation, all the battle's salvage had been given to Harmon by the king as a bonus. Harmon and the remainder of his security platoon caught a ride with *Windswept.*

* * *

"There's a lot of credit in the bay of this ship," observed Evelyn as they stood on the bridge, watching alter reality flash by through the clearsteel portal, close to their arrival in Salvage System. She was not just referring to the boxes of crystals in the shuttle. The bay was full of all kinds of salvage from the battle on the surface of the planet Barlat. There were stacks of rifles, artillery pieces, tanks, and even several of the damaged anti-aircraft systems covering every part of all three bays. They'd been busy gathering during the three weeks after the battle.

"I know," Harmon agreed. "I wouldn't be surprised if some of it has already been repaired over in the bay of the other carrier."

"With that maintenance unit, I don't doubt it," Evelyn said. "Captain Brink said he wants them to mount an anti-aircraft laser system on a tank's chassis. With that kind of mobility, terrain wouldn't limit it like it did the Gritloth."

"He's right," Harmon said. "Before you know it, that man will be commanding a brigade-sized element."

"The Bolts have come a long way from a gang running a few blocks of an overcrowded city," she observed.

"They just need to rebuild their numbers," Harmon said. The Bolts, like all the units involved in freeing the Barlat system, had taken heavy loses.

"Speaking of rebuilding," Evelyn said, "what's your plan for the fleet?"

"I haven't really thought about it," Harmon admitted. "We have enough credit to rebuild the fleet, repair and add ships, and build whatever JoJo thinks the planet needs. I suppose we could look for others like the Withaloo."

"Ma'am, we are coming up on emergence," announced the ship's tactical officer.

Harmon and Evelyn turned back toward the clear-steel portal to watch. When they arrived in-system, they could see *Cube* in place near the gate, where they'd left it. Near it were *Salvage Title*, *Sweet Pea*, a small, strange ship, and one Harmon recognized, though it was damaged even more than *Salvage Title*. Captain Rogers and his ship *Basher* were back in Salvage System.

"Sir, you have a call," said the communications officer.

"Thanks, put it on the screen," Harmon said.

Up on the main screen, Harmon could see the conference room on *Cube*. Clip and Zerith were sitting around the conference table with several others. Zerith had a huge piece of cake on his plate. To his relief, both brothers were there with their mates, also enjoying cake. Cameron and Ralph both had crumbs on their faces as they waved their hands around, telling stories of the recent battles. They'd left to come home to Salvage System a couple of days before the fleet had departed.

Stan looked up and waved with his bandaged stump. "Hi, Commodore, do you want some cake? Bradford made it for me. It's peanut butter."

"When I get over there, I do. I'm not sure what that is, but save me a piece." Harmon smiled.

Hank reached for another piece, and Kyla smacked his hand with her fork. "Save some for the commodore!" Evelyn laughed out loud beside Harmon when Zerith slid his plate a little farther away from Kyla, and Bradford moved to the other side of the table with his.

"Dustin, what brings you to these parts of the galaxy?" Harmon asked.

"Well now lad, that's a long story, isn't it?' Captain Rogers said, pointing his fork. "It would seem that the Fleet admiral decided I couldn't come and help you in the Barlat System when I asked for another leave of absence for me and my kin. Which is strange, because I own me ship, and I explained the situation fully. Instead, our president had him send us, and half the other clan's ships, mind you, to the Yalmordit System to take care of a little occupation problem there. It seems the Gritloth needed to be sent packing, being the bullies they are, and all."

"I hate bullies," Harmon said.

"Aye, that you do, lad. That you do," agreed Captain Rogers.

"Hey, sir," Mike said, "this is Shonflate." He indicated a large toad-like being seated next to him, sniffing the piece of cake on his plate. "He wants to talk to you about a problem."

"A problem?" Harmon asked.

"Yes, sir," the retired senior NCO answered. "It seems a group of pirates have decided they like his system and have moved in permanently."

"They have, have they?" Harmon asked with a grin.

The End...?

# # # # #

About the Author

Kevin Steverson is a retired veteran of the U.S. Army. He is a published songwriter as well as an author. He lives in the northeast Georgia foothills where he continues to refuse to shave ever again. Trim...maybe. Shave...never! When he is not on the road as a Tour Manager he can be found at home writing in one fashion or another.

* * * * *

The following is an
Excerpt from Super-Sync:

Super-Sync

_____

Kevin Ikenberry

Available Now from Theogony Books

eBook and Paperback

Excerpt from "Super-Sync:"

The subspace radio chimed an hour later, just as Lew put aside the holonovel with dissatisfaction. There was no such thing as "happily ever after," no matter how many books she read. No one was going to carry her off into the sunset. Lew reached for the radio controls and felt the thuds of Tyler's boots on the deck in the passageway below. He burst onto the bridge and vaulted into his chair.

He looked at Lew. "Identify the transmission."

Lew fingered the controls and read off the diagnostic information, "Standard Ku band transmission from Earth. Origin point known through Houston nexus. Encryption is solid Johnson Analytics with the proper keys."

Tyler grinned. "Boss."

Lew nodded and smiled as well. "Appears so."

Their mysterious benefactor hadn't called them in more than six months, but every time he'd employed them, the take had been impressive. How he was able to garner the contracts he had bordered on magic. Lew thought the man sounded like some kind of Texas oil baron. Despite the technology, his calls were always voice-only, and there was never any interaction between them and whoever he represented.

Whatever he contracted them to acquire was delivered to a private, automated hangar on Luna. The robotic ground crew would unload *Remnant* and send them on their way again. Anonymous cash transfers always appeared in their accounts by the time *Remnant* returned to lunar orbit. The first mission had earned Tyler's company over a million Euros. The following missions were even more lucrative.

Their benefactor went by a call sign, and they talked in codes meant only for their own ears. It should have been a red flag, but the money was too damned good to pass up. A call from him could *not* go unanswered.

281

Tyler punched a few buttons on his console, and a drawling voice boomed through the speakers, "*Remnant*, this is Boss. Are you receiving?" The transmission ended with a chiming tone that dated back to the early days of spaceflight. The clear delineation of conversation allowed Tyler to answer.

"Boss, this is *Remnant*. Nice to hear from you. How can we be of service?"

A few seconds passed. "Tyler, it's good to hear your voice. I understand you're on a contract flight from our friend in India."

"That's affirm, Boss."

"Roger, you've got a shadow. Are you aware of that?"

Tyler's face darkened. "Roger, Boss. We're aware of the bogey."

By definition, a bogey was an unknown contact with unknown intentions. Should the situation turn bad, the radar blip would become a bandit. Lew checked the telemetry from the unknown ship. There was no change in direction or speed. It was still gaining on them.

"*Remnant*, the trailing vehicle is not your concern. I have a change in mission for you."

Tyler shook his head. "Negative, Boss. I have a contract."

"*Remnant*, I bought out that contract. The shadow on your tail is the *Rio Bravo*, under contract by me to get Telstar Six Twelve. You're going high super-sync."

* * * * *

Get "Super-Sync" now at:
https://www.amazon.com/dp/B07PGS545X

Find out more about Kevin Ikenberry and "Super-Sync" at:
https://chriskennedypublishing.com

* * * * *

The following is an
Excerpt from Book One of the Earth Song Cycle:

Overture

Mark Wandrey

Now Available from Theogony Books

eBook and Paperback

Excerpt from "Overture:"

Dawn was still an hour away as Mindy Channely opened the roof access and stared in surprise at the crowd already assembled there. "Authorized Personnel Only" was printed in bold red letters on the door through which she and her husband, Jake, slipped onto the wide roof.

A few people standing nearby took notice of their arrival. Most had no reaction, a few nodded, and a couple waved tentatively. Mindy looked over the skyline of Portland and instinctively oriented herself before glancing to the east. The sky had an unnatural glow that had been growing steadily for hours, and as they watched, scintillating streamers of blue, white, and green radiated over the mountains like a strange, concentrated aurora borealis.

"You almost missed it," one man said. She let the door close, but saw someone had left a brick to keep it from closing completely. Mindy turned and saw the man who had spoken wore a security guard uniform. The easy access to the building made more sense.

"Ain't no one missin' this!" a drunk man slurred.

"We figured most people fled to the hills over the past week," Jake replied.

"I guess we were wrong," Mindy said.

"Might as well enjoy the show," the guard said and offered them a huge, hand-rolled cigarette that didn't smell like tobacco. She waved it off, and the two men shrugged before taking a puff.

"Here it comes!" someone yelled. Mindy looked to the east. There was a bright light coming over the Cascade Mountains, so intense it was like looking at a welder's torch. Asteroid LM-245 hit the atmosphere at over 300 miles per second. It seemed to move faster and faster, from east to west, and the people lifted their hands

285

to shield their eyes from the blinding light. It looked like a blazing comet or a science fiction laser blast.

"Maybe it will just pass over," someone said in a voice full of hope.

Mindy shook her head. She'd studied the asteroid's track many times.

In a matter of a few seconds, it shot by and fell toward the western horizon, disappearing below the mountains between Portland and the ocean. Out of view of the city, it slammed into the ocean.

The impact was unimaginable. The air around the hypersonic projectile turned to superheated plasma, creating a shockwave that generated 10 times the energy of the largest nuclear weapon ever detonated as it hit the ocean's surface.

The kinetic energy was more than 1,000 megatons; however, the object didn't slow as it flashed through a half mile of ocean and into the sea bed, then into the mantel, and beyond.

On the surface, the blast effect appeared as a thermal flash brighter than the sun. Everyone on the rooftop watched with wide-eyed terror as the Tualatin Mountains between Portland and the Pacific Ocean were outlined in blinding light. As the light began to dissipate, the outline of the mountains blurred as a dense bank of smoke climbed from the western range.

The flash had incinerated everything on the other side.

The physical blast, travelling much faster than any normal atmospheric shockwave, hit the mountains and tore them from the bedrock, adding them to the rolling wave of destruction traveling east at several thousand miles per hour. The people on the rooftops of Portland only had two seconds before the entire city was wiped away.

Ten seconds later, the asteroid reached the core of the planet, and another dozen seconds after that, the Earth's fate was sealed.

* * * * *

Get "Overture" now at:
https://www.amazon.com/dp/B077YMLRHM/

Find out more about Mark Wandrey and the Earth Song Cycle at:
https://chriskennedypublishing.com/

* * * * *

Manufactured by Amazon.ca
Bolton, ON

33610911R00157